Penumbra

A Journal of Weird Fiction and Criticism

No. 7 ☾ Spring 2026

Edited by S. T. Joshi

". . . a voyage in the very penumbra of death."
—Sir Arthur Quiller-Couch

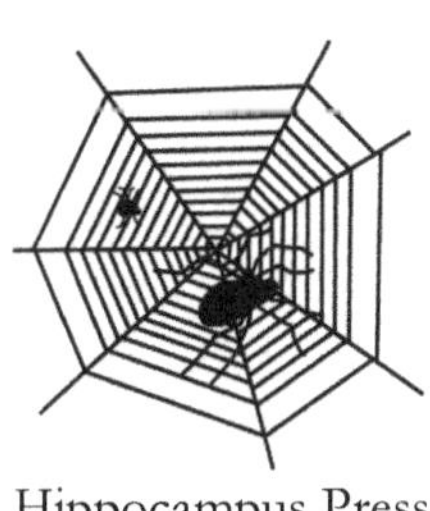

Hippocampus Press

New York

Published by Hippocampus Press
P.O. Box 641
New York, NY 10156
www.hippocampuspress.com

Cover by Daniel V. Sauer, dansauerdesign.com
Hippocampus Press logo designed by Anastasia Damianakos.

PENUMBRA is published semiannually, in Autumn and Spring. Articles and letters should be sent to the editor, S. T. Joshi, ℅ Hippocampus Press. Literary rights for articles will reside with PENUMBRA for one year after publication, whereupon they will revert to their respective authors.

ISBN 978-1-61498-494-8 (paperback)

Contents

Fiction

Nonfiction

Classic Reprint

Poetry

Warlock Corpse

Wade German

I

Some things should remain lost forever; or, if they are ever found, at least left alone. The olden prophets and latter-day seers knew this well. In their sacred testaments and arcane tomes of prognostication, there are many instances of textual lacunae, suggesting that larger omens and oracles have been expurgated or even left unwritten; and both holy and unholy commentators have agreed, after much argumentation, that only rays emitted from the lamp of reason would ever lead our prophets and seers into passing over their own foretellings with discretionary silence. But most of us are not seers; we wander about in the dark without any clairvoyant illumination, and in our blindness sometimes stumble through oblique angles or obscuring veils that occult the profundities of mystery. Some of these occurrences, or encounters, may lead to mystical epiphanies or new worlds of joy; others are the revelations by which we court black morgues of oblivion, affording us only horror. Mine was of the latter kind.

It all began during a routine aerial patrol of the remote mountains that form the northeastern border of Naga-Namkor, when I was a dragon rider of the Naga-Namkorian Empire.

The sector I was responsible for monitoring is a barely inhabited region; it is too bleak and inhospitable an environment for all but the hardiest of creatures. Nevertheless, patrols were conducted regularly as a necessary prophylactic against alien incursions, since recent times had seen probe-like pesterings along that border by motley agglomerations of the uncouth, mutated troglodytes who dwell the blasted wastelands beyond the Ythloryom Mountains.

Having reached the terminus of our route at the northern rim of that sector, we were just turning homewards when Klakalatak, my dragon mount, suddenly raised her snout twice and flared her nostrils to snuff deeply at the gelid air; then she gave a dissatisfied grunt. She had scented something out of the ordinary below. So I slapped her twice at the base of the neck, the signal for her to lead the way, and dragon and rider dove in the direction of a high alpine valley to investigate the anomaly.

As we vectored through the jagged and ice-crowned granite peaks on our landing approach, I soon saw what Klakalatak had scented: a humanoid arm jutting from the snow. We landed beside it, and I dismounted to investigate.

The pristine snow that blanketed the entire valley was slowly turning into slush due to an apparent flash of unseasonable warmth, and rivulets of crystalline meltwater were trickling all around. The arm, and its owner, were locked in a sheet of blue ice just below the liquifying layer of snow. I cleared away the snow and used my sword as an ice-pick to partially free the body beneath.

It was a very well-preserved human—or, as I would later learn, protohuman—corpse. By all appearances he had died here long ago, but not as a result of violence. I imagined that he had perhaps suffered an icy inhumation during some sort of rapid freezing event that occurred in a long-forgotten, primordial age. At any rate, he certainly was not a specimen of contemporaneous, grotesque troglodyte that I first expected to find. I stood back for a moment to marvel at it.

He was dressed like the proverbial caveman, clothed in the skins and furs of a variety of creatures, and wore a necklace of animal fangs and claws. The corpse was short, but not dwarfish; it clearly never had been exposed posthumously to temperatures that allow for natural putrefaction. Its pale, frostbitten skin was thoroughly mottled by black and blue blotches; but underneath all this elemental bruising, it was easy to discern that the corpse was decorated heavily with tattoos of pictographic design. I brushed away the tangled mat of his hair and beard to reveal a sunken, frost-burned face that wore the serene expression of an undisturbed sleeper; and this struck me queerly, where a death grimace would not have been so disquieting. Upon the body I found a knife that was carven not crudely from some kind of bone; around his waist there was a corded belt, tied to which was a bulky leather pouch. I untied and opened it.

The sack contained three long-haired shrunken heads. The eyes and lips of each shrivelled, hideous visage were sewn shut with threads made of black hair; but the threads through the lips were longer and thicker, and were left unclipped to dangle like evil whiskers. At the bottom of the emptied sack I found another, tiny pouch, inside of which was a small set of flat tiles made from wood, each carved with different curious symbols.

I wondered how long the corpse had lain in obscurity, only to lie exposed to new mercies under an indifferent sky. I looked around at the surrounding scape and pondered how the body got there. The terrain was too sheer for climbing; the little valley seemed to be altogether inaccessible, save by flight. I surmised that he could have been dropped there by some prehistoric avian, but eventually decided that he must have been here so long that the very geology had shifted around him of its own glacially slow, epoch-grinding accord to obliterate all trace of his route into the area.

I took up the knife and the pouch with all its contents, then left the corpse where it lay to rot, refreeze, or be plundered by carrion-feeders, however nature would have it. Then we returned to Issykyuul.

I remember how proud Klakalatak had been of her discovery. But I'm sure she would now be mortified to know what a terrible thing she had found.

II

The following day I was met at the entrance to the dragon caves by my old friend Thalaba Kehama-Gebir. Thalaba was a highly respected wizard who had recently risen to some prominence in the Naga-Namkorian court, and acted as a sub-vizier within the queen's security council. After a cordial greeting, he went straight for his point, as had always been his manner. He told me that he was privy to the dragon riders' log and had read of my discovery in the alps. He wanted to know more and had several specific questions. So I added more flesh to the skeleton of my report, describing what I could in detail, and I also mentioned the items I had taken away from the site. He raised his eyebrows at this (I had not included the souvenirs in my report) and said he would like to examine the items at the earliest possible time.

"But first," he said, "you will harness your dragon with a double-seated saddle and take me to the site of this fascinating anthropological discovery of yours. Don't worry; I've already talked to the stable master, and have also taken care of today's patrol schedule; so you are now free to act as a tour guide for an old friend!"

When he had climbed the ladder and was adjusting into the saddle, he also asked me to make no mention of our excursion to anyone. I readily agreed, but asked why it necessitated a vow of silence. He promised to explain on the way.

As we soared over the desert plains heading north in the skirts of the Ythloryoms, Thalaba told me that he suspected the remains I had found were those of an Old World sorcerer, which would be a very rare discovery indeed. Scholars on the subject generally believed that such wizards had made sure never to be buried but burned, due to what then must have been a highly pragmatic fear of necromancy, or the possibility of other vengeful practices upon their corpses. He said that the artifacts I had retrieved, together with the description of the tattoos on the dead body, made him nearly certain that his speculation would be proven accurate.

He continued: "It is the symbols and pictograms that I am most interested in. I have seen such before in an incredibly old grimoire, a tome believed to have been written (*scrawled* would be more accurate!) by a primordial mage, but one whose language is lost to us, and the text therefore indecipherable. But that book contains some of the earliest known examples of the magical symbols and sigils that have come down to us through the corridors of time, and are still used in magical practice today. Some of the curious pictograms and symbols on the corpse, as you describe them, correspond exactly to several in that hide-bound tome. I believe—indeed, I hope!—that what is tattooed on the corpse might provide some sort of a key to deciphering at least parts of that old grimoire."

I nodded, but offered no comment; so true to his old form, Thalaba continued to expound.

"It is believed that the primitive witch covens and other sorcerous clans practiced their arts during a time when the magical forces were at their apogee, since the stars and planets of the old gods were closer to our world then and therefore had greater tidal influence, just as the moons affect the tides. The channels between deities and worshippers were stronger. Ah! The powers of the primordial sorcerers are legendary, almost mythical, in our wizard orders of today! But the magic we practice now is merely a diluted strain of that Old World sorcery; naturally, one desires the keys to unlock the doors to that other age . . ."

"No need to explain further!" I offered from over my shoulder.

He laughed. "But I just might have more to tell when I have seen the corpse!"

When we landed at the site he was ecstatic. "How rare! I believe his origins to be neanderthal, or some other extinct ancestral lineage of ours. And I have no doubt whatsoever that all these tattoos mark him for the relic of a primitive magician."

Then after a long pause, during which he had been poking and prodding at the body, he asked: "Have you ever heard of a *likföt?*"

The query was not rhetorical. We had known each other since youth, and he knew well that I, too, had dabbled in magic studies during college before realizing my talents lay in other pursuits. But I admitted to having never heard of the term.

"In primitive witchcraft," he continued, "it was a suit made from humanoid skin, probably flayed from a magician's corpse by a rival sorcerer, but possibly offered up willingly in receipt of magical favor. It has been written that the wearer of such a suit had access to unlimited wealth; but whether that wealth should be interpreted literally or metaphorically has never been determined. I have often wondered over the magical efficacy of a *likföt;* but of course, in our civilized world, I have no recourse to flaying the hides from mine enemies! Your find presents itself as a rare opportunity to test the potency of the Old World magic. As an experiment, I shall fashion such a suit from the skin of this ancient corpse."

Thalaba had always maintained something of a morbid streak, so I was not much surprised by this. And I confess that I was even a little curious about his unusual plan.

He then asked me how agile Klakalatak's claws were. I replied they were nimble as a knitter's and could thread a needle if needed. He then said the dragon should carry the corpse back to his tower in Issykyuul. When I mentioned how easy it would be to lash the grisly thing behind the saddle, he replied: "No, I think it somehow more appropriate if it were transported in the clutch of a dragon's claws."

And so we returned to Issykyuul, having no inkling that out of the eons iniquity had come at long strides upon us.

III

After helping Thalaba and his butler to transfer the corpse into the tower and up its spiral staircase to a chamber on the third floor, I returned to my quarters, retrieved the artifacts that Thalaba was so eager to examine, then walked back to the tower as the sun began to set.

In that third-floor chamber, which had all the usual accoutrements for a magician's laboratory, the ancient corpse had been laid out on a long table, where Thalaba's apprentice was busy taking notes as part of some cursory examination. Thalaba made some parting instructions to his pupil, then invited me for a glass of Zotarian brandy in his study. As we lounged in our deep leather chairs before the warmth of the fireplace, Thalaba was replete with enthusiasm as he examined the artifacts. He also said that he planned to have the corpse flayed immediately, and that fashioning his *likföt* would take very little time, after the conjuration of a simple domestic spirit to help with the task. When the corpse had been properly flayed, his apprentice would conduct an autopsical dissection of the cadaver. I recall Thalaba saying something about "wonders to be found in the innards that could paint pictures of the lost world," but I was quite tired and beginning to drift; and as Thalaba was clearly eager to get on with his procedures, we quickly finished our brandies and parted ways. I walked home in the gathering night, my mind overflowing with morbid evocations.

And those morbid evocations vexed me throughout the next day and into the evening, so that in order to exorcise my gruesome imaginings and speculations, I decided to pay another visit to Thalaba to see what progress he might have made on his ghoulish project.

As I greeted his butler at the front door, there came a bloodcurdling shriek from the upper floors of the tower. We looked at each other in a startled fright and panic, then bolted inside and rushed up the spiral staircase.

On the third floor we heard sounds of struggle coming from behind the wooden door to the laboratory, which was locked. We were still trying to smash down the door when Thalaba arrived, having dashed down the stairs from his quarters on the floor above.

"This door cannot be forced. Move aside," he commanded. We did so, and Thalaba recited a cantrip that opened the lock. Then all the commotion from inside the chamber suddenly fell quiet as the door swung inward and opened upon a monstrous and prodigious scene, like something out of a dream-phantasy that had somehow manifested and merged into the reality of the room.

Thalaba's apprentice was lying on the floor, a shrivelled and desiccated husk, like some thousand-year-old mummy that wore a hideous grimace on its withered face. It was as if his very life force, the entirety of his animating spirit, had been drained from him. But more terrible to see was a sight levitating nearby, some six feet above the floor: seated cross-legged as if upon an invisible floating cushion was the freshly flayed though very much alive corpse of the primordial warlock.

His skinless sinews, tendons, and muscles glistened wetly with a slick sheen of living blood and thick, red jelly globs and clots of revivified hemoglobin; yet he appeared serene, sitting in the posture of a meditating monk who had attained all the gravity of a remote being altogether outside of worldly concerns.

The butler fled; I now wish that we had done the same. But as Thalaba and I crossed the threshold into the room, the levitating warlock turned his head slightly toward us and opened his eyes, black gleaming eyes; and then his skinless face began smiling slyly, sinisterly at us, revealing teeth that had been filed to triangular points.

Thalaba pushed me aside, shouting: "Stand back, my friend, and do not fear! Just now I am wearing the warlock's very own skin, and the charms of power upon it should protect me against him, as if I were he himself!" And with this, he cast off his robe to reveal that he indeed wore his newly and horribly fashioned *likföt*. But this had no theatrical or magical effect upon the flayed and floating warlock, who watched us with what appeared to be an evil amusement. Then that warlock from out of time stood up on the very air and stepped down an imperceivable stair to stand on the floor before us, chuckling with what soon became a guttural, liquescent cackle. He was mocking us.

Thalaba and I were transfixed in unalloyed horror—then realized we were quite literally frozen, paralyzed; spellbound by workings of the warlock's otherworldly sorcery. I could not flinch, nor even blink—not that I had attempted to try, for it seemed that all idea of motion, the very concept itself, had been banished from my brain.

Now the resuscitated sorcerer held out his right arm toward us and proceeded to peel back the muscle of his forearm so that it fell back in one single flap, like a grisly strip of sirloin, to reveal the arm bones underneath: living bones that, in some immemorial epoch, had been deeply etched with black magic runes. And the warlock now cackled again in a bestial manner, and with his left hand gestured to outline his every limb, his entire body, telling us, in the simplest sign language, that his entire skeleton was similarly engraved with magical sigils: symbols that I understood were more than enough protection against any latent powers afforded to someone wearing the warlock's own stolen *likföt*. Then hell emerged on Earth.

Bound by a supernatural force stronger than black iron shackles, Thalaba still stood motionless and lockjawed, with his mouth half-opened in some aborted magical mid-utterance; then the black stitches that held together the awful suit of skin he wore began to wriggle themselves undone with a highly unpleasant vermicular motion, and dropped to the floor when free. Then the suit itself, like some dreadfully animated spectre, glided off Thalaba's naked body and swiftly crossed the room where it wrapped and grafted onto its original owner.

A moment later, the warlock was shifting his shoulders and waist to make minor adjustments to his newly fitted yet old familiar skin. Then gurgling with what seemed to me a satisfied sigh, the warlock stretched his arms toward Thalaba and slowly began making the motions of someone who pulled an unseen rope toward him.

And suddenly blood began to drip, then seep, in bright crimson rivulets from Thalaba's eyes to stream down his paralyzed face; and I saw the silent fear welling in his reddened eyes. Then Thalaba's throat began to distend and bulge, and there came from him a choking cough; and something rope-like and reddish-pink began to coil rapidly and gather within his mouth, only to flop like a nightmarish tapeworm from the lips; and I realized that his intestines were pouring out from the bloody hole of his mouth. Then other of his entrails began to disgorge themselves: large organs, small organs, multicolored organs for which I knew not the names all spilled forth in chunks and ropy strands to fall with liquescent splatters into a spreading pool of gore at Thalaba's feet.

I could only stand helplessly in witness to the evil and agonizing disembowelment of my old friend, as the expression on his face transitioned from unimaginable pain and suffering to one of utter despair, then disbelieving grief, and finally into the horrible recognition of one who stands before the doors of doom. Then his eviscerated body fell lifelessly to the crimsoned flagstones.

Shocked by the display of malevolent violence, and utterly terrified for my mortal soul, I believed myself about to meet the blackest of black magic fates. But the warlock had paused, and had turned his attention to a table where my collected souvenirs—his own possessions—lay. He gathered them together in the leather bag, then took up the shrunken heads by their hair and strode over toward me and held them before my transfixed eyes. Then in my own head I heard the warlock's terrible voice impossibly utter in the High Speech of old Naga-Namkor: "Old friends." And like some demoniacal jester he laughed in my face. Then he held up the bone knife.

It is too horrible for me to relate what happened exactly next; but soon the warlock stood before the open casement window, overlooking the nighted desert below. Then he began to murmur and croon, and this gained pitch and cadence as he began to sing in the evil tones of his own alien tongue, as if addressing the very evening air and moonlight. I imagined his weird rune to be a sort of venomous gospel music, but eventually realized it for a song of summoning.

For soon, and as if in response, there came the far-off sound of eerily crying winds; then upon those winds, from afar came an alien chittering, which soon became high-pitched screeches; then for a moment those sounds altogether ceased, before there came the tremendous roar of thousands of membranous wings, which burst through the window like a demonian whirlwind to encircle both room and resurrected warlock, some of the wing-tips glancing and cutting my face; then that living cloud of bat-like creatures carried the still-crooning warlock away into some unknown gulf of night. I clearly recall a sense of cool, rushing air; but all other immediate impressions after that are chaotic and inchoate.

There was an indeterminate period of blackness; but I believe the warlock has now sequestered himself in a cavern. There is the crackle of fire, and the scent of something altogether gamey roasting slowly over the flames. But I fear I have no further time for elucidation before my speaking lips, with the same foul-smelling hairs of an unknown beast that have sealed shut mine eyelids, are threaded together in silence forever.

Lines in Late Autumn

Ann K. Schwader

There is a madness woven through the wind
of this strange season neither dark nor light
descending with each final leaf to find
salvation in extinction. As the night
becomes a country all its own despite
our kindled windows, mourning wakes inside
our minds. A feral memory takes flight
across Orion, occultation wide
as raven wingspan stretching to divide
us from the stars we shared. This season holds
no constellation long enough. We slide
past Samhain on November nocturnes cold
enough to silence recollection, yet
its wind remembers all we would forget.

Docent of the Lost Apocalypse

Mark Howard Jones

He walks the broken roads of man, in memory of that brief creature that swiftly came and went half a million years ago. Step after step after step, each taking him further back in time before the remembrance is drowned in the rapidly rising tide of galactic static. He comes to see the cities, now just scars against the sky, each an ossified tarot of wonders and horrors, witness to a history effaced and replaced by myth, rumour and lies, telling of a society with an ash-filled heart and a blackened soul.

Access to artificial memories, resurrected photographs and restored egos told a terrifying tale; but actually to *walk* here, no matter the potential perils that still linger, is a treasure beyond price. He wanders down faceless streets of towering rock, hemming him on either side, straining to listen, to hear all that is left of them, fading voices heard in lonely places. Across ten mountains and beside three moribund oceans, at the edge of the desert of spinning stones, he finds the place; before him lies the point where the gods came down to touch the Earth, where belief is buried and faith flies away. It is still seething and alive, leaking foul dreams and seductive nightmares into the air; the mesmeric language of the gods. And, to their eternal damnation, they *listened.*

Squatting atop the splintered towers of man, beneath a cobwebbed sky that cradled a desultory mortuary sun, commanding the herds of believers who followed in their wake, the gods turned this world into a remnant of nothingness. Empty and lost. An anonymous chronicle of despair, like a lesion circling endlessly against the blackness. The long death of humanity had begun centuries ago but the arrivals from beyond hastened its ultimate destiny as a corpse species.

Beside the track where the last funeral trains ran, he stoops to read something. He is one of the few left who can understand the words. A stone, marked by one of them, their language fading as they descended, the illiterate remnants scratching away to form half-remembered letters, desperate to record their final plea. Words, devoured by the unceasing tide of the present, desperate to declaim their importance to an uncaring universe: the chemical symbol for insanity.

To a scholar of finalities, a collector of exterminations, either self-inflicted or imposed, this world offers up uniquely dark flavours and colours. Their dwelling places are now monuments to failure perched upon milestones of anguish. Upended gods, burning idols litter the rubble fields, still impossibly ablaze from that distant time when the stones turned to glass. If it is possible for an entire race to die a lonely death, then humanity did just that. Many had left the cancerous cities, members of feral tribes, preying upon each other as their numbers dwindled, while others remained, clinging to the broken promises of failing technology. A few tried to leave in their sky-stabbing toys, soon swept aside. The worst of them fell to worshipping the returning gods, pathetic supplicants begging for imaginary mercies.

Exploring their ruined halls and galleries, the shattered shelters, choked with the dust of the dead, he finds the evidences of those thought great and those deemed notable. Their traces barely remain, echoing still in this vacant sphere like wind-blown spores. He first heard of them from hints hidden in the sacred transmissions of the absent mystagogues. Now, as the greyness of twilight grows, he contemplates a final thought, frozen in the crumbling skull of their last ruler—long deposed, long deceased—those faint vestiges becoming unyielding truth. “Seek hope.” Two words, moonstruck nonsense, both a minor resurrection and a confession of failure.

Brushing away the dust-deluged past, he lets the debris of history slip from his long, pale fingers as he decides his time here is over. Turning to depart, he is left with one insistent profanity of thought: if a civilisation falls and there is no one there to hear it, does it make a sound?

Feeling Weird: The Primacy of Emotion and Affect in Weird Fiction

Ben Keene

> We must judge a weird tale not by the author's intent, or by the mere mechanics of the plot; but by the emotional level which it attains at its least mundane point. If the proper sensations are excited, such a "high spot" must be admitted on its own merits as weird literature.
>
> —H. P. Lovecraft, "Supernatural Horror in Literature" 28

1. Introduction

Here is the most influential essay in the study of weird fiction stating that we gauge weirdness by the emotions evoked within us. Some of the most important weird critics of the last three decades have likewise remarked on the roles of fascination (Fisher 8), awe (Miéville, "Weird Fiction" 510–12; "God, that's a merciless question," answers 2–5; Joshi, *The Weird Tale* 91–112), horror (Cisco 7; Joshi, *The Weird Tale* 112–20), terror (VanderMeer and VanderMeer xv) and dread (Fisher 8; Luckhurst 1052) in weird fiction. However, relative to how consistently our emotions are associated with weirdness, the importance assigned to them is quite small. Joel Lane (5–10) and Eugene Thacker (120) are among those to produce idea-driven definitions of weird fiction, focusing on its philosophical power as "the mode of thought most suited to an increasingly unthinkable world" (Coley 298) and almost entirely eliding any affective or emotional component to the weird. I argue to the contrary: affect and emotion take primacy in the weird. This does not mean I deny weird fiction's capacity to make us reflect philosophically or consider our attitudes toward the world. Rather, because it deals in the unfamiliar and unsettling, the weird is inherently subversive and therefore has great potential to make us re-think the world and ourselves. My argument is that, when the weird makes us think, it does so by first making us *feel,* and that this feeling constitutes the fundamental unit of weirdness.

Specifically, I believe the weird is characterized by a combination of compelling feelings with aversive ones: fascination and/or awe and/or wonder and/or curiosity, etc., mixed with horror and/or fear and/or dread and/or disgust and/or apprehension, etc. The supposed oppositionality of, say, disgust and awe makes them seem incompatible at first glance. Nonetheless, such oppositional emotions frequently cooperate in art and in life. For example, Burke interrelates terror and delight when defining the sublime (121–22); Korsmeyer argues "disgust can exert a paradoxical magnetism" (3); for Apter, "excitement is somehow tangled up not only with anxiety but with other unpleasant emotions, such as horror, panic, and disgust" (5); Lacan speaks of jouissance as a "transgression [. . .] beyond the pleasure principle" (183–85).

The intermingling of the aversive and compelling is hardly a new idea within weird fiction either. Miéville describes the weird as a sublime "swillage of [. . .] awe and horror" ("Weird Fiction" 511); though Thacker "neglect[s] [. . .] the real engine of horror—affect" (Newell 10), he nonetheless conceptualizes a "freezing of all affect, resulting in a combined state of dread and fascination" (Thacker 113); Fisher argues that weird fiction evokes feelings similar to jouissance (13) and claims "the weird cannot only repel, it must also compel our attention" (17); Pedersen identifies a "dark wonder" within the weird (327); Lovecraft discusses a commingling of awe and dread ("Supernatural Horror in Literature" 28); Newell defines the weird as fundamentally disgusting, but concurs with Korsmeyer that disgust is paradoxically alluring (197); forum boards for Thomas Ligotti's writing express "horrid fascination" with weird fiction (Aetherwing, answer 3). This is not an exhaustive list.

Considering the frequency of these observations in a kind of writing where *any* consistency is anomalous (Machin 49), the shallowness of our engagement with weird emotions and affects is baffling. It becomes even more confusing upon acknowledging emotion studies' claim that "feelings and emotions are primary when reading literary narrative" (Miall 325). More than that, there is "neuropsychological evidence [. . .] that emotion is at the basis of, and shapes the purposes of, *all cognitive activity*" (Miall 324; my emphasis). Consequently, my use of emotion studies and affect theory throughout this essay should be unsurprising. As such, I must define what I mean by affect, and its difference from emotion. Generally, affect is conceptualized as a force existing "beneath, alongside, or generally *other than* conscious knowing" (Gregg and Seigworth 1). However, affect theory posits a wide range of meanings for affect, not all of which are applicable here. As far as it is relevant to me, affect is a precognitive feeling that, because it is precognitive, cannot be reflected on or rationalised. Emotion is a cognitive and discursive rendering of that precognitive affect; it is affect that has been "owned and recognized" (Massumi 88).

There is certainly an emotional component to my definition of the weird: if I claim to "know the weird when I feel it" (VanderMeer and VanderMeer xvi; Miéville, "Afterweird" 1115), or make judgments about whether certain texts are weird or not, I must have some cognitive idea of what weirdness feels like, even if I cannot fully express that feeling. Nonetheless, as I will argue, the language we use to express our emotions is very imprecise; if I say a weird text makes me feel apprehension and curiosity, this does not capture how my feelings differ from the apprehension and curiosity I might experience before an academic conference. Because we lack the language to precisely determine or understand this weird feeling, it is not wholly reducible to a set of emotions; we must also consider the weird on an affective level if we are to respect the nuance of feeling "weird." Throughout this essay, I refer to a "sensational" weird with the intention that "sensation" should refer to the *mixture* of emotional and affective, discursive and pre-discursive, elements of feeling weird.

As this essay deals in emotion and affect, I frequently assume a personal tone and explicitly draw on my own feelings. This means that several parts of this essay amount to "this is what the weird means *to me*." However, I think this is the most transparent way of approaching something that (as I argue later) is an intensely subjective phenomenon. A sensation-driven view of weird fiction that *didn't* engage with my emotional responses would be fundamentally flawed, and it would be dishonest to phrase my feelings as if they were universal reactions for all readers. Nonetheless, I also broaden my frame of reference, drawing on critical opinions and research studies where possible.

This essay begins with a close reading of three texts: "Little Heart" (Bruce), "Purity" (Ligotti), and "Sun Dogs" (Mauro). My aim in this chapter is not to prove that the weird *is* fundamentally sensational. Instead, I demonstrate the importance of sensations in these texts and thereby show that weird fiction *can* rely heavily on sensational responses. In the succeeding chapter, I use affect theory and emotion studies to argue that our critical responses to weird fiction *are* shaped by our sensational responses. I explore the implications of a sensationally defined weird and argue that this definition is significant because it means weird fiction is intensely subjective and cannot be made to conform to any formula. Most importantly, though, it indicates we can become desensitized to the weird.

2. Broken Boundaries, Bad Parenting, Perversity: A Close Reading

Because I am arguing for the primacy of emotions across all weird fiction, close reading of a few texts has limited usefulness. At best, the close reading of this chapter can evidence the primacy of sensations in the three texts I discuss. Nonetheless, showing that sensations can be integral to a weird tale is a useful starting point. In this section I explore the emotiveness of perversity, vulnerability, and boundary breakdowns in "Little Heart," "Purity," and "Sun Dogs."

My goal is to overcome the limits of close reading by demonstrating the affective power of themes—such as boundary breakdowns or human impotence—that recur in the weird, thereby indicating that the feelings associated with these themes are widely present in weird fiction.

"Perversity" has been associated with weirdness since the 1890s (Harris 1408; Luckhurst 1055; Machin 73; Sheedy). The multiplicity of its meanings makes it a particularly useful term: it can refer to the transgressive, the contrarian, or that which is "perverted" into some strange new form. All three senses are displayed in "Little Heart." The story's first pulse of weirdness arrives when Anna remembers a childhood dream; in it, her father looms over her with "his beak about to pierce the flesh of her cheek," his feathers reeking of "trash" (192). The character of the father—previously kind, handsome, and human—is violently corrupted. Twin senses of the perverse build as the story continues: the "ideal" father Anna remembers is perverted into a bird/man; and this creature is sexually abusive. The father/creature's sexual perversity is described with a physicality that verges on sensuality, a sensuality that inspires disgust: "He licked his lips. He pushed her mother's head down into the feathers and rocked faster as he watched Anna watching him" (193). It is this licking of lips, this controlling of the gaze as if he is proud of his actions, his "gleeful expression" (193) juxtaposed with Anna's inert, bleeding mother that generates the third kind of perversity: contrariness, drawing pleasure from pain. For me, this is the most powerful kind of perversity because it is so inexplicable, because it delights in the transgressive, and because it strikes at the reader's own sense of propriety: this perverse contrariness is a diegetic reflection of the paradox at the heart of the weird, the reader transfixed, maybe even fascinated by Anna's trauma.

The perverse works to a similar effect in "Purity," where the family unit is also debased. The narrator's mother is "perverted" from her gendered role as a guardian of children into a dangerous character plotting the abduction of her son, Daniel. The consequent paradoxicality to their relationship makes it weird. We think the mother should love her son, but the opposite is true; we think there must be a reason for this, but Daniel's sister attests that "it makes no sense" (20); we assume she will at least be ashamed of her inability (or, more likely, unwillingness) to play the "loving mother," but she delights in it. The story ends on the word that encapsulates their relationship: when Daniel asks what the world's third "impurity" is, his mother smiles and declares, "Why, it's families, sweetheart" (21). Superficially endearing but condescendingly deployed, the playfulness of "sweetheart" chilled me with that most powerful perversity, locating pleasure in the repulsive and deviant. Perversity is riddled with nausea yet tinged by a fascination with the nauseating. Its relative prominence in weird fiction is synonymous with the prominence of those attendant feelings.

Vulnerability is another of weird fiction's most prevalent themes. It is interwoven with the human impotence and "anthropoperipheralism" (Miéville, "M. R. James and the Quantum Vampire" 112) explored by weirds old and new alike, Lovecraft's vision of "man's impermanence and insignificance" (Lovecraft, "A Confession of Unfaith" [1922], *Collected Essays* 5.147), and VanderMeer's incomprehensible Area X. In "Little Heart," perversity begets vulnerability. Because the father is initially familiar, Anna and her mother entrust him with their vulnerability; our disgust with the perverted father/creature intensifies when he abuses this trust. This parallels "Sun Dogs." Sadie falls in love with the mysterious June and thereby unknowingly entrusts her body and heart to a hybridized creature; however, Mauro leverages this vulnerability differently.

Before expanding on that thought, however, I should address the "shadow-girl, sun-dog" (30) in the room. June's hybridity is only made explicit on the penultimate page, but Maruo deploys a tonal weirdness when describing her throughout the story, making her sharp and alien: "You had glass shards for teeth, wire for bones; your lips tasted like copper" (27). She is a builders' yard of a person, and the transformation of the body into cold, impersonal material estranges the reader from their own physicality. The body is further reduced to a collage of parts in "I held your bones close" (29), and the vacuity of June's physical form is intertwined with the narrator's love for her in phrases such as "I loved you, somehow, despite your insubstantiality; you cast no shadow, left no footprints" (29). Besides the obvious spectral connotations, the narrator's love is troubled by the doubling of "somehow, despite," repeated invitations for skepticism in the vulnerability Sadie exposes to June. I dreaded the moment Sadie's vulnerability would be exploited, but June proves more trustworthy than her human counterparts. I felt most powerfully weirded when I realized that Sadie chose *well* in making herself vulnerable to the other rather than the human.

When I say that "Sun Dogs" leverages vulnerability differently, then, I mean that vulnerability is used to renegotiate boundaries of kin and other, and to undermine anthropocentrism by subverting our ingrained distrust of the extrahuman. I use "extrahuman" here because June is transcendentally human. Sadie has never "play[ed] well with others" (16); she fled civilization to live alone in the middle of a desert. The ability to entrance her evidences June's preternatural charm. If we define "humanness" by unsurpassed sociability and hierarchical superiority over the "animal," then June, who eclipses anybody Sadie has met, is more human than the men chasing her. Despite June's physical animality, these men figure as animalistic by contrast, roaming the desert in a bloodthirsty pack. This reversal of perspectives is elevated by a corresponding emotional reversal. The unease that Mauro's description has cultivated around June is transformed into sublime joy at almost the same moment her metaphorical difference is actualized: June's "sun-dog" (30) form is revealed when she kills the man who has caught her, but, as she and Sadie flee, Sadie feels that "nothing in my life had been as pure, as perfect as this singular moment of freedom" (31). Because Sadie's emotional vulnerability positions June as kin, and June's brief vulnerability to her captor makes her actions sympathetic, their perfect freedom in the wake of murder does not feel perverse, but instead cements June's extrahuman kinship. Vulnerability acts as an emotional bridge between characters *and* between reader and character, allowing us to re-envision empirical difference through our felt similarities.

Much of this discussion has involved boundaries, which is natural considering vulnerability's relationship to wounding: to feel vulnerable is to perceive the potential to be wounded. Wounding often manifests itself as a boundary challenge: the breaking of the skin barrier or the bursting of an ideological bubble. The loss of a boundary can make one feel hurt and vulnerable. Yet boundaries are also restrictive, and, as in "Sun Dogs," their disintegration can engender freedom or relief. The diverse and apparently opposing emotions signified by boundaries make them a useful case study for this essay, especially considering "the weird's disruptive tendency to breach boundaries" (Greve and Zappe 6). For Margrit Shildrick, monsters inherently pose a boundary problem: they unsettle us because they are "simultaneously same and different, both self and other at the same time" (Gunderson 12). This is true of Bruce's father/creature, whom I refer to as such to highlight his multiplicity. The binary terms we usually conceive identity through (e.g., human:animal or familiar:unfamiliar) are revealed to be inadequate as we find that the father/creature exists in the interstices. Rather than embodying one of these binary terms, he is the "/" between them, unsettling because we literally cannot settle into one way of conceptualizing him. This in-betweenness is true of his physical form (man/bird), but also insofar as he is a mediation between Anna's father and the feathered man from the film her mother starred in (fondness/trauma; trustworthy/untrustworthy; fact/fiction).

Like June, the father/creature is a collage. He is pieced together from film scenes, real moments, Anna's memories, and dreams. These different levels bleed into one another throughout Anna's story, and a powerful weird charge is generated as the boundaries between fact and fiction break down. One of the story's most affecting moments comes when Anna watches her mother's film and sees her mother pluck a "tiny soft black feather" from her thigh (196). Three pages earlier, Anna has recounted the childhood memory of waking up (from her dream of the bird/man sexually abusing her mother) and pulling a similar feather from her own thigh. These scenes recall the "definite weirdness" Mark Fisher observes in the "tangling" of ontological levels (45), fiction seeping into memory. Fisher writes that since weirdness is "fundamentally about a wrongness" (45), it often involves the displacement of things to where they should not be. Here the displacement of the feather memory into film, transposing Anna onto her mother, generates the terror of inevitability: Anna has been marked, and her path will parallel that of her mother's character. Terror and curiosity—because this tangling of levels is certainly curious—intensify when Anna finishes the film and goes into the kitchen. She impulsively smashes her wine glasses, apparently unaware that her mother's character also did this in the movie. However, the terror of her inevitable demise soon collapses into a more immediate dread, any speculative worry condensed into the hereness and nowness of "trash and blood" as Anna smells the father/creature in the hallway (200). The themes of vulnerability and impotence resurface as, barefoot, she cannot leave her circle of smashed glass; despite an initial will to fight, she closes her eyes in surrender as the thing approaches.

On my first encounter with "Little Heart," I misread the next scene. My mistake made it the weirdest thing I have read. In the scene, Anna remembers her real father knocking on her door late at night and demanding that she come out. The real father is metaphorically described as the father/creature, sexually abuses Anna, and she kills him with a shard of broken glass, thereby explaining why he suddenly disappeared during her childhood and why Anna's mother blamed her. Crucially, I missed the opening line, which declares that the scene is a *memory*. In my misreading, the present (henceforth somewhat separated from the remembered dreams and film scenes) became increasingly muddled with the past instead of more clearly delineated from it; the father/creature had returned to visit Anna rather than been determined long-dead; the father's disappearance remained unexplained.

My misunderstanding of "Little Heart" furthered its weirdness by rendering true knowledge forever impossible: it thrust the story further into the interstices of dream/memory/real/film rather than allowing Bruce to fix Anna's trauma as remembered and the monstrous father as a figurative embodiment of it. This not-knowing is central to whatever fascination, curiosity, awe, or wonder we have with the weird: when I feel curiosity or fascination, I am affectively asking, "What is this thing? How does it work/think/happen? Why is it here?"; with awe and wonder, I ask, "How can something so grand, or spectacular, or transcendental exist?" These feelings augment the dreadful or terrifying or disgusting into that which is, in addition to those things, weird. Moreover, as evident in my misreading of "Little Heart," they can be induced by boundary challenges that confuse levels and put things where they are not supposed to be.

Because the compelling aspect of the weird is entwined with affective and cognitive questioning of its subject matter, we may cease to be compelled once our questions are answered. This might explain why critics have suggested that weird fiction can be "literally unthinkable" (Onishi 159) or "echo that which escapes explanation in life" (Manguel xix). Such inexplicability is consistent with the father's dogmatism in "Purity." He never justifies his theory that human thought is impure, despite maintaining that "Without pure conception [. . .] everything is a disaster and will continue to be a disaster" (6). Nevertheless, the success of his supernatural experiments prevents us from dismissing his theory. Instead, the "disaster" he posits becomes a source of apprehension and curiosity. Besides apprehension, the immediacy of this catastrophe—"everything *is* a disaster" (my emphasis)—sparks fear, both insofar as we fear disasters and we fear the unknown. Because the alternative to calamity, "pure conception," is similarly unknown, the reader is left stranded between fears without a point of fixity, unable even to conceptualize one as the negation of the other. Moreover, the father's ideal of "pure conception" is inherently anti-anthropocentric as it assumes humans are convergence points for "THE FORCES OF AN IMPURE UNIVERSE" (19).

Whereas Mauro's anti-anthropocentrism in "Sun Dogs" explores the beauty of togetherness with the other, Ligotti's full-frontal attack on our "humanist illusions" (Lee-Price 7) is more likely to disturb and affront. In his hands, our ideas become abject in the Kristevian sense, a "greasy, greenish liquid" (19) siphoned from the head and left to drain into the sewage. This category mistake whereby the philosophical becomes the "merely" physical is itself a powerful degradation of Western humanism, which has placed mind above body for centuries. There are inevitable emotional implications—shock, rejection—whenever weird fiction overturns our "basic" assumptions about the world in this way. For example, fear, vulnerability, insignificance, and awe are natural responses to Lovecraft challenging anthropocentrism by revealing the smallness of humanity in relation to the outer cosmos ("Letters to Farnsworth Wright" 7). Similarly, I found the mother's conduct in "Purity" disgusting and fascinating because it transgresses social assumptions. Her causeless hatred for David is differentiated from the "motiveless malignity" (Coleridge 315) of non-weird characters like Iago because, whereas a reader may believe that Iago simply hates Othello, the social construction of mothers as guardians for their children makes such a reading difficult to accept here. Without an "acceptable" answer, our fascination with uncovering the "true" nature of her inexplicable hatred remains. However, the final line forever thwarts the resolution of this curiosity by explaining her hatred through the similarly incomprehensible theory of impurity. By writing an ending that renders the knowledge the reader seeks always-inaccessible, Ligotti concretizes intrigue. Fascination and obsession fester in the wound he inflicts on our sensibilities. To continue the metaphor, my disgust and apprehension were integral to my being wounded. Were I impassive to the mother's hatred for Daniel, I would not find her transgressive in the same way. If my disgust is the dagger Ligotti uses to wound my sensibilities, then my fascination is cause for picking at the scab left behind; fascination bids me to return repeatedly to the wounding event, digging at why and how I was wounded, which is bound up with why and how I *feel* wounded. If the weird is a negotiation of the real, as Newell (5) and Lane (5) have suggested, then this negotiation is made possible by our affective responses, and made significant by our emotional ones.

Throughout this chapter, I have discussed perversity, vulnerability, ruptured boundaries, inexplicability and anti-anthropocentrism. Many of these things interrelate: the perverse is often contrary, a seemingly inexplicable mixture of opposites; anti-anthropocentrism involves an increasing porosity to the boundaries that demarcate the human; the flimsiness of these boundaries makes us feel vulnerable. More than that, however, these aspects of weird fiction are united by their affective power, their capacity to move the reader. For example, we are fascinated and disgusted by the extent to which Daniel's mother hates him because her hatred is both perverse and inexplicable. The breakdown of real/remembered/dreamed/filmed boundaries in "Little Heart" is similarly inexplicable and similarly fascinating: our obsession with *understanding* compels us to categorize which ontological level the story's events are occurring on, even when the categories themselves are crumbling. In "Purity," binary categories disintegrate when Daniel encounters intersex genitals for the first time, though the effect here is to perturb him. Nonetheless, he does not forget what he saw but instead recalls it in "a cyclone of images and emotions" (20)—some of those emotions are evidently curiosity and fascination. In "Sun Dogs," our perturbation centers on June. The vulnerability Sadie exposes to her despite her situation beyond the bounds of the human makes June a source of apprehension. However, she comes to characterize the awesomeness of the other as human boundaries are reconfigured and Sadie's vulnerability is validated. In each case, the themes discussed evoke a combination of compelling and aversive sensations. Though some critics have used the philosophical potential of these themes to advocate an idea-driven weird, I will continue to argue that we place critical emphasis on "the importance of borders" (Friedrichsen 132), "the fragility of human nature" (Lane 124), and the breaching of "our epistemic limits" (Onishi 159) because we find these things particularly affecting to begin with.

3. The Theory of Feeling: Proofs for and Implications of a Sensational Weird

Having evidenced the weird's capacity to generate particularly powerful feelings in its readers, I shall now elaborate on the implications of a feeling-driven conception of weirdness. Of course, there is a logical leap here: I have shown that weird fiction is often powerfully affective and emotive, but I have not conclusively proven that all weird fiction is defined by the sensations it brings about. Consequently, the first two subheadings of this chapter apply emotion theory to weird fiction to suggest some of the ways that feelings take primacy when we read. Moreover, many of the things I will discuss as implications of a sensational weird—such as the impossibility of formularizing weirdness, or the necessity of originality in weird fiction—corroborate or explain observations we *already make* of the weird. Therefore, I hope that I am substantiating my position by discussing its implications.

Feeling Is a Form of Understanding

One of Jenefer Robinson's main theses in *Deeper Than Reason: Emotion and Its Role in Literature, Music and Art* is that our emotional responses to a text constitute an "inarticulate [. . .] *understanding*" of it (123). According to Robinson, feeling that Macbeth is terrifying registers a special kind of understanding, "in a bodily and instinctive way that is hard to eradicate," that he is a terrifying character (126). This understanding cannot be replicated by, say, someone explaining to me why Macbeth is terrifying in the same sense that "You can tell me that some comedian is hilarious, and try to explain why, but unless I laugh myself, I do not really understand why he is funny; at best I begin to understand why *you* think he is funny" (127). Furthermore, my understanding continues to develop as I reflect on my emotional responses: Were they appropriate? What caused them? This latter point is exemplified by the previous chapter, an exercise in my comprehending three texts by justifying how I felt about them. Moreover, other scholars corroborate Robinson's theory: Ellis remarks that "emotional processes drive the processing of information rather than being merely responses to it" (17), whereas Korsmeyer claims that "terror is the ground for the sublime because it registers the overwhelming character of its objects" (133). Korsmeyer's observation is particularly relevant because of the analogous relationship between the weird and the sublime (Miéville, "Weird Fiction" 511; Machin 30). Additionally, Lovecraft's work is situated within the literary tradition of "cosmic horror" or "cosmic terror." If terror helps us register the "overwhelming character" of his subject matter, then purportedly cognitive judgments about the "dizzying, disorienting, and alienating sense of being overwhelmed by deep time and/or deep space" (Machin 30) in his work (and weird fiction more widely) are also, in part, sensational judgments.

To put the point most simply, we only truly understand that these things are overwhelming if we feel overwhelmed by them. If Robinson is correct, Machin's judgment originates in his feeling of being overwhelmed, and the critical process of ascribing this feeling to "deep time and/or space" is a means of justifying that feeling as he reflects on it. The overwhelming affect of some weird fiction is the starting point for Machin's analysis, while the emotions evoked by deep time and space are simultaneously an end toward which these themes work—the weird is bookended by sensation. Although this seems somewhat contrived in my analysis of Machin's argument, this is because I want to show how an idea-driven view of the weird effect could be reconceived in sensation-driven terms. Other examples, like Rauth's analysis of how certain descriptive styles can create dread in weird fiction (410–27), or Pedersen's study of four techniques Lovecraft used to inspire wonder (322–26), are much more amenable to my theory because they already imply the primacy of emotions.

Description and "Personal Remindings" in Weird Fiction

A sensational definition of weirdness both informs and is corroborated by Thomas Rauth's account of the "privileged position" description has in weird fiction (408). According to Rauth, the old weird "commonly resorts to failures in trying to describe the incomprehensive and the impossible," its description riddled with gaps that the reader is encouraged to fill (427). The new weird utilizes descriptive failure less, yet Rauth's reading of *The City & the City* reveals that its description remains vague and promotes reader involvement insofar as the reader must interpret its ambiguous or mysterious details (424–27).

Consequently, we can make some general observations about description in weird fiction: "it is characteristic of the Weird to allocate a comparatively large portion of the text to description" (Rauth 408), and the uncertainty or inadequacy of this description coaxes readers to inject their own meaning into the text. These observations are made more salient by David Miall's analysis of emotion in description. Citing a study by Seilman and Larsen, Miall observes that literary texts maximize "personal remindings" (readers are said to have a personal reminding when the text reminds them of something), and that these remindings mostly occur within the literary text's descriptive passages. This is because "descriptive passages (compared with accounts of action or dialogue) may present a degree of uncertainty, challenging the reader to locate a meaning for them through the feelings they evoke" (332–33). Because the weird tends to utilize a "comparatively large" amount of description (Rauth 408), and this description is particularly uncertain, it stands to reason that weird fiction evokes an unusually high number of personal remindings. Since personal remindings involve the allocation of meaning to *feelings*, this suggests weird texts are exceptionally thick with feeling.

Another of Seilman and Larsen's findings is that literary texts are particularly dense with memories of the reader as an actor rather than as an observer or receiver, evoking twice as many actor-role memories as the expository text used in their study (Miall 332). I think the salience of agency in personal remindings makes weird fiction's themes of impotence and smallness particularly significant. Perhaps these themes are so affective because they frustrate actor-role memories, the powerlessness evoked by the text reminding us that we *do not* have the kind of agency we like to identify within ourselves when we read. Assuming our emotional responses help us understand texts, the affective clash between actor-role remindings and feelings of powerlessness may undergird our cognitive analysis of human subjection to "outer" forces in weird fiction. Furthermore, Robinson asserts that "non-cognitive affective appraisals [. . .] fix my attention on those aspects of the story that are of significance to me" (114). This is corroborated by Miall's suggestion that feelings structure the significance we find in texts through personal remindings. If they are right, then the aspects of texts that we deem significant are those that affect us. Our critical interest is drawn to themes like powerlessness because of the affective charge generated by, for example, the clash between actor-role remindings and feelings of powerlessness. Rather than establishing the significance of weird themes and devices through critical reflection, we deem them worthy of critical reflection *because* they are significant to us. We are made aware of their significance by our affective responses, which initially draw our attention to them.

Emotional Re-registration

In *The Philosophy of Horror*, Noël Carroll suggests that horror can be defined in terms of reader response: he claims the genre is centralized around horrifying the reader. As with my account of weird fiction, Carroll's definition is a subjective one, and he tries to "defeat" the charge of subjectivity by basing his argument on features that can be observed within horror texts. Namely, he discusses the role of monsters and claims that horror characters' reactions of fear and disgust are meant to parallel readers' reactions. As an aside, I do not see subjectivity as an inherent disadvantage, as literature (and art more generally) is a highly subjective practice. The argument Carroll suspects others will have with his work—that "he's identified his own reaction by introspection and projected it onto everyone else" (30)—is a valid criticism, but is not applicable here. I began this essay with quotations from numerous critics and readers expressing emotional responses to the weird that resemble mine. The above hypothesis about personal remindings also provides a textual basis for proving whether weird fiction *is* particularly feeling-dense or not.

This is without mentioning that Carroll's proposed solution to the problem fails anyway. He claims to "have approached this issue by assuming that the audience's responses to the monsters in works of horror are ideally intended to run parallel to and often to be cued by the emotional responses of the relevant fictional characters to monsters. This presupposition, in turn, enables us to look to works of horror themselves for evidence of the emotional response they want to engender" (30), thereby avoiding a reliance on introspection. However, this assumption that the audience's responses are meant to parallel the relevant fictional characters' receives little justification. If we are to risk making an assumption of our own, Carroll's admission that he has "not done any audience research" (30) means that his hypothesis is probably based on the similarity between certain horror characters' responses and *his own*. If this is the case, then he is still projecting his response onto a wider audience when he says that the audience's responses are meant to parallel certain characters' reactions, and therefore does not solve the original problem.

So why are we discussing the failed defense of a horror theory? Because we can repurpose it and add something that Carroll lacks: a statement of authorial intent proving the reader is intended to react as the character does. Commenting on the part of "The Raven" where the narrator turns against the bird, Poe remarks that "this revolution of thought, or fancy, on the lover's part, is intended to induce a similar one on the part of the reader—to bring the mind into a proper frame for the *dénouement*" ("The Philosophy of Composition" 23). This is not quite a silver bullet, because the reaction in question is closer to anger than any combination of apprehension and fascination, but it proves that Poe tried shaping readers' responses by having a character parallel those intended reactions.

Affect theory corroborates the effectiveness of this method. Brian Massumi has claimed that "emotional qualification breaks narrative continuity for a moment to register a state—actually re-register an already felt state" (86). So if a reader is already feeling a particular way, and a character expresses similar feelings, this will re-register them within the reader. Knowing this, and knowing that Poe has deliberately used a similar technique, may shed new light on his character's frequent expressions of aversion-tinged compulsion. Viewing Roderick Usher's paintings, Poe's narrator "shuddered [. . .] thrillingly" (55), whereas a "sickly smile" plays across Usher's lips as he is gripped by madness (64); the narrator of "The Pit and the Pendulum" watches the scythe that incrementally approaches him "somewhat in fear but more in wonder" (142); and "The Imp of the Perverse" is almost entirely about "the fierceness of the delight of [. . .] horror" (286). The prevalence of these fear/wonder, horror/delight paradoxes in Poe's works tells us, at the very least, that they were significant to him. Whether by Poe's influence or otherwise, they appear in Lovecraft's work too. When the narrator reads Johansen's description of Cthulhu's city R'lyeh in "The Call of Cthulhu," he finds "awe [. . .] poignantly visible in every line of the mate's frightened description" (*Collected Fiction* 2.51). In the *Collected Fiction* edition of *At the Mountains of Madness,* the narrator and his companion Danforth explore the Antarctic city of the Old Ones for eighty-five pages. Almost every one includes expressions of aversion, compulsion, or both. The two declarations that bookend their trip typify their reactions throughout: "Both of us simultaneously cried out in mixed awe, wonder, terror, and disbelief in our own senses as we finally cleared the pass and saw what lay beyond" (3.70); "For a second we gasped in admiration of the scene's unearthly cosmic beauty, and then vague horror began to creep into our souls" (3.153). In Lovecraft's case, it is almost certain that these characters' feelings are meant to parallel the reader's, as "Supernatural Horror in Literature" claims that "the one test of the really weird is simply this—whether or not there be excited in the reader a profound sense of dread, and of contact with unknown spheres and powers; a subtle attitude of awed listening, as if for the beating of black wings" (28); the weird is only achieved "when to this sense of fear and evil the inevitable fascination of wonder and curiosity is superadded" (27). Lovecraft meant for his readers to experience a mixture of awe/wonder/curiosity/fascination and dread/horror/terror/disgust, so the instances where his characters express these feelings are very likely to be deliberate attempts at re-registration.

Even outside of Poe and Lovecraft—and perhaps because of their influence on later authors—re-registration is common in weird texts. Though I did not look for it when I chose to discuss them, it happens to feature in all three texts discussed in this essay's close reading chapter. In "Purity," Daniel professes "fascination" akin to "a nightmare that exercises a hypnotic power" (12). He also feels "trembling awe" (18) and is glad to find the "atmosphere of ruin and wreckage and of an abysmal chaos" in his father's basement "captivating" (18). "Sun Dogs" is similar, with Sadie's sense of "perfect [. . .] freedom" (31) meant to re-register the allure of the initially aversive other. I have also discussed how the perversity of the father/creature in "Little Heart" and the mother in "Purity" derive affective power from directing the reader's attention to their own interest in that which is disgusting or dreadful or worrying or worse, thereby re-registering such feelings in the reader.

Of course, weird characters proclaiming fascination and terror does not prove that readers feel the same way: re-registration only occurs when the reader is *already* experiencing the feelings the character expresses—a character intimating their guilt does not suddenly make the reader feel guilty. Nonetheless, the frequency with which characters express some perverse fascination or dark awe is textual evidence that, at the very least, these feelings have some recurrent role in weird fiction and, in the cases of Poe and Lovecraft in particular, are probably intended to birth or re-register similar sensations in the reader.

Desensitization

Desensitization is "a decline in cognitive, affective, physical, and behavioral responses to a certain stimulus. Specifically, affective/emotional desensitization is conceptualized as a decrease in negative emotional reactions such as fear, anxiety, depression, or an increase in PTSD" (Conathan et al. 1). Since weird fiction has a particularly strong aversive emotional component, the suggestion that we can become desensitized to it should not meet much resistance. Notably, while most research on desensitization focuses on desensitization to violence, it has also been suggested that people can become desensitized to stimuli related to disgust (Adamczyk 146), fear (Conathan et al. 1), and horror (Alexander and Balfe 1641), emotions that are integral to the weird for Newell (*A Century of Weird Fiction*), Lovecraft ("Supernatural Horror in Literature" 26–27), and Miéville ("Weird Fiction" 511) respectively. The potential for desensitization is also corroborated by my own experience, as I have found myself progressively less affected by weird fiction the more that I've read it. Because we can become desensitized to "a certain stimuli" (Conathan et al. 1), desensitization helps explain why weird fiction must deal in new, varied, and unfamiliar subject matter. As Joel Lane argues, "If the ideas are not strange and disturbing enough to catch the reader off guard, the result is indifference" (7). Besides cognitively familiarizing ourselves with content we encounter repeatedly, we become desensitized to it and consequently feel less disturbed. This helps explain weird fiction's emphasis on "originality and subtlety" (Machin 48). Nonetheless, even if the *specific* subject matter of weird fiction is made extremely varied, desensitization may still diminish our responses to general themes that appear repeatedly in weird fiction, such as those analyzed in the prior chapter.

Naturally, acknowledging desensitization does not mean accepting a sensation-driven definition of weirdness; one must only accept that there is a sensational component to weirdness. Nevertheless, desensitization becomes particularly significant if one adopts a sensational definition because it is now impeding weirdness' defining characteristic, as opposed to only a component of its power. For the sensation-driven weird scholar, desensitization is chewing at the heart of weirdness. For the idea-driven scholar, it nibbles on a finger or two. If I am being dramatic here, it is because the stakes are great: the sensation-driven conception of weirdness defines it as a particular sensational response; if reading weird fiction in bulk dampens that response, then it means we must either refrain from reading too much of it (especially over a short period of time) or accept that in continuing to read we will be getting a neutered version of the weird experience. If we (as a general readership) lean toward the former, it will hamstring the commercial success of weird fiction. If we lean toward the latter, this commercial effect will persist because decreased emotional involvement in weird fiction often diminishes appreciation of the skill employed in writing it (Robinson 124–25) and decreases reader enjoyment (Clasen et al. 355; Chesnokova and van Peer 6).

Furthermore, as covered in the subsection about emotion as a form of understanding, decreased emotional involvement means our emotional understanding of the text will decline. Dispassionately reading about Anna's father coming after her in "Little Heart" is a radically different experience from feeling the terror of him there, in the hall, out of sight but coming, surely, slowly, as Anna resolves herself to resist him—but oh, she cannot! Firstly, and most importantly, the tension that makes this scene so powerful will be lost on a reader who doesn't feel the imminent danger the father/creature poses. Secondly, registering the father/creature as a terrifying figure means I am much better equipped to analyze *why* he is terrifying than someone who had not felt terrified at all. Thirdly, if I am not emotionally involved, I will struggle to aesthetically appreciate how Bruce crafts disgust and horror; for example, the terrible brilliance of her run-on sentences and inescapable rhythm may become more difficult to recognize. This is hardly an exhaustive list of the things lost to a desensitized reader, but I believe it is sufficient to evidence the consequences of our sensational responses being blunted.

The Weird Cannot Be Made Formulaic

The subheading you have just read is not a new idea: several weird critics (Luckhurst 1042; Machin 3) have already reached the consensus that "we cannot expect all weird tales to conform absolutely to any theoretical model" (Lovecraft, "Supernatural Horror in Literature" 28). A sensation-centric definition of weirdness does not contribute a new conclusion to this debate, but it can explain our existing observations. Let us return to how emotions function as a kind of understanding: in feeling that Cthulhu is terrifying, I understand that it is terrifying, and can then rationalize my emotions by reflecting on them. Why do I rationalize my emotions retrospectively? Shouldn't I have an idea of my feelings as I am experiencing them? This is not necessarily the case. Rather, affect theory suggests that affect only exists prior to "conscious reflection" (Massumi 92), as a force "beneath, alongside, or generally *other than* conscious knowing" (Gregg and Seigworth 1). Literary emotion theorists such as Miall and Robinson concur that any "affective appraisal" of a text precedes cognitive awareness of itself (Miall 325–31; Robinson 59); a study by Herbert et al. indicates that our emotional responses[1] to a word begin during the "early stages of semantic analysis," as early as 200 milliseconds after reading it (478). We start working out how

---

1. Some emotion theorists do not use the "affect" vocabulary but instead conceptualize the affective moment as the earliest stage of emotion. Terminology can sometimes conflict, and what Herbert et al. refer to as the beginning of the emotional process would be considered as affect by others.

we feel about words before we are even sure what they mean.

The precognitive nature of affect means that we lack precise cognitive knowledge of what we felt or why we felt it. In Massumi's model, affect can transform into emotion once we have reflected on it and rendered it discursively analysable (88); yet, as Robinson argues, our ability to recognize these affects is limited. English lacks the terms to discursively name all the affects we are capable of (80). Sometimes language cannot capture the subtleties of a feeling or the nuanced ways feelings intermingle. Because we don't have cognitive access to our affective states, our cognitive judgments about what they were or what caused them are "prone to error"—Robinson calls these cognitive evaluations "folk-psychological appraisals" (80). Other factors may interfere with our judgments—I might feel jealous of my brother's new business opportunity, but, since I want to see myself as a good person, I tell myself I am against the opportunity because I am worried about it being risky. These problems make it extremely difficult, if not impossible, to definitively identify what we feel or why we feel it.

This means that single-emotion theories of weirdness are flawed. For example, Newell conceives of the weird as fundamentally disgusting, but, considering the inadequacy of language in describing affects, it seems unlikely that this single term sufficiently describes the entire mess of affects that exist beneath the discursive surface, swimming into and through one another, always conjoining, separating and influencing each other in a dynamic "process" (Robinson 57–99; Miall 324) of feeling. Actually, any discursive rendition of our feelings—disgust, horror, awe, etc.—is an approximation of those prediscursive feelings and fails to capture their affective nuance. This is why I have involved a wide range of emotions in my analysis of the weird. I believe that, on an affective level, we experience some highly nuanced mixture of the feelings that we later come to identify as terror, disgust, awe, etc., hence my focus on the dynamic created by the mixture of aversive and compelling feelings in the weird rather than on any particular emotion within that dynamic.

The constant potential for error when rationalizing our feelings, compounded with the trouble of acquiring precise knowledge about how we were affected, means that schematizing the literary production of specific affects is presently impossible. Furthermore, the difficulty of analyzing affects can explain the consistency with which the weird is deemed "intrinsically problematic for critical discourse" (Machin 13). If the weird operates through mobile, dynamic, and unknowable affects, then it is natural for weird fiction to be critically "slippery" (Gunderson 13; Machin 13; Rauth 408; Webb 83). The fundamental unanalyzability of weird fiction is at the heart of our critical interest in it. It vexes. It compels us to understand but resists understanding. In this respect, weird critics are like weird readers and characters: just as the weird character and reader can seek knowledge in spite (or perhaps because) of a suspicion that this knowledge will unsettle, horrify, disorient, or disturb its possessor, weird critics pursue an understanding of the weird while acknowledging that achieving such an understanding would unravel the mystery that compelled them in the first place. If we "solved" weirdness, we would lose interest in it. Weird criticism is an exercise in acquiring this forbidden knowledge; it is just as perverse as the activity of the reader, we simply explore our perverse fascination on a metatextual level.

Subjectivity and "Personal Histories" of Weirdness

Throughout this essay I have maintained that weirdness is subjective. This follows naturally from my belief that it is primarily sensational—"an emotion is a subjective content" (Massumi 88). The subjectivity of weirdness means that what is weird for one person may not be weird for another. This much is obvious whenever two people disagree about whether a text is weird. However, I feel the historical dimension of this subjectivity has been underexplored. In particular, critics have largely overlooked how the importance of originality in weird fiction impacts older texts that have had their themes, tropes, literary devices, or character archetypes reused by later writers. Even if a text seemed original when it was first written, it may not feel so to readers of today. Joel Lane criticizes these later writers, remarking that "the so-called Cthulhu Mythos has suffered badly from familiarisation: when the elder gods start to feel like drinking buddies, it's time to say goodbye" (7); yet he does not follow the idea through to its conclusion: the implications for Lovecraft. For example, pop culture references and adaptations familiarized me with Lovecraft's work long before I had read any of it. And it seems fair to me, on one hand, to recognize the unparalleled critical and authorial influence of Lovecraft on weird fiction, and on the other hand to say I don't *feel* a tale such as *At the Mountains of Madness* is weird. My first impression of the shoggoth came from pop culture, where it was fully explained to me and depicted with dubious potency—a teddy bear compared to the creature Lovecraft wished to shape in his reader's imagination. With a nigh cuddly image of it fixed in my mind as I read the story, how was the shoggoth supposed to horrify or fascinate me?

This is without even mentioning the relationship critics have traced between instances of 'golden age' weird fiction and the First World War (Miéville, "Weird Fiction" 513–15; Rauth 412; Joshi, *Evolution* 61). Some writing, Lovecraft's included, generated part of its weirdness by exploiting the fears, concerns, and fascinations of its particular era—speaking to the spirit of the age. That age is long gone, and we are hardly likely to react to the fiction of the 1920s in the ways that readers of the period did. The sensations evoked by "canonical" weird works may dissipate with time, and, by the other side of that coin, we may unearth hitherto neglected works that are coincidentally *more* evocative in the present. Weirdness requires constant reappraisal. When I say that I don't find *At the Mountains of Madness* weird, then, I am not denying that many would have found it weird when it was written, or that many find it weird now. I simply object to the notion that an author or work should be considered weird across all times, across all places, across all traditions, and to all people. If critics insist on being concrete and objective, the most they can do is to trace a web of influence between texts and authors historically referred to as weird: Poe and Hawthorne influenced Lovecraft, Lovecraft influenced Derleth, and so on. It is readers who decide which texts (and, by extension, authors) are weird to them—that is to say, each of us develops a *personal* history of the texts and authors we find weird.

Besides its historical significance, the subjectivity of weirdness means that people will react differently to certain weird tropes and devices. For instance, I have repeatedly referred to Rauth's analysis of description as producing dread in the weird. I won't dispute the emotive power of description, since Miall (333–34) provides evidence supporting such a conclusion, but who is to say the emotion will always be dread? Rauth justifies his feelings in this way, but couldn't somebody else respond to weird descriptive techniques with apprehension or fear or other similar but different emotions? In fact, Rauth acknowledges that the descriptive techniques common in weird fiction have "a highly subjective and divisive" effect (415). This goes for most observations of the weird's form or content. Turnbull identifies "visible interconnections between humans and nonhumans across micro and macro scales" as weird (275), Freeman is weirded by the presentation of "a familiar object from an unfamiliar angle" (1125), and I find human impotence particularly weird; but these themes will not be felt equally by everyone, and both the kind and degree of their affectiveness can vary based on their significance to the reader. As critics, we can propose things that we find weird or that we think others may find weird, but it is readers who decide what feels weird to them—that is to say, each of us develops a personal register of the themes and literary techniques we find weird.

Finally, the subjectivity of weirdness may explain how it manages to "surreptitiously (and not so surreptitiously) attach itself to the corpus of many writers who [. . .] would not define themselves as writers of weird fiction" (Machin 16). If weirdness is identified through the reader's response rather than the author's intention, then it is quite reasonable for a reader to find something weird even if it wasn't written with weirdness in mind. The only requirement is a difference in personal registers of what is weird and what is not.

Final Thoughts on the Implications of a Sensational Weird

Affect and emotion are important elements of all literature, constituting a first-hand understanding about how aspects of a story might be horrifying, or funny, or fascinating. Furthermore, they attract our attention to the elements of the text that are significant to us, thereby directing our critical processes. The peculiar quantity and uncertainty of description often exercised in weird fiction make it especially dense with personal remindings—ergo, especially dense with feelings. Moreover, a sensational definition of the weird explains our present observations about its critical slipperiness, its attachment to authors who would not self-describe as weird, and (so as to mitigate desensitization) the necessity of "originality of content and style" (Lane 7) in weird fiction. Some critics have argued that the weird is defined by the disillusionment it expresses with the everyday (Lane 5), or the questions it raises about humanity's position in the universe and the borders that surround us (Gunderson 12). Nonetheless, as I have sought to establish, our thoughts are guided by our feelings and our attitudes are shaped by our sensations. Not only does sensation determine much of the significance we find in weird themes such as borders and impotence, but affect is precognitive and is therefore our first point of contact with the weird text, influencing our subsequent cognitive processes. Therefore, it must be said that sensation takes primacy when reading the weird, and its participation in our cognitive observations deserves more critical attention than it has hitherto received.

4. Conclusion

Our sensational responses are important on at least three levels when we read weird fiction. First, our initial affective appraisals of the text focus our attention on the things that are significant to us

(Robinson 126). Because I am unsettled by the in-betweenness of Bruce's father/creature, I find his transgression of fact/fiction and man/bird boundaries worthy of further critical reflection. Second, our sensations constitute an instinctive understanding of the text (Robinson 122–31). Because I am disgusted by how Daniel's mother treats him in "Purity," I am well equipped to cognitively analyze why their relationship is disgusting and can do so by justifying my feelings. Somebody who did not feel this way may not even realize that the mother can be read as a disgusting character, and will instead have a different understanding of her. Third, our emotional responses make our critical observations significant. Rauth argues that the special ways description can operate in weird fiction are important because they induce dread (427).

Our sensations have these three types of significance in all modes and genres of writing. Weird fiction is differentiated from other kinds of writing because we associate it with specific ways of feeling (dread, fascination, terror, awe, disgust, wonder) and not with specific subject matters (ghosts, monsters, death), though some critics associate it with more general kinds of subject. In this sense, weird fiction is similar to horror, which is defined by its capacity to "rais[e] the affect of horror in audiences" (Carroll 15), and dissimilar to a genre like high fantasy, which is defined by its grand adventures and/or monsters and/or magic, etc. Just as a monster might horrify some people but not others, accepting the centrality of sensations in weird fiction means acknowledging that weirdness is a subjective phenomenon that is felt differently by different readers. Furthermore, in the same way that our qualitative evaluation of a horror novel will be impacted by how much it horrifies us, the intensity of our fascination and terror significantly influences how much we enjoy and aesthetically appreciate weird fiction. Perhaps most importantly, however, a sensational definition of weirdness suggests that reading weird fiction in bulk detracts from our experience of it as we become desensitized.

This last observation may be critically and commercially problematic, but it is not a problem with a sensational definition of weirdness per se. The biggest issue with such a definition is that, because it makes no formal or stylistic specifications of weird fiction, it doesn't cleanly differentiate the weird from other modes like the Gothic, which might also be said to fascinate and terrify us. Worse still, an academic conference might be the object of my curiosity and apprehension—does that make it weird? This problem arises because of the breadth of emotions I have considered. My lack of specificity should not be surprising, considering the difficulty of accurately recognizing or understanding our affective states; emotion is, by nature, an imprecise rendering of affect. However, my lack of discursive specificity belies the *particular* affect brought about by weird fiction. I might say I felt curiosity and apprehension in response to a weird text *and* in response to an academic conference, but in both cases the actual feelings differ greatly even if I use the same terms to describe them. I feel different kinds of apprehension and curiosity; the problem lies with the imprecision of our emotional vocabulary. Though I believe there is a sensation we associate with the weird, which colors our experience of it and distinguishes weirdness from, say, Gothicism, I only have the language to approach this sensation in vague terms. This vagueness means that my definition can be improperly co-opted to suggest that academic conferences are weird. Nonetheless, I am pleased! I am pleased my definition is vague, pleased that we cannot truly "get to the bottom" of what we are feeling or why we feel it. Pleased that the great mystery of weird fiction cannot be "solved" for the foreseeable future, pleased to know I have reason to remain curious, interested, fascinated. I am happy to keep saying, "I know it when I feel it" (VanderMeer and VanderMeer xvi).

Works Cited

Adamczyk, Lidia, et al. "Parents Are Less Disgust Sensitive Than Non-Parents, and Child Presence Has No Effect on Parent Disgust Sensitivity." *Parenting* 24, No. 4 (2024): 144–53.

Aetherwing. "TLO Member Interview: Aetherwing." Interview by Phillip Stecco. *Thomas Ligotti Online*, 15 April 2009, www.ligotti.net/showthread.php?t=2788&highlight=purity (Accessed: 2 May 2025).

Alder, Emily. "(Re)encountering Monsters: Animals in Early-Twentieth-Century Weird Fiction." *Textual Practice* 31 (2017): 1083–1100.

Alexander, Abigail, and Myles Balfe. "Horror, Experimentation and Enhanced Interrogation." *Deviant Behavior* 42 (2020): 1628–44.

Apter, Michael J. *The Dangerous Edge: The Psychology of Excitement*. New York: Free Press, 1992.

Bruce, Georgina. "Little Heart." In *This House of Wounds*. Pickering, ON: Undertow, 2019. 185–202.

Burke, Edmund. *A Philosophical Enquiry into the Origin of our Ideas of the Sublime and Beautiful*. 1757. Oxford: Oxford University Press, 1998.

Carroll, Noël. *The Philosophy of Horror; or, Paradoxes of the Heart*. London: Routledge, 1990.

Chesnokova, Anna, and Willie van Peer. "What Literature Does to Our Emotions, and How Do We Know? Empirical Studies Will Tell." *Synopsis: text, context, media* 25 (2019): 1–10.

Cisco, Michael. *Weird Fiction: A Genre Study*. New York: Palgrave Macmillan, 2022.

Clasen, Mathias, et al. "How Stephen King Writes and Why: Language, Immersion, Emotion." *Orbis Litterarum* 78 (2023): 353–67.

Coleridge, Samuel Taylor. *Lectures 1808–1819: On Literature.* Volume 2. Ed. R. A. Foakes. Princeton: Princeton University Press, 1987.

Coley, Rob. "The Horrors of Visuality." In *Photomediations: A Reader*, ed. Kamila Kuc and Joanna Zylinska. London: Open Humanities Press, 2016. 290–310.

Conathan, Devin, et al. "Rethinking Emotional Desensitization to Violence: Methodological and Theoretical Insights From Social Media Data." *Proceedings of the 8th International Conference on Social Media & Society*. 28–30 July 2017, Toronto *ACM Digital Library*, doi.org/10.1145/3097286.3097333 (Accessed: 3 May 2025).

Ellis, Ralph D. *Curious Emotions: Experiencing and the Creation of Meaning*. Amsterdam: John Benjamins Publishing, 2005.

Fisher, Mark. *The Weird and the Eerie*. 3rd ed. London: Repeater Books, 2016.

Freeman, Nick. "Weird Realism." *Textual Practice* 31 (2017): 1117–32.

Friedrichsen, Dennis. "Breaching the New Weird: Worldbuilding and Atmospheres in China Miéville's *The City & The City*." In *Komparatistik: Jahrbuch der Deutschen Gesellschaft für Allgemeine und Vergleichende Literaturwissenschaft,* ed. Alexandra Müller et al. Bielefeld: Aisthesis Verlag, 2022. 127–49.

Gregg, Melissa, and Gregory J. Seigworth. "An Inventory of Shimmers." In *The Affect Theory Reader,* ed. Melissa Gregg and Gregory J. Seigworth. Durham, NC: Duke University Press, 2010. 1–25.

Greve, Julius, and Florian Zappe. "Introduction: Conceptualizations, Mediations, and Remediations of the American Weird." In *The American Weird: Concept and Medium,* ed. Florian Zappe and Julius Greve. New York: Bloomsbury Academic, 2020. 1–11.

Gunderson, Marianne. "Other Ethics: Decentering the Human in Weird Horror." *Women, Gender & Research* 26, Nos. 2–3 (2017): 12–24.

Harris, Wendell. "John Lane's Keynotes Series and the Fiction of the 1890s." *PMLA* 83 (1968): 1407–13.

Herbert, Cornelia, et al. "Buzzwords: Early Cortical Responses to Emotional Words During Reading." *Psychological Science* 18 (2007): 475–80.

Joshi, S. T. *The Evolution of the Weird Tale*. New York: Hippocampus Press, 2004.

———. *The Weird Tale*. Austin: University of Texas Press, 1990.

Korsmeyer, Carolyn. *Savoring Disgust: The Foul and the Fair in Aesthetics*. Oxford: Oxford University Press, 2011.

Lacan, Jacques. *The Four Fundamental Concepts of Psycho-Analysis*. Tr. Jacques-Alain Miller. New York: Penguin, 1994.

Lane, Joel. "This Spectacular Darkness." In *This Spectacular Darkness,* ed. John Howard and Mark Valentine. Leyburn, UK: Tartarus Press, 2016. 1–12.

Lee-Price, Simon. "Black Matters: The Cosmic Horror of Thomas Ligotti." *London Conference in Critical Thought.* 30 June–1 July 2023, London (Unpublished) *Buckinghamshire New University Repository,* bnu.repository.guildhe.ac.uk/id/eprint/1869 (Accessed: 30 May 2025).

Ligotti, Thomas. "Purity." In *Teatro Grottesco*. London: Virgin, 2008. 3–21.

Lovecraft, H. P. *Collected Essays.* Ed. S. T. Joshi. New York: Hippocampus Press, 2004–06. 5 vols.

———. *Collected Fiction: A Variorum Edition.* Ed. S. T. Joshi. New York: Hippocampus Press, 2015–17. 3 vols.

———. "Letters to Farnsworth Wright." *Lovecraft Annual* No. 8 (2014): 5–59.

———. "Supernatural Horror in Literature." In *The Annotated Supernatural Horror in Literature.* Ed. S. T. Joshi. 2nd ed. New York: Hippocampus Press, 2012.

Luckhurst, Roger. "The Weird: a Dis/orientation." *Textual Practice* 31 (2017): 1041–61.

Machin, James. *Weird Fiction in Britain 1880–1939*. Cham, Switzerland: Palgrave Gothic, 2018.

Manguel, Alberto. "Foreword." In *Black Water: The Anthology of Fantastic Literature,* ed. Alberto Manguel. London: Pan, 1983. xvi–xix.

Massumi, Brian. "The Autonomy of Affect." *Cultural Critique* 31, No. 2 (1995): 83–109.

Mauro, Laura. *Sing Your Sadness Deep*. Pickering, ON: Undertow, 2019.

Miall, David S. "Emotions and the Structuring of Narrative Responses." *Poetics Today* 32 (2011): 323–48.

Miéville, China. "Afterweird: The Efficacy of a Worm-Eaten Dictionary." In *The Weird: A Compendium of Strange and Dark Stories,* ed. Ann VanderMeer and Jeff VanderMeer. London: Corvus, 2011. 1113–16.

———. "'God, that's a merciless question': China Miéville's Interview from *Weird Tales.*" Interview by Jeff VanderMeer. *JeffVanderMeer.com,* 2008, www.jeffvandermeer.com/blog/2009/06/16/god-thats-a-merciless-question-china-mievilles-interview-from-weird-tales (Accessed: 2 May 2025).

———. "M. R. James and the Quantum Vampire: Weird; Hauntological: Versus and/or and and/or or?" In *Collapse: Philosophical Research and Development,* ed. Robin Mackay, Volume 4. Falmouth: Athenaeum Press, 2008. 105–28.

———. "Weird Fiction." In *The Routledge Companion to Science Fiction,* ed. Mark Bould et al. Abingdon: Routledge, 2009. 510–15.

Newell, Jonathan. *A Century of Weird Fiction, 1832–1937: Disgust, Metaphysics and the Aesthetics of Cosmic Horror*. Cardiff: University of Wales Press, 2020.

Onishi, Brian. "Weird Ecologies and the Uncanny in *The Happening.*" In *Philosophy, Film, and the Dark Side of Interdependence,* ed. Jonathan Beever. London: Lexington, 2020. 157–73.

Pedersen, Jan B. W. "Weird Fiction: A Catalyst for Wonder." In *Wonder, Education, and Human Flourishing: Theoretical, Empirical, and Practical Perspectives,* ed. Anders Schinkel. Amsterdam: VU UP, 2020. 318–31.

Poe, Edgar Allan. *Selected Tales.* Ed. David Van Leer. Oxford: Oxford University Press, 1998.

———. "The Philosophy of Composition." In Poe's *Essays and Reviews.* Ed. G. R. Thompson. New York: Library of America, 1984. 13–25.

Rauth, Thomas. "Forms and Functions of Description in the (New) Weird." *Anglia* 141 (2023): 407–30.

Robinson, Jenefer. *Deeper Than Reason: Emotion and Its Role in Literature, Music, and Art.* Oxford: Clarendon Press, 2009.

Sheedy, Alessandro. "Perverted by Language: Weird Fiction and the Semiotic Anomalies of a Genre." Ph.D. diss.: Tasmania University, 2017. University of Tasmania, doi.org/10.25959/23239916.v1 (Accessed: 2 May 2025).

Thacker, Eugene. *Tentacles Longer than Night: Horror of Philosophy.* Vol. 3. Winchester, UK: Zero Books, 2015.

Turnbull, Jonathon. "Weird." *Environmental Humanities* 13 (2021): 275–80.

VanderMeer, Ann, and Jeff VanderMeer. "Introduction." In *The Weird: A Compendium of Strange and Dark Stories,* ed. Ann VanderMeer and Jeff VanderMeer. London: Corvus, 2011. xv–xx.

Webb, Toyah. "'Her Brains Are All Over Her Body': Jeff VanderMeer's Avian Weird." *Animal Studies Journal* 11 (2022): 80–101.

A Rose for the Sleepwalker

James Ulmer

A front had swept through town the previous night, and I'd gone out for a walk that morning in the cool, clear air, watched a pair of fish hawks circling, riding the blue currents high above the rooftops and trees of the neighborhood. As I was returning home, the phone rang. I threw the deadbolt behind me, stepped quickly across the room, and, recognizing the number, snatched up the receiver at once.

"Hey, Garrett. What's up?"

His usual habit was to call in the evening, after a glass of wine or two, so I was a little surprised to hear from him.

"Glad I caught you," he said. "I know this is a strange request, but is there any way you can drive up here? I need to talk to you."

I heard the note of urgency in his voice at once, though he was trying to disguise it. For more than thirty years, as I'd moved back and forth across the country, anywhere I had the opportunity to pay the rent and paint for a while, he'd lived in the same five-bedroom house in a shady, wide-lawned community north of Atlanta. No matter where I was, he'd always kept in touch. His son and daughter were grown now and out on their own, and three months ago his wife, Elaine, had died unexpectedly after a brief illness. The fact is, I was worried about him.

"Sure," I said. "Are you at home?"

"No. I'm at the cabin."

I'd been to his house before but never to the cabin. I wrote down the careful directions he gave me and told him I was on my way.

I headed north to I-10, then caught 75 heading up into Georgia. A mix of curiosity and concern kept my foot heavy on the gas pedal. I reached the outskirts of Atlanta in less than five hours but lost some time on the crowded beltway that circles the city. Once north of town, I exited on a northbound interstate and began the steady, gradual ascent into the mountains.

The North Georgia Mountains are an extension of the Appalachians, branching off south and west before leveling out in a series of rolling foothills. I had never seen that part of the state before; the countryside was wild and beautiful. That day, the leaves of the massive white oak and mountain ash trees climbing the steep ridges were splashed with fall color, the old-growth forest punctuated by the occasional straighter, darker shapes of pines. Streams rushed down from the high ground rising from the roadway, the cold, iron-scented water chilling the air, and I lost count of how many bridges I crossed. I turned off on a sequence of state roads, each one smaller, narrower, less traveled than the last. As the afternoon wore on, I found myself more and more grateful for Garrett's meticulous directions: I would not have wanted to be lost in those mountains with the darkness closing in.

At last, putting my battered Honda in low gear, I turned off on an undulating local road that climbed a steep incline in a series of hairpin turns, the narrow, twisting blacktop shaded by the branches of enormous oaks. In exactly three-quarters of a mile I reached a gravel drive framed by a pair of fieldstone pillars, the rusted chain connecting them lying on the ground. I pulled up the drive, motor groaning, and parked under the raised A-frame cabin next to Garrett's silver Lexus SUV.

Emerging from my car into the declining daylight, I looked up to see him stationed above me, silhouetted at the edge of the overhanging deck, a hand raised in greeting.

Ten minutes later Garrett and I sat on his deck, a rustic teak table between us, looking west over the tops of the trees that fell away at our feet down the nearly vertical descent. The light was dropping quickly now, casting a red wash over the multicolored leaves. A bottle of zinfandel, a wine he particularly liked, stood open on the table. I'd picked up two bottles of it on my way out of town.

I poured myself a generous portion, then him. He drained his glass at once without bothering to taste the wine. I filled it again and braced myself for what was coming.

"First of all," he said, "thanks for driving all the way up here. I realize you probably have better ways to spend your weekend."

My eyes traveled over the sweep of oaks and sycamores so different from the wind-bent cedars and stretches of black needlerush in the marshes along the coast.

"Glad to be here," I assured him.

"You may change your mind when you hear what I have to say. I have a rather strange story to tell you."

I shrugged. "Try me."

He leaned back in his chair. Patches of sunlight and leaf-shadow covered him in a harlequin design. A sudden breath of wind stirred the treetops, and the pattern shifted and flowed over him. The autumn cold, bringing with it an intimation of ice and winter, began to rise out of the forest.

"About a month after Elaine died," he began, "I started having dreams about her. The odd thing is, I've never been one to remember my dreams, and if I ever did, I never paid the slightest bit of attention to them. But these dreams were so *real,* nothing strange or disjointed about them. They didn't seem like dreams at all. Usually we were just talking, exactly as we always had, and when I woke up and realized that I was alone, it felt as if she had just stepped out of the room. The only incongruous note was that Elaine was always much younger than she was at the time of her death. She looked exactly like she did when we first met—twenty-three and just off the train from Louisiana. What do you make of that?"

"Maybe that's the way you want to remember her."

"Yeah," he said, unconvinced, "maybe. But you know that Elaine was always a beautiful woman her entire life. She knew how to take care of herself."

That was true. She did. She was.

I reached for my wine and studied my friend over the rim of my glass. So far, there was nothing unusual in what he was telling me. Of course a man who misses his dead wife dreams about her. I was silent, waiting; there had to be more. We sat facing the trees. The sun had moved to our right by then, and the leaf-shadow nodded and swayed on the wall between us in the fading light. Soon the sun would drop into the branches, the wind would stop, and dusk would thicken, erasing shadows in the general gloom. Floating above the reach of forest, a thin crescent of moon defined itself in the gradually darkening sky.

"After a few weeks of this," he continued, "I woke up unexpectedly one night in the kitchen. The digital clock on the microwave read *2:13*. I had no idea how I got there, but the feeling was the same. One instant, she'd been standing against the wall, looking intently at me, about to speak—and when I woke up, she was gone. Nothing but shadows and darkness."

The picture was disturbingly vivid.

"You were dreaming. Sleepwalking."

"I was sleepwalking," he replied, "but I wasn't dreaming. When you sleepwalk, you're deeply asleep, but you're not in REM sleep. Your eyes are open, and you see everything in front of you exactly as it is. You grasp a doorknob, turn it, and push open the door to enter a room. You avoid walking into the furniture, pull out a chair, perhaps, to sit at a desk. Apparently, this is often accompanied by night visions."

I took another taste of the wine. "You mean you also see things that aren't there?"

Garrett smiled thinly. "Yeah, that's how my doctor put it. Normally, I would've accepted an explanation like that. But then, some things happened which began to convince me otherwise." He shifted uncomfortably in his chair. "I have a theory about this. I mean, why, under the circumstances, should we assume that we're seeing everything accurately, precisely, but that this one element is a hallucination? Does that make sense to you?"

I didn't know how to answer that. At the time, none of this made sense to me. Fortunately, Garrett didn't wait for a response.

"I believe that what we're seeing—*who* we're seeing—is actually present; that when we're in that particular state, we see things that our eyes can't register during normal waking consciousness." He leaned forward and tapped the table emphatically with his index finger. "But that doesn't mean they aren't there. And when those presences know that we can see them, it makes it easier for them to find us."

We both took a moment then to finish our wine in silence, to fortify ourselves: he for the telling, me for the taking it in. The sun had dropped into the trees by then, and the west was smeared a brilliant crimson, the thin striations of clouds a deep, somber purple. Above that riot of color, the first stars flickered above the crescent moon in the darkness. I rose without a word, walked inside to the kitchen, drew the cork from the second bottle, and returned with it. I filled our glasses and placed the bottle on the table.

Resuming my seat, I asked, "Are you suggesting that Elaine was actually there?"

He nodded. "She was. I'm sure of it."

"What happened to convince you of that?"

"Two things. Three, really. First of all, my doctor checked me into a sleep clinic. I don't suppose you've ever been to one of those?"

When I shook my head, he continued.

"They hook you up to a machine and record your brain wave patterns as you sleep. They also monitor your breathing and film you so they can correlate your brain function to any possible movement you make—talking in your sleep, whatever. My doctor told me that in most cases of sleepwalking the problem simply stops on its own without any need for medication, but given the suddenness and severity of my case, he wanted more information. That was fine with me. By that time, I was waking up in a different room in the house every night."

It was dark now, very dark in that mountain forest far from the lights of any town. I could barely make out Garrett's features across the table from me, but I could feel him thinking. After a moment, he began again.

"A few days later I went back to review the results of my session. The doctor ran the video at fast-forward, slowing the tape to comment when I rolled over in my sleep or my breathing changed. Then something unexpected happened. There was a moment of static on the tape. The picture crackled, went snowy for a second or two, then cleared again, and in that brief interlude I saw a figure standing by my bed. I'm not sure what the doctor saw. He apologized for the poor quality of the tape and said it happened all the time—which is something I've wondered about since—but there was no mistaking the identity of the figure. It was Elaine."

A pause ensued as I struggled with that.

"She stood to my right, looking down at me as I slept. The camera was behind her, shooting from above, so all I could see was the back of her head and a sliver of profile. But it was definitely her. She was wearing one of those flannel hospital gowns that tie in the back."

"That's impossible," I said.

"Right. But it was her."

I considered the possibility that grief had unhinged my old friend or that his mind had imposed on the chaos of static and white noise the thing he most needed to see. But I kept those observations to myself.

"What do you think she wants?" I asked.

"I don't know. I've been asking myself that same question." He drained his glass, and I refilled it and topped my own. "My doctor was rattling on about prescribing a sleep-aid, about my 'recovery,' but I was barely listening. I now understood that my problem was not a medical one, and that I couldn't stay in that house. I came up here to think, to try to get away, but it hasn't worked. That's when I called you. You're the only person I know who would listen to my story without assuming that I was delusional."

I felt a little ashamed when he said that.

"What do you mean, it hasn't worked?"

"You remember I said that three things had happened?"

"Of course."

He pushed back his chair and stood. "Well, let me show you the other two."

Garrett disappeared inside and returned in a moment, something long and thin pinched between his thumb and first finger. He laid it ceremoniously on the table: a long-stemmed rose, black in the nearly moonless night.

"Pick it up," he said.

I did. Bringing it closer, I saw that it actually red, still fresh and sweet-smelling.

"On my way up here," he said, "I stopped and put a dozen red roses on Elaine's grave. When I arrived, I found that"—and he pointed to the rose in my hand—"lying on the kitchen counter."

"But how did it get here?"

"You tell me. No one has been here since January, nine months ago, shortly before Elaine was diagnosed. The place has been locked up tight."

I put the rose down at once.

"And then there was this," he said.

He reached into his shirt pocket and placed something next to the rose. I saw a flash of gold in the darkness and a chain coiled up like a snake on the table.

"Go ahead," he said. "Take a look."

A pendant hung from the chain, a gold heart with a dark red stone in its center, the large stone outlined in smaller diamonds.

"The stone is a garnet," Garrett said, "her birthstone. I gave that to her shortly after Chance was born. It was her favorite piece of jewelry. She was wearing it around her neck, as she'd requested, when they closed the coffin lid on her and nailed it down. When I arrived here yesterday evening, it was lying next to the rose on the counter."

I never sleep well in a new place, even in the best of circumstances, but that night sleep was impossible. The implications of Garrett's story were enough to keep me wide awake, listening to every creak and groan in the cold, drafty cabin. From somewhere out in the darkness, an owl sounded its eerie, interrogatory call, repeated, insistent.

It was hours after midnight when I heard a latch click open and footsteps pass my door. Rising from bed as silently as I could, I felt my way down the shadowy hall to the front room. The crescent moon had long ago passed over the roof and disappeared into the trees behind the house, leaving the front of the cabin as black and lightless as a vault. As my eyes adjusted to the darkness, I saw Garrett standing in profile, staring straight ahead. There was nothing in front of him but a blank wall and the interceding darkness, but everything in his posture—the tension in his shoulders, the way he seemed to lean forward as if drawn into a whispered conversation—suggested an exchange, an appeal. I heard a faint word—*yes*—not his voice, and then he extended a hand, a gleam of gold in his palm. That hand never moved, but as I watched, the gold disappeared link by link—the chain and heart, I realized—as if the fingers of a hand I couldn't see had gradually closed over it.

Startled, I retreated to my room and locked the door.

The next morning I said nothing to Garrett about the night's excursion. Unless he'd woken up, he wouldn't remember what had happened anyway, and I was in no mood to discuss my suspicions. Before I left, I invited him to visit me. I felt that if he could just get away for a while, he'd be fine. The beaches, I told him, were glorious in the fall, with the vacationing families gone and a mellow warmth still lingering. I suggested that he stay at least a week. We'd go to the sea every day, eat flounder and shrimp at a place I knew along the river in the blowing shadow of old live oaks draped with Spanish moss. He told me he looked forward to it, but even then I knew he'd never come.

One evening ten days later, I got a phone call from an Atlanta exchange. I assumed it was Garrett calling from an unfamiliar number, but the voice on the phone identified itself as Chance, Garrett's son. He'd gone to the house to check on his father and found him lying on the floor of his study, dead of a heart attack.

I attended the funeral at the nineteenth-century Episcopal church in the town where he'd lived for so many years. The solemn event, with its stained glass and candles, the sense of ceremony like a secret handshake, seemed unreal to me. As I was leaving, walking across the lot to my car through the pale November light, his son approached and asked me if I had a minute. He then informed me that the cabin had been left to me.

"That's not right," I said. "That cabin should go to you and your sister."

He shook his head. "He wanted you to have it as an artist's retreat. He was very particular about that. Ruthie and I have been well taken care of, believe me."

Chance handed me a manila envelope that, I later discovered, contained the deed to the property and a letter addressed to me. In the letter, Garrett thanked me for being his friend.

It took me weeks to return to the cabin. I knew that taking possession of the place would mean that I'd have to accept that Garrett was gone for good. We'd known each other since we were kids, and I realized that it was unlikely that I'd live long enough to make another friend like him. At last, one late December afternoon found me standing on the deck where we'd had our last exchange, cold in my warmest sweater, looking out at the desolate prospect of miles of empty gray forest, the trees stripped of their autumn colors. I saw at once that he'd been right about the potential of the cabin as a studio. Plate-glass windows everywhere took in the view; there was morning light at the back of the cabin and late light in the front, so I could move my easel around the space like a sundial.

I began to plan out the first canvas I'd paint there, a portrait of Garrett sitting on the deck telling his story, the brilliant autumn landscape falling away at his feet. I imagined a woman with a single long-stemmed rose standing behind him, abstracted, her face turned away, partly obscured in shadow as she gazed off at something outside the picture frame.

Silence and darkness fell over the landscape by slow degrees. I sat up for a while, remembering. A single lamp burning on an end table cast a circle of light on the floor and a second one, drawn slightly out of shape, on the A-frame's slanted ceiling. One summer night when we were twelve, I'd slept over at Garrett's house, and we'd crept down the dark staircase at 2 A.M. and snuck outside together. A dense green scent, undiscernible by daylight, rose from the fragrant lawns. We had both come to suspect that some vital secret had been hidden from us, something we couldn't have named, though all we discovered that night was a raccoon making its humpbacked retreat across a neighbor's back yard, the porch light casting its enormous, distorted shadow over a wooden privacy fence . . .

Finally, sometime after ten, I switched off the lamp, waded through the darkness to the bedroom, and lay down on the comforter. I fell immediately to sleep.

Hours later, in the silent last quarter of the night, I found myself standing in the empty front room of the cabin with no memory of how I'd arrived there. Starlight glinted coldly on the black plate-glass windows. My attention was drawn to a shadow on the wall, and as I watched, the shape detached itself and began to coalesce, to take on dimension until a figure, a woman, stood before me—back turned, a shimmer of tarnished golden hair. When she swung around to face me, I saw at once who it was, and a rush of ice crawled down my spine. She wore the garnet pendant at her throat, the one I'd seen returned to her, black in the lightless dark.

She was beautiful but wrong: breathless, not alive, her unblinking eyes fixed blankly on my face. She seemed inhuman somehow, as unconscious as a flower. I told myself that I was dreaming, but there she stood, five feet in front of me.

I took a step back.

"Why are you here?" I asked. "What do you want?"

I saw her black lips move in the shadows, so I know she answered me. I recall a blurred, lisping whisper, the voice of a sleeper speaking in a trance, but her words have gone back into oblivion.

My heart was racing, and then I found I was awake, fully awake, staring in the darkness at the empty wall.

I left the mountains at dawn. I'll never paint there, as Garrett had hoped I would, and I'll never under any circumstances go back. It's been ten months now, and I haven't walked in my sleep since that night. Instead, I walk the long open stretches of beach along the sea when the sun is high. At times a crowd of gulls will pass over me, calling out plaintively, and I am covered in a cross-stick of wings and shadow, terrified and certain, in that instant, that some presence will arrive from the darkness. I feel then that I am about to remember what she said, but perhaps it's just as well that I haven't.

Larvae of the Sarcophagus

Wade German

Thou little fly, that burrows six feet deep
(Two miles by human scale!) through blackest soil
To plant thy eggs, which soon begin to roil
The mouldered earth where carrion beetles creep,
A coffin, cauldron-like, bubbles below;
Thy insect larvae now consume their meal
With undeniable, ferocious zeal.
O mindless feasters! thou shalt never know
These graveyard corpses once were seeds of ghosts,
Who transcendental, gaze into their plots
As into mirrors—horridly, to see
Their faces swarm, their bodies teeming hosts . . .
They turn their backs, then leave the loathsome lot—
The cemetery of reality!

Brass Tacks

Scott J. Couturier

> Guilt manifests in a myriad of powerful guises. It stalks us, surely as a wild beast; devours inexorably from within, like a parasite; drives us to total self-betrayal in service of some nominal "greater truth." What limit, then, to the power it may impress on inorganic forms, to say nothing of organic forms newly expired?
>
> —Doctor Marvello, *Treatises on Iniquity*

Abe toyed with the rim of his empty coffee cup. Around and around his finger ran, porcelain squeaking faintly. Over-caffeinated, one of his legs bobbed up and down with restless vigor, tip of his shoe fixed rigidly on the tile floor. He kept seeing the same image, muzzle-flash followed by the kid's expression of surprise and despair. His mark—and not even a major one, just $5000 in cash. He still hadn't gone to pick up the money.

The waitress, a middle-aged woman named Laurine, came over, her dark eyes scanning him head to foot. "Need me to top that off? Or you had enough?" She glanced down at his bobbing leg.

Abe grunted, pushing the cup toward her. "I feel bad about it," he said aloud, hardly believing the words as they escaped his mouth.

"Bad about what?" Laurine asked in a cautious tone, knowing the question was a risk. Her face took on a severe expression.

Bang! Was the gun louder, that flare more dazzling? The look on his victim's face . . . *victim?* "It's nothing," Abe said, pulling out his wallet and tossing a few crumpled bills on the Formica tabletop. "I feel bad about something I shouldn't feel bad about. That's all."

Now she offered a faint smile. "What'd you do, kill somebody? I'd feel bad about that if it were me."

He stared at her in disbelief, gaze finally lowering to the empty cup. "It's nothing. I did my job like always, no questions, cash on the barrel. I just did my job." Abe's smooth, expressionless lips hid his clenching teeth.

"We all do what we gotta to survive," Laurine agreed. The place was empty except for him, her, and presumably a cook in back, though Abe hadn't seen any such person. A silence hung on the air like a mask over something terrible; not even any flies, and the fluorescent lighting shone pure, without accompanying hum. Abe looked up at Laurine, taking in her false eyelashes, the generous smear of red on her lips. He'd come here a few times after finishing jobs; sometimes they even flirted. But tonight he could tell she was a little afraid of him. Truth to tell, he felt afraid of himself.

"You know, killing someone isn't bad if the person's bad. And if there's money in it, well, all the better. Sometimes justice comes right out of a gun." He pointed his fingers, moved his thumb like a hammer striking. "Bam! Always one clean shot. I don't waste time, don't like seeing others suffer. Just pay me, and the job gets done. Know what I mean?"

He'd let slip a few things to Laurine before, enough for her to think he was an undercover cop or private investigator. Now, understanding dawned in her eyes, and she actually tottered back a half-step. "You've gotta be joking with me, right?" she said, almost pleading. "I mean, I don't have to go call the cops, do I?"

A shiver ran through him. "No," Abe said, "not tonight, anyways." He stood and loomed over her, his six-foot-four frame hung with a heavy black coat. "In fact, I doubt we'll be seeing each other again." He threw a ten on the table, turned, and pushed through the glass door, wincing as the little bell chimed overhead. Out into the night, sweet and enveloping . . . the moon hung high, flushing the streets with silver marred by streetlight ambiance.

Abe reached down to the concealed holster at his right hip. Empty. He'd left the gun in his target's hand, a perfect suicide frame-up. Guy was supposedly wanted for a lot of things, but Abe found him before the law did. Five thousand dollars, blood money, tithe from the potter's field. He slid his fingers along the leather, then turned and went in search of his car, marine mist billowing around him in tumultuous white shrouds.

Earlier, he'd taken a bus to the nearby town where his mark was staying. Hiding in the bushes by the man's motel, Abe waited for hours, through the fall of freezing dusk. He remembered how moisture had beaded on his face, he sat so perfectly still, like a frog on a lily pad or statue in a cemetery. The target—Peter Marwood—had made someone in the upper echelons angry enough to put a price on his head. Something about cutting drugs with embalming fluid to sell more packets, pocketing the change himself.

Scum. Pusher. Piece of human waste. Abe waited just five minutes after sunset before entering the room and making the kill.

Post-hit, he mocked the corpse up to look like a suicide, but the whole time his hands shook uncontrollably, the sight of Peter's ruined face, his mouth gaping in forever-unspoken protest, searing his mind like a brand. Usually a drink or three would steady his nerves after a difficult job, but whiskey had proven insufficient. So he went with his instinct and headed to the diner instead.

Now Abe could never go back; he'd practically confessed to Laurine. *And I thought she and I might have something,* he reflected as he reached his rented Lexus and popped the locks. *But who am I kidding? Married to the job for me means married to Death. And it's not wise to cheat on her.*

Something odd had happened on the bus ride back into town. Abe heard sounds coming through the floor, as if someone were climbing along the undercarriage. Other passengers noticed it too, but no one said anything. Then, when the bus stopped downtown, he swore he'd seen a shadow fall down and slip off into the urban jungle. Had someone hitched a ride by clinging to the vehicle for nearly an hour over rough backroads? *Guess that's one way to handle not having the fare,* he'd thought.

As he drove toward the airport, again and again Peter's agonized face flashed through Abe's mind. The kid had whimpered as he went down, then gurgling out a half-heard word through a mouthful of blood. One of his messier shots, but he'd been taken aback by how young Peter was. Young and pale-faced, haunted by some kind of sorrow; not the look of a hardened, or even softened, criminal. Also, Peter had no kit with him, no gun, no nightsuit, nothing to indicate he was an operator of any kind. Yet Abe set everything up as instructed, propping the body against the wall, securing the gun in its already-stiffening hand and making the splattered brains look related to the shot. Nothing to worry about: he'd killed a hundred people, what was one more? But guilt, like a spreading venom, festered in Abe as he navigated through the mist-woven streets. He'd been reflecting on his life lately, coming to some unpleasant conclusions about himself. But this job—he'd just killed an innocent kid, *knew* he had.

Should he even go pick up the money? Just put his foot in the tank and head for the West Coast instead, to a safehouse he knew . . . could he look his boss in the eye without accusing him of killing an innocent? For that matter, what about all those other kills? It's not as if Abe did a deep dive on his victims, before or after. *Victims!* Now he had multiple victims! Abe gulped as a droplet of sweat trailed over his Adam's apple like a dagger-tip. He was out of the city now, heading toward the airport. No one else was out on the road, just the restless mist that coursed over the hood of his car, pulsing into the cab through the heat/AC vents. Was it getting harder to breathe? Was he having a panic attack? More than a few of his marks experienced them on realizing their fate. Ahead he could see the airport lights shining up into the hazy night sky, looking like solid columns of lurid, luminous marble. For just a moment he lost all sense of time and space, the Lexus seeming to hover in a netherwhere of coiling vapors.

Then he was at the gate, passing through, waving to the guard (the first person he'd seen since leaving the diner). He did jobs in this city often, since the gangs here were opposed to his boss—and his boss's boss. But somehow he knew he wouldn't be back this way. In his mind he saw the hotel room as he'd arranged it, Peter dead and slumped against the gore-smeared wall with mouth agape, pistol clutched in his rigor-mortis grip. Even as he surveyed the memory, Peter's one remaining eye cleared of death's blear, the wide-blown pupil contracting as it focused on Abe with a horrid hatred, a mania of vengeful wrath.

Abe had ditched his kit in a prearranged spot; there was nothing in the Lexus to incriminate. He left it with an employee at the entrance, went in with his meager luggage, and approached the appropriate gate. It was several hours before his plane left, so he arranged himself as he often did with a newspaper covering his eyes, hands crossed over his broad chest. Normally he would fall asleep within moments, but now his thoughts were too troubled to permit even the slightest vestige of dream-whimsy.

An hour on, he slid the newspaper aside when two security employees walked past, talking to each other; each carried a heavy flashlight that could double as a cudgel. "Someone's out on the tarmac," he heard the woman say to the man, "we need to check it out." On they went, Abe thinking nothing else of it, introspection again fixating on the mock suicide scene, or rewinding minutes before to the flare of his gun, the look of awful surprise on Peter's face. Peter—usually he would have forgotten his name by now. Was this the end of his career? He'd seen other hitmen go soft, wearying of all the amassed death. That's why he took the jobs he did, clear-cut morally, never involving women or children. After twenty years of delivering lead, as he liked to call it, he barely had enough saved to keep a roof over his head. If another appliance busted he'd need to start taking jobs of a whole different caliber. Wasn't that why he came all the way out here for a measly $5000?

"What's a life worth?" his boss once asked him. "You tell me what it's worth, Abe."

Young and stupid, with only a few notches on his belt, Abe had frozen, then said, "I don't know, sir."

"Well, I'll tell you. It's worth whatever someone is willing to pay." And he'd laughed, Abe laughing nervously alongside him.

That was many years, many bodies ago.

Perhaps Abe did doze for a bit; the next sound he heard was a muffled voice announcing that his flight was ready for boarding. He pulled the newspaper from his face and halfway stood up, only then noticing a speck of blood on the lower left breast of his jacket. "How could I have missed that?" he muttered to himself as he scrubbed it off with his thumb. Had Laurine noticed? Maybe it blended in with the black leather. But if she had . . .

The flight itself proved unremarkable in any respect, save that Abe continued to be haunted by visions of the killing. They would ebb and sink and dissipate, so that he finally felt capable of closing his eyes. And then—the flare of his gun, the stink of powder and blood and urine and shit commingling. For distraction he looked out the window at the passing night, half-quarter moon lowering below the horizon just as sunlight started welling in the east. He hadn't slept, and felt like shit; usually he took a nap after a job, but just look at him now! Abe waved a hand over his face and smelled something coppery, remnant of the blood wiped off his jacket. The rumble of wheels announced a snack cart at his side, but Abe shut his eyes and pretended to be asleep until the stewardess moved on.

That poor kid, he thought. *And they'll think he did it to himself. His family will put him in the ground believing he took his own life.* Unfathomably, he felt a prickle of tears gathering in his squinched-shut eyes.

Fuck no! You didn't cry at your own son's funeral. No way are you going to break down over some dead sucker who deserved what was coming to him. You think the bosses would put you on just any dumb kid? Have a little faith, have a little faith, have a little faith. So the mantra was repeated as he sped through the dawn, sleep evasive, and every so often the copper stink of blood flitting over his nostrils.

Arriving in his home city, Abe disembarked after trying to make himself look presentable in the cramped bathroom. Someone had been sick in there, puke spilling down the side of the gray plastic suction toilet. The smell reminded Abe of other bodily fluids. *He shit and pissed himself, like a little kid. What's more, he did it before I shot him. What kind of criminal shits and pisses themselves at sight of a gun?*

Abe went home—a squat two-story with its own yard, even a few trees—and tried to get some sleep. For the next fourteen hours he tossed and turned in bed, waking to a news report on TV about a man inspectors found clinging inside his plane's left-rear wheel well. The stowaway looked dead to them, so they called for an ambulance to come retrieve the body, but it was gone when they returned. A manhunt in the surrounding area was ongoing.

Abe shivered as he sipped at a cup of too-hot coffee. He felt something besides guilt today, an even more unwelcome visitor: fear. Of what exactly he couldn't say, though the news report rattled him so much he decided to skip town, all on his own volition. He was repacking his bags when the phone rang.

"Yeah?" he said, picking it up and answering without looking at the caller ID. Only five people had this number.

Silence for a moment. Then his boss's voice, familiar but with an inflection he'd never heard before. "Abe? That you?" he demanded. "We gotta talk, you and me."

Abe stood there, naked except for his boxer shorts, and nodded into the phone. "Of course," he added, realizing the boss couldn't see him. "If it's about not picking up the money, I just wasn't feeling well. Decided to come back here and sleep it off. Must be food poisoning, or one of those twenty-four-hour viruses."

"What happened on the job, Abe? You never let me down before. Not once in all these years. So what happened to the kid? You snitch on us, or what?"

Abe's body shot cold, the deep cold of a meat freezer he'd once hidden in for almost a day in pursuit of a mark. "What do you mean?" he asked in a thin, baffled voice. "I did the kid, set it up like I always do. What's the problem?"

"Owner broke into the room today when no one answered. He found it empty, Abe. No body, no blood, no gun. Bed was even neatly turned down. Tell me you took him somewhere else and did him, left him in a ditch or something." Was there panic in the boss's voice? Abe took three deeps gulps of air before he could reply.

"I did him," he said at last, voice shaking. "Shot him in the left side of the head—he was left-handed, you know I read every dossier down to teeth and brass tacks. I set it up like always, like *always,* and left without anyone seeing. No way he was alive; no way anyone but hazmat could scrub all those brains off the wall."

"Well," the boss said, in a resigned voice, "it does seem we have a problem. You're telling me you did the job, but there's no sign the job's been done. I know this was little fish for you, but hey, that's no reason to insult my intelligence by making up stories. You know what happens to storytellers in this organization, Abe. You've helped me out with plenty of them."

"What do you want me to do, sir?" It was an automated response, emerging from his military past. "Go back and kill the kid again?"

"Too late for that. He's gone, vamoose, flown the coop. The whole operation is a scrub, Abe. And you know what? It might be a good idea for you to leave town for a while. We don't know how this will play out yet. After what the kid did—"

"What did he do, sir?" Abe asked spontaneously. "Youngest one I've ever hit. It's not worth five thousand dollars if I can't get him off my mind."

"Developing a conscience now? Guy's out there peddling contaminated drugs! You read the file, which shows the little shit's age."

"Took the job before scanning his bio deets." *I trusted you,* he added in his mind, *to know my limits.*

"Not on us then, is it?" the boss countered. "Teeth and brass tacks, heh. He's younger than your usual, but you said you needed work, and this was the first job I had. But you can rest easy, since the kid's alive; figure you went soft on him because he just learned to shave last week. Unless you can explain how the body went missing?" His tone shifted again, acquiring a lascivious hint. "You know, we make provisions for our best agents. I've never had to intercede on your behalf, but whatever pervert stuff you may get up to, it's forgiven preemptively. Just be honest, Abe. Honest Abe. Heh, now isn't that funny?"

Abe's grip on the phone tightened. "You still haven't told me everything. Contaminated drugs are peanuts. What did that kid deserve to die for?"

"You know, Abe? I don't like this new tone. Remember I don't have to tell you anything, except who to kill and when to kill them. It's never been a problem before, though sometimes I do make up stories so you'll feel proud."

Abe almost said something that would have cost him his head. Instead, he drew in a deep breath, glanced at his mostly-packed suitcase, exhaled, and asked, "You want me to skip town over this?"

"Consider it charity. Here you are, lying to me bald-faced, saying you did the kid when there's not a drop of evidence. His car was still there, but he could easily jack another one. Best thing for everyone involved is for you to just vanish for a minute, go to the fucking islands or something and sweat it out in the sun. If the kid's dead, well, we'll know soon enough. If he's not, we'll know even sooner. *Capisce?*"

"Capisce," Abe answered, and hung up the phone. He then went to the bathroom and splashed water on his face. Staring at himself in the mirror, he was amazed to see livid red veins in his eyes. *As if I haven't slept at all, or just smoked a whole joint.* He started shivering again, this time with a kind of nameless apprehension. The kid's body was gone. It was missing. No blood or brains on the wall, no sign of him at all. How was it possible? Did that mean—

Abe stiffened as he heard a creak, a *footstep,* come from downstairs. This was followed by the rustling sound of someone seating himself in the plush chair by his front door. Moving so fast he got out of breath, Abe crammed his remaining clothes and passport into the suitcase, muffling the clasps with his hands as he snapped the lid shut. Then, without missing a beat, he was out the back door attached to his bedroom. This led to a rickety iron stairwell that ran down into the weedy backyard. Sprinting, gasping, Abe leapt the low stone wall ringing the yard and made for the garage, where he kept his old truck gassed up in case of emergencies. Hopping in the cab, he turned the engine over and gunned it down an alleyway toward the main road. In his haste he hadn't even grabbed a gun; no matter, there were two handguns strapped under each seat in the truck. Abe breathed easier for just a moment before remembering the creak downstairs, the subtle rustle of a body sinking into the chair by the door. Most likely the boss had decided he was too big of a liability. Probably sent out some greenhorn to deal with him, a sort of twisted initiation ritual. *Not this time!* he thought, laughter bubbling loathsome on his lips.

Abe made it to the airport, bought a ticket, and went someplace else. Someplace equatorial, where he could sip drinks out of coconuts as he'd seen in the movies, spending what was left of his cash without care. He kept away from phones, knowing the boss would send someone for him; best to pretend he didn't exist, and hope it took. Meanwhile he tried to enjoy himself, though visions of Peter's murder ran on a loop in both his waking and unconscious mind. Sometimes he smelled the stink of gunpowder; at other times he felt a thin mist of blood spray over his cheek. And his jacket: Abe had scoured the breast for some hint of the bloodstain, but found nothing. In spite of all evidence to the contrary, he knew he'd killed the kid. Killing people was his business. But—there was no body, meaning no crime had been committed. So why should he feel guilty at all? *The snake devours it own tail,* he mused, drowning his unease in wave upon wave of fruit-flavored tequila drinks topped with miniature umbrellas.

After two weeks his funds started running low. Then, to his surprise, Abe discovered a fresh deposit from the boss's account. It came with a note: "Hope you're enjoying the sunshine. No sign of the kid yet, alive or dead. Come back when you're ready, and we'll talk. No reason to ruin a good business relationship over a misunderstanding."

Abe puzzled over the message for an entire afternoon. So the boss knew where he was . . . but then, he'd ordered Abe to get out of town. The note's familiar tone at least meant he'd called off the hit. Abe could still hear that creak from the living room downstairs, vivid in his memory as Peter whimpering. Maybe the boss never had it out for him in the first place. Maybe . . .

He took the next plane back, sleeping almost the whole trip, though his dreams remained unsettled.

Arriving back in the city, Abe found a car waiting for him. A Mustang this time, very nice; the boss must really want to get on his good side. Maybe they'd finally found the kid's body. Abe had decided the motel owner must have discovered the corpse, panicked, cleaned the room, and disposed of the remains before the police investigation. It was the only scenario that made any sense. Either that, or Peter had survived somehow . . . *boom, splash!* Brains painting the wall in curlicues of gore. A hollow head almost caving inwards, one eye shot clean out. The body falling . . . *the body.* And again those waves of remorse, of regret not just for killing Peter, but for almost everyone he'd turned a gun on in his long tenure. The self-deceptions he usually employed to perceive himself as an agent of good were systematically dismantled; not prone to self-examination, Abe had found plentiful time to abstract beneath the Caribbean sun. One way or another, he was out of the business, out of it for good. No more faking suicides, planting guns, lying to himself. The boss would argue with him, probably threaten him, but it was his life and his rules, god damn it. Time for the killer to take control.

He pulled into the entrance of his driveway. Flanked by two pedestals of cement, topped with crouching griffins; a medieval affectation, left over from the early days when he'd worn a leisure jacket while on the job. He'd even had one of those fake crests drawn up for himself, intending to have it embroidered on his breast pocket. However, events soon disabused him of that early naïveté, and he'd traded in his entire wardrobe for a black coat, black shirts, and black pants. The outfit of an executioner. Not a conscious decision, but then his life never felt like one he'd chosen. That first kill was just for some pocket money, so he could feed his kid . . . the second kill was easier, but then the mark had been a mass murderer. By the tenth he'd constructed a mythology of justice around his actions. Shooting Peter had shattered his delusion, cracking for years now; the kid's look of terror, of resentment at his cruel fate, radiated in Abe's brain like a fever-germ. He'd never live it down, never take another life, not even in self-defense. *Especially not in self-defense.*

In the midst of this maundering self-pity, Abe suddenly froze, slamming on the brakes. Looking ahead, he saw the final slant of evening sunlight shining through the bay windows fronting his integrated living room/patio. This light seemed to glow on a head of tow-colored hair, faded yellow like old straw. In a flash he was transported back to the motel room, leveling the gun while Peter's eyes bulged out like a hanging man as he stumbled backwards, the kid making wordless protestations before the trigger was pulled and the bullet loosed. It entered through his left eye, blew out the back of his head. The body went down like a ragdoll, a useless broken thing; more strings he'd cut, a candle blown out by a scythe. Peter had convulsed, twitching in his death throes, chunks of brain dripping down the wall like jelly. His pale blond hair was caked in red.

No one came back after that; no one survived that. But there could be no doubt who Abe saw sitting in his living room, halfway turned from the window, gun held at the ready in his left hand. It was the same chair he'd heard someone settle into—the exact same .38 caliber he'd planted on Peter. Abe's mouth went dry as he reached down to clench the grip of his new snub-nose, only useful at short range. He could sneak around the back, go up the iron spiral stair, though that would undoubtedly alert Peter. No question the kid had staked himself out in the living room with pistol in hand, waiting for Abe's return. The only question was why he'd positioned himself so carelessly in front of the window, easy prey if he had a scope with him. But all Abe had were his vacation clothes, a couple of useless souvenirs, and the snub-nose. He got out of the car, stood and swayed as he stared at the gun in Peter's hand, held tightly in a grip that looked wrong somehow, twilight making it difficult to tell what exactly alarmed him. Perhaps the absolute rigidity of the fingers? Almost he turned on the headlights, but that would spoil the element of surprise.

Abe drew out his gun and crouched low, creeping towards his prey. No doubt he would kill the kid this time, kill him deader than any man who ever lived. Of course he'd felt wrong about the job; he'd done it wrong. Peter had survived somehow and come after him. Did the boss know? Maybe they were working together. The deposit, and the jovial note summoning him home . . . Closer now, and no question it was Peter. Abe could see his cheek and the side of his nose, make out the characteristic curve of his jawline, oddly swollen. He forgot the names of his kills, but never their faces. Only of late had they started haunting him.

Just then Peter trembled and bent sideways, propping his head against one of the chair's upholstered wings to peer out the window. Abe swore and raised his gun; then, at seeing the face, he shook and sweated profusely, stumbled backwards, raised the snub-nose to his own temple, and fired a single universe-ending shot.

The boss steepled his fingers, going over the report again. A half-drunk bottle of Scotch sat at his left elbow. He was trying to understand how one of his best, most loyal men could have done something so completely out of character.

Why would Abe kill himself? He just wasn't the type. And why, oh why, did he go and stash Peter Marwood's body in his house? The state of advanced decay indicated the corpse had sat in the chair for the full two weeks Abe was abroad on a company-funded holiday. In fact, an eruption of post-mortem gases had lolled the head to one side, making it seem as if the corpse leered out the window with its sole putrid eye. An autopsy of Peter found a bullet in his skull, the exploded brains seeming to have been crammed back inside; it matched the gun clutched in his decomposing hand. Meanwhile, the bullet in Abe's brain came from the snub-nose the boss had thoughtfully stowed in his new car's glove compartment.

"I told him to let me know if it was pervert stuff, that I wouldn't judge," the boss muttered to himself as he lit his twelfth cigar of the day, also pouring out another dram. "No wonder he was feeling guilty. And that dead kid in the window, staring out from a face all coated in maggots . . . guess poor Abe just couldn't take it anymore."

Pathmate

Manuel Pérez-Campos

Do not despair, Countess, of thy beauty,
that it has brought a hundred suitors
to thy court—accomplished warriors
all, yet unsuccessful in their plea.
Few are willing to love so utterly—
that witnessing on thy palm the harbingers
of grief when pillaged by the horrors
of thy fanged sins—would yet remain with thee.

'Tis not alone beauty he should love,
but its denial, too—for one implies
the other, and, in one form, together move.
This thou seek'st: the gentleness of eyes
unfounded in deceit; and, though not found,
is better than the folly they propound.

The Rock Brought Shlock

Edward Guimont

In a 10 December 1932 letter to R. H. Barlow, apparently in response to comments by Barlow on upcoming H. G. Wells film adaptations, H. P. Lovecraft mentioned that he had not seen the 1919 adaptation of Wells's 1901 novel *The First Men in the Moon* (*OFF* 45). It is somewhat surprising that Barlow even knew of it, as Lovecraft was not alone in missing out on it; for decades it has been considered a lost movie, with nothing but a few set photos remaining (Gifford 102–3). But Abdul Alhazred's famous maxim, "That is not dead which can eternal lie" (*CF* 2.40), applies to lost films as much as it does to ancient gods. Prime examples are the several 1960s episodes of the British science fiction staple *Doctor Who,* wiped by the metropolitan BBC but with copies discovered decades later in the hands of private collectors, or former BBC studios in countries that had been British colonies at the time, such as Nigeria and the UAE (Kistler 81–82). Indeed, the Spanish-language version of the 1931 *Dracula* adaptation, which Lovecraft hated, was considered lost for decades—as was the 1933 film *Berkeley Square,* one of his favorite films (Migliore and Strysik 12–15). And now, thanks to Kino Lorber, another film—if not entirely lost, at least long snared in the tangle of rights issues—has finally been made accessible after decades, one with its own Lovecraftian connection: the 1963 B-movie *The Spacewoman Brought Terror,* an extremely loose adaptation of "The Colour out of Space."

Lovecraft was famously a stickler about movie adaptations—disliking *Dracula* and *Frankenstein* (both 1931), though being more sanguine on two based on Wells sources, *Island of Lost Souls* (1932), an adaptation of *The Island of Doctor Moreau,* and *The Invisible Man* (1933)—and proclaiming that he would never allow any of his own works to be adapted to film (Migliore and Strysik 2, 6; *OFF* 18, 57). Obviously, film adaptations were eventually made; Peter Cannon's alternate-history *The Lovecraft Chronicles* even includes an amusing segment detailing a 1930s serial based on "Herbert West—Reanimator" produced by Hal Roach Studios (Cannon 82–85). The actual 1985 film adaptation of *Re-Animator* played a major role in opening up Lovecraftian pastiches, as during development, director Stuart Gordon's lawyer was the first to determine that Lovecraft's works were in public domain, and therefore there was no need to seek licensing from Arkham House (Gaspard 103). This was certainly not the case in 1963, when *The Spacewoman Brought Terror* appeared—although whether that mattered at all was part of the controversy behind the film, leading to years of legal issues and critical amnesia.

The film's origins lie in a major historical development. On 16 June 1963, the Soviet spacecraft *Vostok 6* was launched, orbiting the Earth for three days with its sole cosmonaut crew before returning safely. That occupant was Valentina Tereshkova, who had become the first woman in space, beating the US in another early space milestone.[1] This new Soviet victory in the Space Race stung, coming as it did not only less than a year after John F. Kennedy had publicly committed the US to beating the USSR to the moon by 1970, but immediately after NASA had publicly rejected accepting female astronaut candidates.[2] This made Tereshkova a figure of inspiration around the world, especially for women interested in science and science fiction (Strausbaugh 160). As recounted in the documentary *An Adventure in Space and Time,* one such woman to take inspiration from Tereshkova was Verity Lambert, a young Brit-

---

1. In a bit of synchronicity, Tereshkova was born on 6 March 1937, just a little over a week before Lovecraft's death.

2. The second Soviet woman in space was Svetlana Savitskaya, who in the early 1980s became both the first woman to fly into space multiple times and the first woman to perform a spacewalk. In contrast, the first American in space, Sally Ride, would not fly until 1983.

ish television producer. Lambert was beginning to develop a new educational science fiction show that would debut on 23 November that year, to be called *Doctor Who*.

Doctor Who also drew inspiration from the 1953–57 *Quatermass* serials by Nigel Kneale, whose Lovecraftian themes have been well documented; after leaving *Doctor Who* in 1965, Lambert would eventually produce the 1979 film *Quatermass IV* (Kistler 2–4; Migliore and Strysik 86–91; Gifford 85–86). *Doctor Who* follows the adventures of the nameless alien Doctor, who travels across space and time with various human companions in his TARDIS, a time- and space-travel machine that is bigger on the inside and permanently stuck in the external shape of a London police call box. Science fiction historian Alan Kistler has noted that a predecessor of the TARDIS is the "Time Locker" from the 1942 story of the same name by Lovecraft's epistolary acquaintance Henry Kuttner, which is both a door to the future and bigger on the inside than seems from the outside (Kistler xiv). In the 1970s, Brian Lumley wrote a series of Lovecraft pastiche novels featuring his character Titus Crow, who travels through space and time in a "time-clock." In a 1984 interview, Robert M. Price made the connection between the clock and the TARDIS, but Lumley stated that the idea had instead come from the "coffin-shaped clock" from "Through the Gates of the Silver Key," leaving open the possibility that that also might have been a TARDIS inspiration (Price 55; *CF* 3.277).

One of the original actors cast by Lambert for *Doctor Who* was Jacqueline Hill, who would play the London schoolteacher Barbara Wright, inadvertently swept up with the Doctor to become his adventuring companion. Hill had previously been in the 1957 BBC adaptation of Lovecraft aficionado Rod Serling's teleplay *Requiem for a Heavyweight;* notably, Hill convinced the director to cast as her character's husband an unknown young actor named Sean Connery (Kistler 38–40). However, what drew Lambert to Hill was that she had just played Tereshkova—of a sort—in the Anglo-American science fiction film *The Spacewoman Brought Terror*. In the film, Hill played Soviet cosmonaut Olga Kovalenko. While Kovalenko was most directly inspired by Tereshkova and the film meant to capitalize off her flight, the name—and several character details—were drawn from fictional female Soviet aviators in two recent films, Janet Leigh's Olga Orlief from *Jet Pilot* (1957) and Katharine Hepburn's Vinka Kovalenko from *The Iron Petticoat* (1956). This demonstrated not only the rushed development of *Spacewoman,* but its liberal approach to 'inspiration'—setting up its litigious future.

The Space Race began with the Soviet launch of the first satellite, *Sputnik I,* on 4 October 1957 and its follow-up, *Sputnik II,* on 3 November, done to commemorate both the fortieth anniversary of the communist revolution and the Soviet contributions to the International Geophysical Year (IGY), an international agreement for scientific exploration. This led to a sudden reaction in the West, including the formation of NASA on 29 July 1958. Beating NASA to the punch in responding to *Sputnik,* however, was Roger Corman, with his film *War of the Satellites.* Riding off the panic over the Soviet launches, Corman began production on the film in December 1957—just after the explosive failure of the first American satellite launch attempt, *Vanguard*—and released it to theaters in May 1958. In this, Corman won his own B-film space race. The first successful US satellite, *Explorer I,* was launched in February 1958. The excitement over *Explorer*'s launch led to a cinematic attempt to capitalize on it: *Space Master X-7,* which came out that June. This film—whose working title was *Missile into Space*—had a somewhat Lovecraftian plot of its own, about a space probe returning an alien fungus to Earth. Its co-writers had earlier worked on the scripts for the more respectable films *Conquest of Space* (1955), *Forbidden Planet* (1956), and *Invasion of the Body Snatchers* (1956).

It therefore made sense that when Tereshkova's flight made a major sensation—and spurred on by the failure to take similar advantage over the prior crewed spaceflight milestones of Yuri Gagarin (1961), Alan Shepard (1961), or John Glenn (1962)—Corman lobbied American International Pictures (AIP) to fund a film to capitalize off her moment in the cultural zeitgeist. The director chosen was Reginald Le Borg, a prolific workman who had directed several Universal horror B-movies in the 1940s, and would immediately go on to direct *Diary of a Madman,* an adaptation of Guy de Maupassant's "The Horla," starring Vincent Prince. But perhaps most relevant in his corpus was the cheap yet bizarrely compelling 1961 *The Flight That Disappeared,* something of a cross between *Airport* and a *Twilight Zone* episode. En route to Washington, a plane carrying three scientists is taken into space, and then an alternate dimension, by time travelers who never lived in the first place, because their future was destroyed by advanced nuclear weapons the three scientists would pitch to the government. Sent back into the past, the scientists decide to abandon their plans and potentially alter the future—a plot that might not have been out of the realm of Lovecraft's appreciation. With director chosen, given the subject and quick turnaround, Corman and AIP logically turned to *War of the Satellites* screenwriter Lawrence Goldman, who turned in a draft script for a film titled *The Moon Missile.* This was changed to the more Cormanesque *The Spacewoman Brought Terror,* not just to increase the salaciousness, but out of fear of confusion with the 1958 cult classic *Missile to the Moon,* itself a remake of the 1953 *Cat-Women of the Moon* (Warren 108).

This is where the story of *Spacewoman*'s story becomes a story in and of itself. *War of the Satellite*'s art director, Daniel Haller, would go on to helm two of the first direct Lovecraftian film adaptations, *Die, Monster, Die!* (1965; also based on "Colour") and *The Dunwich Horror* (1970) (Migliore and Strysik 244). Haller and Goldman shared their interest in Lovecraft during the early years of working together on AIP films, but Goldman gave no indication that *Spacewoman* was originally meant to adapt any Lovecraft film, let alone "Colour." Details remain unclear, but August Derleth would later claim to Clark Ashton Smith and Ray Bradbury separately that someone at AIP, either a lawyer acting officially (Smith) or unnamed production figure acting unofficially (Bradbury), realized this was a Lovecraft adaptation that had been made without the approval of Arkham House. Corman and Goldman never commented, but Le Borg and Haller would later offer a brief rejection of this as a Derleth fabrication. According to Derleth, once AIP negotiated for the use of "Colour" as inspiration, the filming proceeded without any change to the existing script—only an additional credit to Derleth and Arkham House in the final film for providing the rights and "consultation."

If this is the case, then the poor-quality script has no one to blame but Corman and Le Borg, as the finished movie contains numerous scenes where exposition is given by narrator or obvious pickup recordings (sometimes clearly by a soundalike), and several shoddily filmed second-unit scenes stitch in background detail. In this it is not dissimilar to the 1960s B-films of Coleman Francis, particularly *The Beast of Yucca Flats* (1961). Whether this stitch-up of disparate elements worthy of Herbert West was the by-product of the rushed production, or the insertion by Derleth of his (and Lovecraft's) fingerprints, remains unclear. But whatever the production quality and the looseness of the adaptation, there remains at the core an interesting concept.

The film opens with a scene set at the "Space Flight Complex" in Alabama, apparently meant to be the Marshall Space Flight Center in Huntsville where Wernher von Braun worked. Suitably, a German-accented "Professor Von Kerman" (Martin Kosleck) speaks to a crowd of reporters, announcing that the USSR has successfully landed a three-cosmonaut capsule, the *Lunik 21,* in the Moon's Eratosthenes crater.[3] In the early twentieth century, the astronomer

3. "Lunik" was the nickname given to the Soviet *Luna* series of space probes, a combination of *Luna* and *Sputnik.* All the Lunik/Luna probes were uncrewed; the actual *Lunik 21* landed the remote-control Lunokhod 2 rover in Le Monnier crater in 1973. In a case of reality being stranger than fiction, years after the end of the Cold War it was revealed that the CIA "kidnapped" *Lunik 2* in 1959 to reverse-engineer its design secrets, which in 2024 was announced to be the basis for an upcoming movie of its own (Strausbaugh 78–79).

William Henry Pickering believed that Eratosthenes contained living plants and herds of insects whose life cycles and migrations could be observed from Earth in the form of shifting color hues in the crater. The teenage Lovecraft believed this as well, charting his efforts to map the lunar vegetation of the crater in his amateur astronomy magazines (Guimont and Smith 90–111), although Goldman may have been unaware of Lovecraft's youthful endorsement of Pickering's theory. Professor Von Kerman notes that "Just as the crater's Greek namesake proved the Earth was round, Eratosthenes may now prove that Earth is not alone as a refuge for life in this cosmos."

From Kerman's proclamation we are shown a matte painting of Eratosthenes, with a spindly cylindrical spacecraft—already anachronistic by the early 1960s, particularly in contrast to the lunar module depiction in the following year's *First Men in the Moon* adaptation—already landed. The lunar crater is one of two paintings done by esteemed space artist Chesley Bonestell, who contributed similar scenes to the George Pal–produced films *Destination Moon, The War of the Worlds,* and *Conquest of Space*—and through illegally used art from his collaborations with von Braun and Willy Ley, *Cat-Women of the Moon* (Warren 160; Newell 158–70). Bonestell's work on *Spacewoman* was some of his last film work, and he considered it of poor quality compared to his earlier cinematic contributions; but even a poor Bonestell is still a Bonestell. In addition to Eratosthenes, Bonestell contributed a painting of the mutated Gardner farm with its alien life for the film's climax.

Lunik 21 is shown lifting off from Eratosthenes, with a voiceover announcer from "International Wireless News" (Paul Frees, emulating the famous voice of Orson Welles) stating that radio contact has been lost with the craft, and radar observations showed it losing control and deviating from its flight path as it approaches Earth. Instead of landing in Siberia, the announcer states that Aerospace Defense Command shows it falling over the Matanuska Valley Colony in Alaska's southwest, which will be impassable due to "recent snow road blockages." This conveniently allows for a plausibly remote location still within the United States that could match the rural remoteness of nineteenth-century Massachusetts from "Colour," much as the earlier *The Thing from Another World* (1951) relocated the titular Thing's space crash from Antarctica to Alaska (Warren 49–51). It also, perhaps by coincidence, reflects the 1923 Soviet science fiction novel *Aelita,* where a Soviet spacecraft to Mars returns to Earth, crashing on the shore of Lake Michigan (Tolstoy 161–63). *Aelita* was adapted into the first Soviet blockbuster film the next year, with its constructivist set design inspiring films from Fritz Lang's *Metropolis* (1927) to the H. P. Lovecraft Historical Society's *The Call of Cthulhu* (2005). *Aelita* itself was loosely remade in the US as the 1951 B-movie *Flight to Mars* (Siddiqi 278–80; Warren 34). Likewise, having an updated version of "Colour" replace the meteorite with a space vehicle makes sense, given that the original story was probably influenced by rocket pioneer Robert Goddard, and in turn influenced rocket designer Jack Parsons (Guimont and Smith 119–21).

The perspective now switches to the "Arkham Farm," where the Gardner family—parents Nathan (Nahum from the original; played by Nelson Eddy) and Aimee (Nabby [Abigail] Gardner; Marguerite Chapman), oldest son Thad (Thaddeus; Teddy Martin), teenage son Martin (Merwin; Tommy Kirk), and the show-stealer, a yelping Cardigan Corgi farm dog named Broccoli (playing himself—and obviously with no equivalent in the ailurophile Lovecraft's original)—tend to their farm. From off-screen, Nathan tells his wife, in dialogue seemingly recorded after the fact, that he is glad the latest shipment of ammonium nitrate fertilizer arrived before the snowstorm closed off the roads. With a loud booming noise, the family rushes out to see the crash of the Soviet lunar ship, conveniently off-screen from the camera. Notable among the cast is that Kirk would play a Martian spy in next year's AIP beach party film *Pajama Party,* and that Chapman had played Betty Kearney in the 1940s serial *G-Man Ghoul,* with its several plot parallels to "Herbert West," as well as Martian scientist Alita in *Flight to Mars* (Warren 34).

But most curious is Nelson Eddy's appearance. Born in Providence but moving at a young age to Philadelphia, Eddy became an opera singer there and in New York, before a 1933 performance in Los Angeles set him on a role appearing in Hollywood musicals, transitioning to TV after World War II. *Spacewoman* was one of his last acting appearances (and one of the few non-musicals) prior to his death in 1967. It is apt that this rare acting turn for him was in a Lovecraft adaptation, as Nelson was also the cousin of Lovecraft's friend Clifford M. Eddy, Jr. As a result of his leaving Providence as a boy, Nelson was not close to Clifford, and it is not even clear that Nelson knew the family connection to the source material (Guimont 9). But it is a curious link, nonetheless.

On the Arkham Farm the Gardners run to the *Lunik,* where from off-screen they rescue only the female crew member, who introduces herself as the scientist Olga Kovalenko. Thad and Aimee introduce themselves, establishing that they relocated from Wisconsin to Alaska in the Depression and are one of the few farming families that remain decades later. This may seem like Derleth's influence—but in reality, the Matanuska Valley Colony was an actual New Deal program, established in 1935 with the relocation of several hundred farming families from Wisconsin, Michigan, and Minnesota. However, the project collapsed rapidly, with only a handful of initial settlers remaining by the 1960s (Shortridge 597; Miller 48–49). While the specific state from which the Gardners originated may have been an appeal to Derleth, it was still logical, and the choice of the colony meant that there was a remote and largely abandoned farming region to work with. One reason for this abandonment was that the valley had been formed by a glacier, and as a result had quite rocky outcroppings—a suitable replacement for the blasted heath of the original story (*CF* 2.367–68; Shortridge 584; Miller 72–74). An immediate outbreak of measles on the establishment of the colony, leading to its evacuation, also provides an interesting parallel to the history of Innsmouth (*CF* 3.195; Miller 84–85).

The Gardners tell Olga that, because of the recent snowstorm, the phone line is down, so they cannot call Aerospace Defense Command. Coming out of her shock, Olga asks what happened to the *Lunik* and the two pilots. Nathan tells her that the ship sank into "the pond" (used to provide water for the farm's livestock) after breaking the ice, and they were lucky to get her out in time—shades of the *Icarus* ship from the first *Planet of the Apes* film five years later (with its script by Lovecraft fan Serling). Olga starts to tell a fantastic story about how having landed in Eratosthenes, they discovered glowing, strange-colored lunar plants in line with Pickering's observations, and retrieved samples for the Academy of Sciences in Moscow. In reality, the Soviet astronomer G. A. Tikhov had established an institute for theoretical study of astrobiology at what is now the Fesenkov Astrophysical Institute in Kazakhstan, but it was dismantled after his death in 1960. However, neither Tikhov's work nor its discontinuation would probably have been known to Western filmmakers in the early 1960s (Briot 175–85).

In a curious anachronism that speaks to the rapid scientific progress of the 1960s, Olga states that by examining the Eratosthenes plant life through a microscope, she could see similarities with the foraminifera—shelled microorganisms—discovered by "Soviet expeditions to the deepest parts of the Pacific, proving that our lunar neighbor was once linked to the deep ocean of primeval Earth, and that some of our most ancient life still lives on our cosmic companion." This almost seems like a reference to R'lyeh from "The Call of Cthulhu." But it instead draws from an actual theory, proposed in the nineteenth century, that the moon was flung out of the early Earth and that the Pacific Ocean is the remnant of its origin. Ironically, the actual lunar samples returned from the Apollo missions at the end of the decade were partly responsible for the ultimate debunking of the theory (Guimont and Smith 139). Its usage in *Spacewoman* is certainly permissible, given that Lovecraft himself cites it in *At the Mountains of Madness* (*CF* 3.100)—and the author himself knowingly used outdated astronomical theories in a childhood story about the far side of the Moon (*Letters to Rheinhart*

Kleiner 49–50). Meanwhile, the expedition referenced by Olga is probably meant to be the charting of the Challenger Deep by the Soviet research vessel *Vityaz* in 1957, as part of the same IGY as the *Sputnik* launches (Kort 137–38).

As told by Olga, whether in Moscow or Kazakhstan, and originating on the moon or the Pacific, the analysis of the Eratosthenes life is not to be. On the *Lunik*'s return flight to Earth, the two pilots began acting erratically and turned on each other. Aimee suggests they were fighting over Olga, who dismisses the attack on the professionalism of Soviet cosmonautics. Olga insists that it was the effect of the lunar plants on the men. Young Martin, an avid follower of the space program, suggests that the lunar plants will probably die due to the combined shock of freezing water and Earth's gravity, and Olga agrees (so much for their supposed deep-Pacific origins!). That night she and Thad discuss their upbringing, with Olga having grown up on a collective farm, and both of their fathers being World War II veterans who fought the Nazis. Could a détente between the two youths be in development?

Olga is given the bed in Thad's room, who sleeps on the couch. The family is woken up in the morning by the barking of Broccoli, who has run down to the pond, taking the place of the Gardners' well from the original story (*CF* 2.371). Overnight, the barley crops near the lake have grown to twisted dimensions and forms, given good effects in Bonestell's background matte shot, and we are told—and perhaps thankfully not shown, given the limited effects budget—what the cattle now look like, having drunk from the water provided from the pond. Barley and cattle, incidentally, were accurately chosen as being in line with Matanuska colony farming (Miller 102–10). The twisted crops, now turned into vine and thick brush and glowing with an unearthly light—for which the audience has to take the word of the Gardners, given the black-and-white color palette, albeit with a helpful quasi-electric hum added in for the glow's noise—have blocked off access to the road. Even without the snow, Gardners, and Olga could no longer escape if they wanted to.

To be fair, the matte painting by Bonestell is impressive, and the glow and its sound is effective for the limited budget. But it is here where the movie falls apart. According to interviews given by several crew members and AIP personnel decades later—safely after Derleth's death—this is where the typical litigious bluster of the Arkham House founder came to have a major impact. The plan was to have the zombified cosmonaut pilots, assimilated into the lunar plant life, rise from the water to attack the family. While this makes for the interesting fact that *Spacewoman* almost originated the trope of zombies caused by a space probe laying siege to a farmhouse half a decade before George Romero's *Night of the Living Dead,* it is perhaps a blessing in disguise, as it avoids similarities to *The Beast of Yucca Flats, The Thing from Another World,* and *Invasion of the Body Snatchers*. Unfortunately, it does cause the ending to feel rushed and anticlimactic. Critics of Derleth will say that with the potential lawsuit over *Spacewoman* allegedly being an unauthorized adaptation of "Colour," Corman and AIG were unwilling to dedicate the planned amount of money and time to it but didn't want to throw out the money and film that had already been shot. Derleth and his supporters, as well other several other neutral parties—notably Isaac Asimov in a column in the magazine bearing his name fifteen years later—would argue that it was just a by-product of Corman putting out a rushed, low-effort product to capitalize on a contemporary event, and that if anything, the Derleth lawsuit was a convenient excuse.

In any event, the climax of the film shows several shots of the Gardners walking through their mutated farm, and Thad using a shotgun to save Olga from attack from a mutated cow. With the brief glimpse shown, it is probably a blessing that the majority of the cheap cow puppet is offscreen. Retreating to the farmhouse as Martin announces the plants are seemingly attacking them with intelligence (shades of the trees from *The Wizard of Oz,* perhaps, or the later *Evil Dead*), Olga realizes that the plants are driven off by the ammonium nitrate fertilizer—referenced earlier in the movie by Nathan in offscreen dialogue, indicating that the earlier mention was a retroactive addition. Martin notes the lack of nitrogen on the moon. The *Lunik*'s fuel tanks contain nitric acid—a detail that derived from the then-current Soviet *Vostok* spacecraft of Tereshkova and dating back to German missiles from World War II. Nathan notes that he still has a stock of farmers' dynamite—anachronistic by the 1960s, but something that early twentieth-century farmers would have had on hand. The Gardner men, aided by Olga and Broccoli the dog, manage to make it to the farming shed while evading the plastic tube lunar-plants, retrieving the dynamite and tossing it into the pond, where off-screen Nathan tells the family (and the viewer) that they should rupture the underwater tanks of the *Lunik,* releasing the nitic acid. An explosion from beneath a farm pond miniature, relatively high quality for a Corman production, demonstrates the end result, and Olga tells us from offscreen that the plants should die off "now that the core of the infection is burned."

The next morning, a helicopter from Aerospace Defense Command arrives, unloading both the "Soviet Ambassador" (unnamed and unspeaking, and played by an unidentified actor) and "General Mitchell" (Robert Emhardt). Professor Von Kerman from the introduction is absent—evidence toward those who point to it being filmed after the fact, as an effort both to salvage the runtime and to provide some legal differentiation to satisfy Derleth. It is agreed that the *Lunik* will be raised and returned to the Soviet Union with its dead cosmonaut heroes. Olga and Thad say farewell but promise to meet again—next time in Moscow, similar to the ending of the 1966 film *The Russians Are Coming, the Russians Are Coming,* about a Soviet submarine running aground on a New England island. Olga promises General Mitchell that the scientific knowledge gained from the expedition will be shared across the world (as were the data from both the Apollo and actual Soviet Luna missions). The sharing of knowledge is particularly important, because the film ends with Olga warning General Mitchell and the Soviet ambassador against any future missions to the region of Eratosthenes, or the moon overall—an echo of not only the warning against the return to Antarctica in *At the Mountains of Madness,* but the injunction to "Keep watching the skies!" from *The Thing from Another World* (*CF* 3.11–13; Warren 52; Guimont and Smith 277).

Given the abrupt ending to an already cheap movie, it is not surprising that *The Spacewoman Brought Terror* is not only an overlooked, but also until recently a difficult to find entry in the corpus of Lovecraft adaptations. Because of the potential legal issues, showings and official releases were extremely rare until long after Derleth's death, with a notorious case being versions printed in Rhodesia during its unrecognized unilateral independence from Britain in the 1970s. Beyond the legal and quality issues, there is the fact that it is also a movie released shortly before John F. Kennedy's assassination featuring Soviets winning his challenge to reach the moon. It also was overshadowed by two other, more direct adaptations. On the one hand was *First Men in the Moon* (1964), co-written by Nigel Kneale, with its Soviet-American lunar expedition encountering the remnants of the Victorian steampunk mission from Wells's original novel and its run-in with mysterious insectoid Selenites, overtaking *Spacewoman* as a reaction to the early Space Race and unexpected lunar life discoveries.

1965 would see *Die, Monster, Die!,* the more straightforward Corman-produced "Colour" adaptation. *Die* was directed by *Spacewoman*'s co-writer Haller, who was reportedly (and understandably) unhappy with how the first film came out. In the aftermath, AIP negotiated with Arkham House to get the right to adapt "Colour," but whether out of legal issues or vindictiveness on the part of Derleth, this specifically did not include any retroactive right to adaptations, leaving *Spacewoman* in legal limbo. This was detailed in a 28 October 1965 letter from Arkham House artists' manager Robert Goldfarb to Derleth, but as it is part of a collection of Derleth's correspondence that went up for auction online in 2017 for more than $400,000, it is beyond my ability to refer to the source text directly. While *Die* is also not a straightforward "Colour" adaptation, it is more faithful than *Spacewoman,* though it does incorporate some of the earlier movie's changes—Arkham being relocated outside the continental US; a contemporary 1960s setting; and the meteorite being given space-age changes, in this case radioactivity (Migliore and Strysik 50–51).

Despite its relegation for decades to the gray market of convention showings and illicit copies on the level of *The Star Wars Holiday Special, Spacewoman* did have some impact. From 1959 into the early 1960s—and popularized by an ostensibly nonfiction 1960 essay by science fiction author Robert A. Heinlein—the urban legend of the "lost cosmonauts," alleged space explorers who died in orbit and were covered up by the Soviet regime, proliferated. The lost cosmonauts gained additional popularity with the film *Countdowns* (1967) and *Apollo 18* (2011) (Strausbaugh 163–72; Guimont and Smith 136–37). Soviet spaceflight historian Thomas Ellis shared with me some of his research on both Tereshkova's reception in the West and *Spacewoman*'s role, however scant, in the propagation of the lost cosmonaut myth. Likewise, at NecronomiCon 2024, I discussed the upcoming *Spacewoman* remastered re-release from Kino Lorber with film buff David T. Zeppieri, and it was mentioned during the final night screening of Haller's *The Dunwich Horror*. With *The Spacewoman Brought Terror* receiving a legal, widespread release for the first time since its rushed completion more than six decades ago, there will hopefully someday be enough attention for it to receive its own panel, if not an actual screening, at a future NecronomiCon.

Works Cited

An Adventure in Space and Time. Directed by Mark Gatiss. BBC Two, 2013.

Briot, Danielle. "The Creator of Astrobotany, Gavriil Adrianovich Tikhov." In *Astrobiology, History, and Society: Life Beyond Earth and the Impact of Discovery,* ed. Douglas A. Vakoch. Heidelberg: Springer Berlin, 2013. 175–85.

Cannon, Peter. *The Lovecraft Chronicles*. Poplar Bluff, MO: Mythos Books, 2004.

Gaspard, John. *Fast, Cheap & Written That Way: Top Screenwriters on Writing for Low-Budget Movies*. Studio City, CA: Michael Wiese Productions, 2007.

Gifford, Denis. *Science Fiction Film*. London: Studio Vista, 1971.

Guimont, Edward. "Some Notes on a Necroentity: Reflections on NecronomiCon Providence 2024." *Dead Reckonings* No. 36 (Fall 2024): 8–9.

———, and Horace A. Smith. *When the Stars Are Right: H. P. Lovecraft and Astronomy*. New York: Hippocampus Press, 2023.

Kistler, Alan. *Doctor Who: A History*. Guilford, CT: Lyons Press, 2013.

Kort, V. G. "Scientific Research of «Vityaz» During IGY." *International Hydrographic Review* 37, No. 2 (1960): 137–41.

Lovecraft, H. P. *Collected Fiction: A Variorum Edition*. Ed. S. T. Joshi. New York: Hippocampus Press, 2015–17. 4 vols. [*CF*]

———. *Letters to Rheinhart Kleiner and Others*. Ed. S. T. Joshi and David E. Schultz. New York: Hippocampus Press, 2020.

Migliore, Andrew, and John Strysik. *The Lurker in the Lobby: A Guide to the Cinema of H. P. Lovecraft*. San Francisco: Night Shade Books, 2006.

Miller, Orlando W. *The Frontier in Alaska and the Matanuska Colony*. New Haven: Yale University Press, 1975.

Newell, Catherine L. *Destined for the Stars: Faith, the Future, and America's Final Frontier*. Pittsburgh: University of Pittsburgh Press, 2019.

Price, Robert M. "An Interview with Brian Lumley." *Crypt of Cthulhu* No. 19 Candlemas (1984): 52–55.

Shortridge, James R. "The Collapse of Frontier Farming in Alaska." *Annals of the Association of American Geographers* 66, No. 4 (2008): 260–88.

Siddiqi, Asif A. "Imagining the Cosmos: Utopians, Mystics, and the Popular Culture of Spaceflight in Revolutionary Russia." *Osiris* 23, No. 1 (December 1976): 583–604.

The Spacewoman Brought Terror. Reginald Leborg, dir. United Artists, 1963. Kino Lorber remastered Blu-Ray release, 2025.

Strausbaugh, John. *The Wrong Stuff: How the Soviet Space Program Crashed and Burned*. New York: PublicAffairs, 2024.

Tolstoy, Alexei N. *Aelita*. 1923. Tr. Antonina W. Bouis. New York: Macmillan, 1981.

Warren, Bill. *Keep Watching the Skies!: American Science Fiction Movies of the Fifties, Volume I: 1950–1957*. Jefferson, NC: McFarland, 1982.

Summer Time Gone

Ngo Binh Anh Khoa

The cloudless sky ignites with hues
That dim the blinking stars—
Where blues meet yellows, greens join reds
To paint the skies afar.

The silence shatters with the cheers
Of those that came to see
The summer's fireworks and partake
In the festivity.

Each face there shines, all flushed with joy,
Touched by the vibrant light,
Except for one, a visage pale
That hides from mortal sight.

The vampire boy has come to hunt,
Urged by his torturous thirst,
For he no longer could resist
The urge brought by his curse.

He's finally dared to leave his lair
Beneath a vacant house;
Now, cloaked in shadow, he moves forth,
As quiet as a mouse.

His gleaming eyes would roam and find
A lone man standing near.
Masked by the bustlings all around,
His footsteps none could hear.

But as the boy's about to strike,
The fireworks have him stunned
With orbs of yellow and of red
Like tiny scattered suns.

Unconsciously he reaches out
As if to grasp their warmth,
But only emptiness would greet
His fingers, clawed, deformed.

The voices of the gathered souls
Become just background sounds
As he stares at the blossoming light,
His mind by memories bound.

He was alive once, young and free,
Undamaged and unsoiled.
One moment of misplaced trust, though,
Left all that innocence spoiled.

A woman who was known to be
His mother's longtime friend,
Passed onto him her dark disease
To which there is no end.

His sickly body ceased to change,
And his mind ceased to grow
While those around him aged and died.
Grief was all he would know.

That grief became disgust and fear
Aimed at himself alone,
For he knew his disease could spread.
The cure—just one is known.

Years came and went, and he would hide
In darkness underground,

Subsisting on the blood of rats
And any insect found.

But with each day that later passed,
The curse demanded more
Until the blood of pests could not.
Quench his thirst like before.

Thus, he's decided to come out
To try and grab a bite,
A tiny bit, he tells himself,
Enough to last the night.

He's found his mark. He's made his move.
He's had a solid plan,
With which he's almost made off with
The lone, oblivious man.

But now his mind is filled with thoughts
Of colors, warmth, and light,
Which shower his frail, filthy form
With radiance—alien, bright.

When was the last time his dull eyes
Were filled with such fine hues
Instead of shades of black and gray
While his mind drowned in blues?

Some memories of the distant past
Outpour inside his head,
And for a moment he pretends
That his heart is not dead.

The thirst that always torments him
Becomes a muted ache
As the young boy there stands and stares;
His limbs unsubtly shake.

Right here and now he's just a boy
And not an exiled beast,
Repulsed by those once of his kind,
Whose anguish never ceased.

Right here and now he's just a boy
Lost in the bygone days
When his small hands were gently held,
And colors blessed his gaze.

His vision never leaves the skies
Till darkness once more reigns.
The vanished stars reclaim their spots
And softly blink again.

The crowd disperses gradually
Until there's only one—
A lost and lonely child that once
Was someone's treasured son.

He stands within the veil of black,
Devoid of sights and sounds,
A hand on his unmoving chest,
His mind in silence drowned.

What more is he still waiting for?
The boy himself knows not.
He stays as if time will reveal
To him that which is sought.

The hours idly pass until
From out the glowing east,
A flood of gold starts to outpour,
Unhindered once unleashed.

But it has yet to reach his place,
And there forms a divide
Between the light and dark, where he
Is meant to pick a side.

Should he remain bound to the shroud
Where shadow stretches, cold?
Or should he choose cremation with
The warmth of radiant gold?

The dark retreats as light spreads out
Before his pondering gaze
Until its reach is inches from
The border of his space.

To leave and live, or stay and die?
The question haunts his head–
A guillotine that looms and gleams,
Held by a fraying thread.

His hand's again upon his chest,
Unmoving as before.
But then, his mask of porcelain cracks,
A rattle to his core.

To leave and live? A tasteless joke
That births a mirthless smile.
He does not live, not anymore—
Has not for quite a while.

The boy is hungry, sick, and cold,
So weary of the world.
All he now yearns for is to rest;
His eyes are further blurred.

Deliberately he reaches out
To grasp the pouring warmth.
Enveloping heat embraces him,
Engulfing his frail form.

The final thought to cross his mind
Is how relieved he is
To be wrapped in the cleansing light,
Released from his abyss.

Angelystor's Shadow

Ellen J. Greenham

The Llangernyw Yew, also referred to as the Angelystor tree, is dated to between 4000 and 5000 years old and stands in Sy Cynog's churchyard in Conwy, Wales.

"I knew you would come back."

"It terrifies me that I have."

Stepping back from the splintering doorframe against which he leans, the man moves just enough to let her through and not enough for her to avoid brushing up against him, his gaze fixed ahead to the world outside. She waits mute behind him, while he continues his watch as if she had never arrived. Cars disgorge their blind human cargoes to wander around and kick up the sun-rusted dirt, bewildered, it seems, and then they leave. Countless years of them coming here, tourists to this now silent town of Gwalia that sits undigested by endless rusted rock and heat. When she first came long ago, that first day he *saw* her, he knew she would return. Now she is here, and he will not let her leave.

His thoughts run mercenary to the notion of why she came back, while her mind turns to the uncanny ground just beyond reach that has dogged her for most of her life. Something beneath the shabbiness of the room evades her knowing, this room with its yellowed wallpaper departing in one paralysed sheet from a corner above the fireplace, unable to softly fold and descend upon whatever happens to lie beneath it at the time. It has been departure-ready for some time, a remnant corset keeping this shanty trussed and tied from within as defence against a devouring world. Raising her hand to her throat in search of preventing an unnatural escape, she steadies her breath that he might not hear.

With his back turned upon her and blocking what little is left of the light of the sun, his form offers no vulnerability, his disregard proclaims no kind of animal trust. He is simply where this time of day always finds him.

Soft lights pulse into existence in other windows of other such shanties, signifying an ordering of some dry kind, a reluctance of life to leave altogether. Surrounding those heartbeats, nothing other than red dust and more dust and the pretense of streets. There had never been a need to order this settlement into something resembling a place of human habitation, but it spread out that way anyhow.

She came here once before, but not at dusk, rattling into town in one of those cars of the curious. They come in two kinds—the kind that come to see the house on the hill of some other country's now long-dead president, and the kind who come to see the headframe and abandoned shanties, remnants of the way, it is recorded, people used to live. But records never capture essence and never mind the people who still live here; they seem to be more an inconvenience for the fact that their houses cannot be invaded and investigated. But she, she was peering through the grimy window from the back seat of a pale blue Holden Sunbird with a knowing already there; she was out of that car and stirring up the dust with her small feet long before the grown-ups even opened their doors.

He watched her then from the deep recess of his home, standing in the shadows at the back of the narrow hall into which the front door had stood open, just as it does now. Squinting in the sun, her fair hair curling erratically at the ends, she surveyed the town in a manner unlike other children he had seen. Then she turned and peered into his house, through that open door and down the length of the passageway to where he stood. He knew she couldn't see him, and he knew that she knew he was there, standing on the oriental runner with its threads coming loose like fibers of sinew and muscle on a half-chewed bone.

Reluctant to turn away from the invisible visibility she sensed, the child was lax in heeding her mother's call. Turning to answer, she took a few steps, turned back, and looked again. He could feel her mind reaching out towards him, no, down into him and willing him forward, willing him out into the light so that she might see what kind of creature prowled in the shadows. She was unsettlingly knowing; she was something latent in the form of a child. He retreated further still, and he watched her for the rest of the day.

The inescapable dust of a terrain brought forth when life first stirred in salt water and did not yet know what it would become, somehow, this girl understood such age. The secret things dormant beneath the dry where this ancient land labours to contain itself.

There was some kind of intent for this place at Creation, some kind of knowing that got lost, derailed from the order of things and spun into the fabric of the roiling, molten mass below, only to be spat out of there too. Belonging nowhere at all, it seeped up and into the world after the mine came, the sweat of men unearthing it without knowing, dredging it out from where it might have otherwise never been found; and one little girl years ago without knowing how to name it, understood it.

"You can sleep out there," tilting his head towards the back of the shanty. "There's a room by the kitchen." His gaze never shifting from some unfixed point outside, his body refusing to turn and acknowledge hers, he adds, "Don't go walking at night."

With no words in her mouth reaching for articulable form, she picks up her bag and walks to where he directs. One threshold crossed, this next seems a finality that in crossing will set her irrevocably within these walls. The curve of a doorknob, disrupted by dents telling of some rough handling or other, is cool in her hand, its black paint worn thin and chipped from use. The rusted mechanism heralds entry into a small enclosure, corralling just long enough for a narrow iron bed and an old wooden wardrobe at its foot on the facing wall. Beside the bed, a makeshift table, an old crate, its splinters rising in wait for departure.

The walls are hessian-lined, the window grimy and shut. Spaces between the floorboards open large enough for spiders and scorpions and all manner of crawling things, but not for snakes, there will be no serpents here. The wardrobe smells as if it hasn't been opened for uncountable years, black hooks in its bowels, no rail, no hangers.

The bed compresses like dull wadding as she sits, wondering why she came. Something has scooped out memory, replacing it with an emptiness that is not empty at all. Turning her head to look out the window for light, she finds the crystalline blue of day so well removed from the sky, she cannot recall its brilliance. Before her is a strange hue as if it were faded by age and neglect.

She stares at that sky beyond the glass forever, it seems, and yet it does not change. She cannot find her thoughts, each time trying to secure her mind on something she knows, only to find it slips into oblivion. Must be tired, she thinks, then realizes she is not.

Rising from where she sits, in leaving the room her substance seems to trail away behind her in a way that only the unwilling virgin bride could ever understand, but leaving this room is the only way to leave this shanty, it is the only way to enter the kitchen to eat or enter the outhouse to expel or enter the passageway of Oriental sinew running the spine of this chamber, to speak to him. She already accepted the outcome of this room when she made the decision in the city to return.

She had not even seen him that day in 1978, she just knew he was there. Now he is not there.

"Hello?" Her voice falling dead in the air, did it come out at all? "Hello, are you there?"

Nothing. He has left the front door open, and standing where he had been when she arrived, she finds no recollection for how she got here. Did she drive? Did she get a lift from those nice tourists who met her on the road? They had seemed so concerned that she was alone, that they were all so far away from Kalgoorlie. Extending a foot over the threshold, then remembering his words, *don't go walking at night,* she obediently draws it back in. Nothing to do but go to bed and sleep.

The dawn light creeps over him like a suffocation, a denial of his substance.

The door by the kitchen opens and wraithlike she moves, her feet dragging as if the room will not let go. It is like pulling a knife through honey and a strange kind of corn-silk rasping tears at her somewhere inside. She notices without noticing and, walking through to the kitchen, cold and hungry, begins a search for sustenance. Old pans, chipped crockery and mismatched cutlery, a rusting colander, and empty containers with the last greasy residue of something organic, some sort of unknowable ichor. There must be something to eat. Searching the dusty shelves, she disturbs nothing other than the flaking husks of long-dead insects, all the time wondering where he has gone.

This cannot be happening, there must be something to feed the gnawing inside her. There is nothing. Standing up from where she has been bent over searching dark corners in the dresser cupboard, she strides along the gristly runner to the front of the crumbling domain and turns to the only other door she has seen.

The only other door. Struck by the clarity of this thought, she notices now there is no back door, just a wall to mask something evasive outside. There is only one way in or out. Her hand on the doorknob to an unseen room, the resolve she thought that she had evaporates to something with no name and no place in the linguistic code. This must be where he sleeps, it can be no other room in this four-chambered enclosure.

A powdering of dust drifts in the air about her as she loosens the door from its frame. Yes, a bedroom. Sparse, the walls papered and intact, the iron bed made to accommodate two, its counterpane once ornate lace and brocade of white. To the right of the window looking in from under the shanty's front porch, a dark-stained bureau stands opposite the bed. On it are the brush and comb and mirror of a lady, silver and ivory and fibrous bristles—these are the objects of no man. Hanging from a hook on the back of the door, a blue flannel work shirt grimed at the collar and neglected. This room, god, this room is cold. How can he sleep in here and not feel the cold? It is as the cold of caves and stone that wait for life to lie still, so that it might seep into the places where bone cannot grow. He is not here.

She will wait—what else can she do? She will wait in the collapsing embrace of the armchair in the shabby sitting room with a fireplace and no fire and she will wait for him to return from wherever it is he has gone. Perhaps he had gone out to get food, she had arrived unannounced after all, though not, she now thinks, unlooked for.

He watches her. She sits and waits. Waits for him to return when he had never left. Waits for the memory that has been taking hold since that first day she came. He knows she does not know what she waits for, he knows she does not know what it is, buried so far down that it seems impossible to reach. He watches her now as he watched her then when eight years old and full of the knowledge of a buried world. It filled her eyes with knowing that day when she heeded her mother's call only to wander off on her own again. She knew what danger was and she had stayed away with success for so many years since.

All the latent power of what she is sitting coiled in that rotting chair. It is dusk once more before she comprehends what time has passed, her last breath exhaled in the act of sitting. How many dusks have there been?

Somewhere indeterminable outside, a noise drifts in through the eternally open door as if from chill heights and plunges straight down into some inexplicable depth. Startled, she sits up and listens. That did not happen last night. Rising and not thinking, forgetting his warning, she finds herself standing on bare earth and looking for the source. The steam winder at the headframe, that noise, awful and alluring.

From within lengthening shadows at the open door where he has always been, he watches her, outside, vulnerable again. Outside, where he told her not to go, where he knew she would go. How long has he waited for this?

"I told you not to go outside at night." Splitting the air his voice carves up what remnant safety was left.

Turning more slowly than defence under threat should determine, she *sees* him for the first time since her arrival. *Gods, how long have I been here?* She sees him as she had sensed him that child's day when she stood in the empty dark of the kitchen, wide-eyed and screaming inside for the fearful thing to be gone and yet never leave her, all in one heartbeat.

"Did I ever leave this place?"

He stares beyond her, shadows behind his eyes ignite in the smouldering dark of a night that has at last arrived.

"Did I?" But she knows she did. She must have, she remembers getting in the car with her mother, driving away and leaving this dusty, troubling place behind. A vacancy opens, ready to swallow what little is left of the child who gained wisdom and the woman who walked like a ghost into vibrant life for the decades that came after.

"You left, and then you came back, and now you are here." Stepping out from the shanty he walks past her and begins the climb to the top of the hill.

Overwhelmed by a desire to reach out and touch him, she follows. She does not want to stop him taking her to where she knows he must, she wants to take from him as much as she can before they get there. One last task. It is as if the age of the world has moved so far beyond her it has become a babbling decrepitude, worn out and still living, gutted and still pulsing, mewling in the last gasp of something it has moved so far beyond it will never get back to where it once was.

One more task for the winding engine. One more load for the cart. One more journey down into the open pit, to the secret place so that it may be lost forever, so that in the forgetfulness of the world he will no longer be alone.

Young Strickland's Career

J. D. Beresford

[First published in Beresford's collection *Signs and Wonders* (Golden Cockerel Press, 1921).—ED.]

No doubt the story of the future is written, so far as the future is an expression of present potentialities. We boast our foreknowledge of planetary history, and can prophesy with fine accuracy the occurrence of every major and minor eclipse or occultation in the solar system. But in the most precise science there remains always at least one element that is undefinable and unknowable. The regular traffic of planets about the sun might one day be upset by the coming of an unknown visitor from the deeps of space. The materials of our knowledge are so limited. And in human affairs we know so little of the materials. Nevertheless, it may be that to the universal consciousness the future is a foretellable expression of our present potentialities.

I remember how my friend Strickland used to harp on that theme eighteen years ago. I was incredulous; a stickler for free-will. I could not bear the thought of anything like a cut-and-dried programme of human development. But my one really convincing retort to all his arguments was to reply, "Oh; on broad lines, perhaps. On the very broadest lines."

Strickland's attitude just then was so obviously influenced by his desires. He had married at forty, had one child, a boy, and was oppressed by the fear that he would not live to see his son's future. Strickland was obsessed with that idea for a time. He even went so far as to consult mediums. And a man of forty-five who will consult professional mediums about the future cannot be quite sane.

His sole excuse for that lapse was the plea that astrology had failed him. He had had two very expensive horoscopes cast, and they had been most grievously at fault concerning the first three years of little Strickland's life. Both forecasts had been gloomy with regard to those early years, prophesying a delicate constitution, unusual trouble with infantile complaints. And one horoscope shrugged its inspired shoulders at the critical period of teething, and continued with a kind of cynical despair, as if the astrologer were a little ashamed of the way he was earning his ten guineas: "Should he, however, survive . . ." And the truth was that little Strickland was quite a fatiguingly healthy child. His appetite and his craving for exercise, even at the age of eight weeks, were, admittedly, almost abnormal.

So Strickland lost faith in the pattern of the stars, and tried mediums, who were not so nervous of the magistrates in those days. If he had stuck to one clairvoyante he might have laid his restless inquiry, but, unhappily, the first lady he visited misread her client's hopes, and mapped out a successful business career for his little son; and Strickland, who had already fulfilled that destiny in his own life, and had ambitions to see his son leading a "really sensible Government," took another opinion. The second prophetess, pathetically anxious to please, no doubt, saw young Strickland as a Bishop; the third was a shade nearer to the mark with an Admiral; but the fourth—a charming young woman, recently engaged to be married, and collecting a trousseau by her last professional efforts—made the boy a Poet.

After that Strickland bought a crystal, and tried to see the future for himself.

I laughed at him then, of course; and even now I feel inclined to laugh at those first foolish inquiries of his. But his very earnestness should have saved Strickland from anything like ridicule; and I am glad to remember that I did not laugh when he told me of the one and only vision that came to him through the crystal—it was, by the way, an unusually fine specimen, as big as an orange. He picked it up second-hand, somewhere in Soho.

As I see it, one of the most intriguing features of Strickland's experience is the fact that he had ceased to probe his son's future when the vision came. The boy was seven years old then, and had a little sister of two and a half who had partly diverted her father's attention. And Strickland had probably outgrown the fear of his own premature death; though it may be that his passionate longing for assurance as to the glory of his boy's career had not so much spent itself as been thrust back into his sub-consciousness. Superficially the difference in him was quite obvious. The change of his tone, for example, when he spoke of his son. Even the manner of reference. The tender enunciation of "My little boy" had altered to "That young rascal of mine," just the proudly modest description of the ordinary father.

And when the vision came, neither he nor I related it in any way to his ancient search. . . .

He came to my rooms one evening after dinner, produced the crystal from his pocket, and tossed it over to me.

"A present for a sceptic," he said. "I've finished with it."

I might have thought that he was clearing up the lumber of his old fancies if it had not been for his manner; but the garment of his initiation still clung to him and affected me with the strangeness of its mystery.

I shuddered.

"What did you see?" I asked.

"Oh! don't say you believe in it," he said; "after all your jeers at me."

"Did you see anything?" I insisted, nursing the crystal in the cave of my two hands. I stared into it and saw the faint pink of my magnified palm. No vision came to me; yet I was aware of some potency in the thing.

"Perhaps some reflection, some translation of one's sub-consciousness. . . ." I ventured.

Strickland sneered. "By God, I hope not," he said.

"What were you—looking for?" I asked.

"For nothing. I wasn't looking for anything," he said. "I picked the thing up by the merest accident. I was going to give it to the little girl—as a plaything."

"And then . . ." I prompted him.

"I saw a picture in it. It snatched my attention. I wasn't thinking. . . ."

"And the picture?"

"Hell. Just hell. The real thing; none of your picturesque flames and torture. It came out at me, as it were, and it was—well, the abomination of desolation, nothing more nor less than that."

"But . . ." I began.

He interrupted me. His eyes were fixed on the vision of a future that had become a fragment of his past. "A waste," he said, in a low, thoughtful voice. "A dead, horrible waste . . . all black and pitted and furrowed . . . it looked as if there had been some awful, blasting eruption . . . or as if the whole earth had been scorched and blighted by some unimaginably vast fire. But, oh! the terrible gauntness and death of it all."

He paused and threw his head back with a queer laugh before he continued in a new tone, "It was just a silly nightmare, that's all. And it had its inevitable element of the grotesque. In the middle of that waste there was a scarecrow, a live scarecrow—digging. Digging turnips, if you please. Oh! it was bosh, of course, absolute bosh. I shall have forgotten all about it next week. But I couldn't give the crystal to the little girl after that. You can keep it. Tell me if you get anything. . . ."

So I kept the crystal, and sometimes stared into it. But no vision came to me.

It was in the late autumn of 1919 that Strickland got permission to go out to France. The war had made an old man of him, although he was little over sixty; and he begged me to go with him. "I should like you to help me," he said. "I have a feeling that we might, perhaps, hear something about that young rascal of mine. 'Wounded and missing,' you know, always leaves one with just a hope."

The first beautiful release of peace was passing then into that restless craving for immense action which affected us all so strongly at that time; and the feeling was aggravated in my case by the realisation of impotence. I was too old to help.

I accepted Strickland's offer, eagerly. . . .

I do not believe that he remembered his vision when, after a week's fruitless inquiry, we came one afternoon to the historic desert that had once been beautiful France. Certainly, he made no reference to his old experience; but he was almost senile. I noticed a difference in him, even in that one week.

But I remembered; and I had a fit of cold shivering that I could not control when we came out on to the awful plain that they now call The Plain of the Dead, and saw the figure of that one demented peasant, dressed in the grotesque relics of two nations' uniforms.

He was digging feverishly with his pointed spade, and I heard the ring of it as it struck.

It was not a turnip that he wrenched up.

The thing rolled towards us. . . .

Young Strickland's head had always been a queer shape.

Re-enchanting the World: The Modernist Weird Fiction of Mary Butts

James Goho

Mary Butts (1890–1937) grew up in Dorset, England, near the Badbury Rings, which became her place of sanctuary as a youth and may have seeded her lifelong sense of enchanted, mystical landscapes. In her article on supernatural fiction, "Ghosties and Ghoulies: Uses of the Supernatural in Fiction" (1933),[1] she reminisced that "a great part of her imaginative life was elicited by it and rests there" (*AR* 350). That Iron Age hill fort is located on the southwest of the English Channel known for the Jurassic Coast whose cliffs retain fossils illustrating geological history over tens of millions of years. These primal sites were enhanced by an array of works by William Blake in her childhood home, Salterns, an eighteenth-century house overlooking Poole Harbour. Thomas Butts (1757–1845), Mary's great-grandfather, was an important patron of William Blake, and the house contained many of Blake's works. Blake's visions of the luminous in the world may also have contributed to her view of the supernatural underlying the natural and built environments. After her father died, to Mary Butts's loss and regret, her mother sold off most of Blake's works.

A well-known member of the Modernist movement, Butts was routinely reviewed positively as an author in England during her life (Kessler 207). However, after World War II she vanished from the literary scene for decades. Starting in the 1990s and continuing into

1. The *Bookman* (London) originally published this essay in four installments from January to April 1933. The reference to "Ghosties and Ghoulies" may come from a traditional Scottish prayer: "From Ghoulies and Ghosties / And long-leggedy beasties / And things that go bump in the night, / Good Lord, deliver us!"

the 2020s, McPherson & Company republished many of her books. Her short stories are beginning to appear in collections of weird fiction, such as Melissa Edmundson's *Women's Weird: Strange Stories by Women, 1890–1940* (2019) and James Machin's *British Weird: Selected Short Fiction, 1893–1937* (2020). The *New Yorker* published her short story "The Master's Last Dancing," centered on the 1920s in Paris, on 30 March 1998. Her literary work is also receiving critical attention again, for example, Roslyn Reso Foy's academic study *Ritual, Myth, and Mysticism in the Work of Mary Butts* (2000), Mark Valentine's "Inner Bohemia: The Mystical Fiction of Mary Butts" (2012), Amy Clukey's "Enchanting Modernism: Mary Butts, Decadence, and the Ethics of Occultism" (2014), Merve Emre's laudatory essay "Modernism's Forgotten Mystic" (*New Yorker,* 20 December 2021), and many others.

Butts admired the work of such writers of supernatural fiction as M. R. James,[2] Walter de la Mare, May Sinclair, Margaret Oliphant, and Arthur Machen, with whom she shared a sense of the mystery found in certain landscapes (Valentine, "Inner Bohemia" 27). In "Ghosties and Ghoulies," Butts impressionistically scanned English strange stories. Her essay is concise, and she skims over much of the history of supernatural fiction, focusing on the British tradition. It is more an expression of her approach to supernatural fiction and her personal beliefs about unusual or supernatural experiences than an analysis of the genre that H. P. Lovecraft achieved in his "Supernatural Horror in Literature" (1927) or the comprehensive history and aesthetic appraisal of the literature in S. T. Joshi's two-volume *Unutterable Horror: A History of Supernatural Fiction* (2012, 2014).

Butts praised those authors who, in her opinion, "seek [. . .] without explanation, the consciousness of a universe enlarged" (*AR* 337). More specifically, she defined "supernatural" as a quality in literature that elicits "a stirring, a touching of nerves not usually

2. Butts published her laudatory essay "The Art of Montague James" in the *London Mercury* in 1934 (*CE* 198–213).

sensitive, an awakening to more than fear—but to something like awareness and conviction and memory" (*AR* 335). She thought the best supernatural stories spark a truth of life that often remains hidden or forbidden. These experiences were often associated with a place or certain environs. Yet the luminosity she sought could shine forth in normal spaces as well: where a waste ground shifts unexpectedly into a field of goldenrod, or a modern building vanishes to reveal the cave of Pan, or a calm copse of oaks transforms into the wild frenzy of the Bacchae. This was how she assessed supernatural literature. She strived to express it in her works. It was the expression of something beyond our everyday perception of the world. She always felt there was some magic in the world. For her, the "supernatural" existed. Occasionally this elusive quality shone through our normal perceptions of the natural and built environments. For example, in her "Mappa Mundi"[3] (1937), an everlasting enchanted Paris, beyond the "mere shell" of Paris that we observe (in the mechanistic sense), takes a young American into its shadows (*CS* 284).

In addition to her literary talents, Butts was notorious for her early lifestyle of parties, drinking, and drugs. For example, Evelyn Waugh mentions a hedonistic party at "Mary's" in an entry in his diary of 15 September 1925 (Waugh 221). The occult also fascinated her. Yet modernist writers such as Ezra Pound and Ford Madox Ford praised her work (Ashbery in *CS* 8). She lived in France for six years, where she befriended Jean Cocteau, who illustrated her prose piece *Imaginary Letters,* printed in Paris in 1928. There she fell deeply into the world of drugs and the occult, including a stay at Aleister Crowley's infamous Abbey of Thelema at Cefalu in Sicily. After about three months she fled (Clukey 79), rejecting Crowley's methods and views (Matless 340). In 1930, Butts's mother rescued her from Paris. From 1932 onward, Butts

3. "Mappa Mundi" means map of the world and refers to a European medieval map of the world. It includes more than physical characteristics, including mythological, biblical, and exotic figures.

lived in a cottage in Sennen, Cornwall, near the Sennen Hedge, a standing stone (menhir) site. She christened her cottage "Tebel Vos, House of Magic" (Valentine, "Inner Bohemia" 29). At this ancient site she discovered the enchanted landscape she had always strived to find and illuminate through her fiction. David Matless deems Mary Butts a "mystic modernist" (339).

Key aspects of her fiction are the return of an ancient past that was enchanted, shape-shifting environments, a sensitivity to natural places, and visionary experiences. Butts's style challenges readers. Her fiction merges impressionism with expressionism; that is, she tries to capture the wonder of the hidden world through the inner turmoil or elation of the human experience with our inadequate language. She experimented with methods to break down the cognitive boundary between human beings and the external world increasingly found in modern technological, mechanical, and industrial societies, that is, to reintroduce a direct sense or feeling of a mystical world different from our scientific, instrumental view of the world. She often deployed unusual similes in her works. In *Armed with Madness* (1928),[4] the character, Carston, "goes down a white road sprung like an arrow across the moor that filled the lowlands like a dark dragon's wing" (*TN* 129). She also used stream-of-consciousness techniques and sentence fragments that disrupt a normal reading experience. Her prose can be abrupt and clipped at times. However, her style can also be elongated and elegant as if the world shifts and lengthens.

Kessler says Butts's prose is often "syntactically eccentric," and a page may "call for rereading" (210). The concluding sections of *Armed with Madness* illustrate this aspect of her prose in both structure and language. The novel's structure shifts from chapters to sections generally headed by the names of characters in capitals. In

4. Butts wrote this novel during World War I. It ends with the inscription: *"Cornwall—London 1918–1919."* During her time in London she aided the anti-conscription organization, the National Council for Civil Liberties (Radford 132).

these concluding sections, the characters leave the Gault House and travel separate ways; for example, Felix goes to Paris and Scylla goes to London. These sections seem to represent the disintegration of that community and present a microcosm of the decay of the modern world. The narrative voice swings from free indirect discourse to interior monologue to third-person narration. Readers are challenged because the novel's point of view keeps shifting. One section includes a scene, or perhaps a short libretto, with lines and methods of delivery for the characters. Another tells of extreme violence inflicted on Scylla by Clarence, who is shellshocked.[5] He is one of the survivors, or walking dead, from the Great War. Charles Taylor says the war was "a gigantic slaughter of young lives" (492). It was a slaughter that haunted the lost generation in Europe. Shellshocked characters appear in many of Butts's works, because part of her literary mission was to document the conditions of her generation. Such characterizations also suggest that the disenchanted world of violence, alienation, and hopelessness triggers PTSD (post-traumatic stress disorder). Kessler argues that Butts's idiosyncratic style reflects her striving to express something that is hidden, something she feels more than conceives.

In her Sennen cottage Butts devoted herself to writing, powered by her imagination, her transcendent appreciation of the natural environment, and the nearby haunting structures from the past. Amy Clukey argues that for Butts "magic and aesthetics provided a means to stave off the psychological and spiritual devastations of modernity" (78). Mary Butts's oeuvre includes five novels: *Ashe of Rings* (1925), *Armed with Madness*, and *Death of Felicity Taverner* (1932), followed by two historical narratives, *The Macedonian* (1933) and *Scenes from the Life of Cleopatra* (1935). She produced three

5. Butts's "Speed the Plough" (1921) is a short story about a shellshocked veteran of World War I, which Lawrence Rainey calls a masterpiece. In "The Golden Bough" (1923), Butts reshaped Sir James George Frazer's myth of the ritual death of a leader to the reality of the walking dead of "wounded young men" on the streets of London (*CS* 92).

collections of short stories: *Speed the Plough and Other Stories* (1923), *Several Occasions* (1932), and *Last Stories* (1938). A childhood autobiography, *The Crystal Cabinet,* was published shortly after her death in 1937. She wrote other shorter works such as the pamphlets published in 1932, *Warning to Hikers* and *Traps for Unbelievers* (Blondel, *AR* viii). These two works express her love of nature, the need to preserve forests and sacred places, and her pleas to restore our spiritual or mystical awareness. She was also a prolific book reviewer for the *Bookman*, the *Sunday Times*, the *Daily Telegraph,* and others (Blondel, *AR* viii–ix).[6] Highly regarded literary journals of the time, such as the *Little Review* and *Transatlantic Review,* published her fiction. In this article I will focus on a selection of her short stories that exemplify her search for and attempts to recreate an enchanted, mythical world, along with a discussion of two of her novels, *Ashe of Rings* and *Armed with Madness,* which feature similar themes.

Butts wrote to challenge the overwhelming atmosphere of "disenchantment" in the world. She wrote to express that "reality outside the observation of the senses" (*AR* 350).[7] "Disenchantment" is the cultural rationalization and devaluation of myth and religion in modern society, as coined by Friedrich Schiller and elaborated on by Max Weber. Butts reacted against what she called "dogmatic materialism" (*AR* 334), which for her meant the rule of scientific explanation for everything, the disavowal of myth, and the disdain of ancient beliefs. Yet she was not anti-science, as she knew of and appreciated the concrete benefits that advancing scientific discoveries brought. Butts expressed an overwhelming feeling of loss through an overly pursued materialism.

In *On the Aesthetic Education of Man* (1791), Friedrich Schiller studied history, politics, and science and concluded that art should have a greater role in societies. In the "Sixth Letter," he mourned the loss of myth, magic, and wonder, which he argued flourished in

6. Mary Butts's reviews are included in her *Collected Essays* (2021).
7. In *Armed with Madness*, the character Picus asks "[w]hether a true picture of the real is shewn by our senses alone?" (*AR* 123).

the past and which he saw as reaching its zenith with the ancient Greeks. Schiller decried the de-divinization of the world and the accompanying loss of a harmony between the human and the natural. Moreover, he argued that the modern state submerged individuals and exalted empiricism, reason, and utilitarianism. Specialized knowledge and skills fragmented and alienated individuals from themselves, others, and the world. It dis-enchanted the world. For Schiller, the cure was through the study of aesthetics and education in the arts, which would rekindle a sense of wholeness and contact with nature. He argued that the sense of wonder needed to be revived. Schiller recognized the benefits achieved in his time, yet he claimed the "prize of humanity" belonged to the Greeks (18).

As if responding to Schiller, Butts strived to portray wonder found in nature in her fiction. She also believed that the disenchantment of nature was harmful to human beings. Early in her life she indulged in occult practices and transcendental magic as she worked to understand and express her inner awareness, but she abandoned those practices and found that the true expression of enchantment would be through her art. In *Ashe of Rings,* Butts transformed her experience near the Badbury Rings into a novel of the continuing mystery and enchantment power of ancient Neolithic sites. A house and the prehistoric earthwork are the Rings of the title. Anthony Ashe, the patriarch of the Ashe family, says, "We are a priestly house, like the Eumolpidae" (*AR* 20), who were one of two families charged with the care of the festival at Eleusis (Bowen 39). This links the Ashe Rings to the Eleusinian Mysteries of Demeter and Kore, the most revered of all ancient Greek mystery religions (Bowen 34). In the novel, the earthwork is the arena of a contest between members of the Ashe family, with one side representing the disenchantment of the world and Vanna, Anthony's daughter, representing enchantment.

Max Weber revived Schiller's notion in his *Charisma and Disenchantment: The Vocation Lectures* (1919). He argued that the scientific process mechanized[8] our picture of the world. The advance of scientific methods and rationalization "meant that, in principle, there are no mysterious incalculable forces intervening in our lives, but instead all things, in theory, can be *mastered* through *calculation*" (18). This was the process of disenchantment. The German word used by Weber, *Entzauberung*, literally means demagification, as suggested by Richard Swedberg and Ola Agevall. For Weber, the effect of this process was a world with no mystery. It was predictable, rationalized, and freed of the numinous. Sara Lyons argues that Weber's thesis was that the rise of science and modern capitalism, along with destruction of traditional communities, removed mystery from the world and, thus, its meaning. "Nature lost its visionary gleams and was exposed as a purposeless mechanism" (Lyons 873). What remained was a world primed for exploitation. Moreover, the lives of people were diminished to a pure materiality, causing a "pervasive sense of alienation, nihilism, and ennui" (Lyons 873).

Karen Armstrong argues that myth "looks into the heart of a great silence" (4). That great silence is the unknown, or what at first we have no words to express. It is as if one must find a way to leap over the language ravine between humans and the rest of nature. Armstrong says myth is an imaginative art form that helps us make sense of an unknown world. This is similar to the notion that it is through artistic expression that myth is reawakened. As Butts contented, there is an element of experience (an experience that is hard to describe precisely because of the limitations of our language) that goes beyond ordinary perception, which is framed by our language system. Mythic narratives help express that experience. Butts believed that our language systems limit, determine, and prescribe how to experience the world. Algernon Blackwood wrote that "an expansion of normal consciousness" would bring back the numinous vision of nature (xiv). Butts shared Blackwood's view.

---

8. E. J. Dijksterhuis titled his influential history of science *The Mechanization of the World Picture* (1950).

A young American, Currer Mileson, is transported into a hidden nature in Butts's short story "Mappa Mundi." In the story, Paris becomes a mystical city or exhibits its true nature hidden beyond the human constructions. The tale entrances readers with its unusual phrasing, which reflects the twisting streets and shifting structures of the city similar to Machen's view of London expressed in *Far Off Things* (1922) and other works. Butts wrote that there was a *noli me tangere* (do not touch me) veil that warped one's view of the city. She envisioned the old gods, for example Isis, as if they yet wandered the streets of Paris. And she brought to life old myths, such as the Minotaur hiding in the labyrinth of Paris streets. Butts conveyed a sense of magic roaring through the streets with an expressionistic style focusing on the reactions of the characters when they faced "bridges [that] have a spring to them like a bent bow," and where "one finds [s]hadows" on the "moon-candied stones, cat-black and sharp" (*CS* 285). That is, "on the other side of shadows there is another country" (*CS* 291).

Paris appears as overlapping realties. The young American goes over to that other country. He becomes a shadow dimly seen at times in a distant lane, at the end of a bridge over the Seine, or as a shadow thrown from one tree to another. He was past "hailing distance from shore" (*CS* 286). The female narrator muses that perhaps we are all *"eidola"* (*CS* 283), that is, the latest to arise from the womb of Isis upon which Paris is superimposed. The narrator searches for that young American through the shadowy streets of a shape-shifting Paris. This is akin to what Butts saw as the core of some supernatural fiction in her "Ghosties and Ghoulies," where a "place becomes another place" but in fact "it is two places at once" (*AR* 342). Arthur Machen also believed we were obscured from the beauty and dreadful mystery of the universe. Yet it does occasionally appear, for example, to Lucian Taylor in *The Hill of Dreams* (1907): "All London was one grey temple of an awful rite, ring within ring of wizard stones circled about some central place, every circle was an initiation" (115–16). These ancient rings of Britain haunt many works by Mary Butts.

At the end of "Mappa Mundi," a Paris police agent visits the nameless narrator in her rooms for the second time. He asks again about the strange disappearance of the young American. She challenges him that it seemed "to be a little ghost of evidence that he was still occasionally seen" (*CS* 290) and goes on to say that Mileson met a "shadow, who has drawn him into the shadows. [. . .] He may come to no harm there" (*CS* 291). He was in an enchanted place "only just outside the gates of Paradise" (*CS* 291). This story illustrates Butts's notion that in some supernatural stories the people experiencing a strange, uncanny experience may have their "consciousness enlarged" and move "into another state of existence" (*AR* 343).

Another story illustrating the transformation of an ordinary urban environment into an enchanted place is "Brightness Falls" (1932). The title is from the Thomas Nashe poem "A Litany in the Time of Plague," first published in 1600. Here it seems that Butts illustrated the differences between those who are firmly set in the disenchanted world and hold that all happenings and things can be explained through reason and careful observation and those who experience something different, something that seems to defy the mechanistic picture of the world. In this story, a piece of London is transformed, as happens to Paris in "Mappa Mundi." The story also reflects Butts's feministic viewpoint and concern with the dominant patriarchal society in England during her lifetime. In general, her female characters appear to be more amenable to magical or enchanted experiences than males, who sometimes ridicule such happenings, as occurs in "Brightness Falls."

The unnamed male narrator of the story tells Max's version of an inexplicable experience of his wife Parmys and her friend Cynthia. These two women chanced upon a magical site on the green behind the Lincoln's Inn[9] in Central London where they

9. Lincoln's Inn has a private garden separated from the adjacent Lincoln's Inn Fields, which is the largest public garden in London.

experienced another reality beyond the ken of the narrator and Max. But Max saw something that he tries to tell to the narrator, who is dismissive. Both he and Max are skeptical of enchantment and myth. Max ends up refusing to acknowledge the actuality of an unusual scene he witnessed. He dismisses it because it does not fit into his conceptual scheme. Max says the explanation for it "lies in some kind of hypnosis" (*CS* 147).

The narrator becomes irritated at Max's delay in describing what happened behind Lincoln's Inn, but Max's delay reflects his hesitation in experiencing again what happened. It started with a phone call from Parmys asking him to come immediately. She sounded as if the "sea beginning to rise before the wind" (*CS* 152). She told Max they must go to the green lawn at the back of Lincoln's Inn because it was "one of those places" (*CS* 153). There, Parmys appeared like "an archaic goddess stored with raw power" (*CS* 154). Cynthia "moved like a lost star" (*CS* 154). Parmys's voice changed to a sound "like strings of gold and silver" (*CS* 155). Max could not stay with them because "they were half in, half out of another world" (*CS* 155). The old London scene changed and Parmys and Cynthia appeared beneath a towering fountain on long terraces beyond which a wooded country seemed colored "like spring" (*CS* 155). After their experience, they were "like children, enchanted, drenched with some abnormal radiance" (*CS* 156), as if they had been reborn. Max denies his experience, thinking he had been tricked. He wishes Parmys's "nature would take a proper feminine course" (*CS* 148). He shuns the doors of perception that seemed to open for the two women, and the male narrator agrees with his assessment. William Blake wrote that if "the doors of perception were cleansed, everything would appear to man as it is, Infinite—For man has closed himself up, till he sees all things thro' narrow chinks of his cavern" (166). This is what Max and the narrator do. "Brightness Falls" expresses the sense of a place sliding from the disenchanted to the enchanted. The phrase "brightness falls" has a double meaning: it suggests the fall of light and its dissolution. Yet it also suggests that people can be re-enchanted.

In his recent book, *Cosmic Connections: Poetry in the Age of Disenchantment* (2024), Charles Taylor suggests that post-Galilean sciences propelled the process of disenchantment. It solved many scientific problems and ushered in new forms of technological control, which have accelerated more quickly in modern times. He revives the claims of Schiller and Weber, arguing that human beings have become estranged from the world; hence they have lost a feeling of belonging and meaning. Taylor attributes this to the positivist tradition that disdained any sense of connections between human feelings and our understanding of the world. In the positivist view, he argues, we, as individuals, are alone in an immeasurably vast cosmos, alienated and disconnected from anything, including other human beings. But he is not anti-science; he knows the improvements in life achieved through science, along with the dangers. He may echo the character Picus in *Armed with Madness,* who asks "[in] what lies the scientific triumph but that its formulas work?"[10] (*AR* 123).

Arthur Machen decried the increasing trend toward materialism and industrialization that he saw in England. In his introduction to *Notes and Queries* (1926), he wrote "there is no possibility of happiness in the hell of industrialism" and lamented the loss of enchantment (xi).[11] Yet, as Taylor argues, that old world of

---

10. In quantum physics, the elegant equations do work, but they also mean something about the quantum world, that is, reality is quantized. The structure, composition, and "laws" of the quantum level are vastly different from our everyday perception. It is where matter may behave like a wave or a particle, two or more "particles" may be correlated regardless of the distance (entanglement), and a quantum may be in many potential states simultaneously up to being measured, but it is not magical. The equations depict that microworld where the "normal conception of reality does not apply" (Greenstein 118). Much of modern technology is based on quantum physics (Lees 41).

11. Butts echoed this when she referred to the "hells of materialism" (*CE* 328).

experiential myth as the guide to life is gone. There is no return, and there is no abandoning of industrialization or science. Like Schiller and Taylor, Butts believed enchantment can be achieved through art. Taylor contends that the arts are not mere frivolities or amusements or distractions from the real purpose of being; rather, they are a primary way of apprehending the world, where we may find a harmony with existence, where we make a cosmic connection. Cosmic connections that Butts experienced and tried to communicate in a language that is inadequate but yet might approximate those connections.

Butts felt the mystical actualized in certain places. In *Ashe of Rings,* she wrote about the enchantment of a Neolithic earthwork. She believed that something outside of the normal resided at such sites and that some people experienced the wonder embedded there. It was beyond appearances and more "than the atomic structure common to all things" (*AR* 350). These sites seem akin to portals through the perceived world into another reality that is accessible to some people directly, which they try to express in our language's limited ability. In *Ashe of Rings,* "Mappa Mundi," and "Brightness Falls," Butts tackled the problem of expressing experiences outside of the normal. Ludwig Wittgenstein recognized this problem. In *Tractatus Logico-Philosophicus* (1921) he wrote: "There are, indeed, things that cannot be put into words. They *make themselves manifest.* They are what is mystical" (89). He argued that we are constrained by our language. Trying to break the "boundaries of language" or escape "the walls of our cage" of language is "hopeless," yet he "deeply" respected the effort ("A Lecture on Ethics" 44).

Mary Butts struggled to escape the cage. She struggled to express what she experienced in certain places. In "Ghosties and Ghoulies," she called such a place a *temenos* (*temenoi* in the plural), from the Greek *temnein* (cut off, sever), which refers to a ground surrounding a temple or a sacred enclosure (*AR* 349).[12] These places

12. All etymologies and definitions are from *The New Shorter Oxford English Dictionary* (Oxford: Clarendon Press, 1993).

are where one may experience what she called "mana," that is, an energy or knowledge beyond and outside ordinary sense perception (*AR* 349). She noted Eleusis as an example of such a place where people could be initiated and "have their souls strengthened by contact with reality outside the observation of our senses" (*AR* 349). She elaborated on that energy in her essay "Traps for Unbelievers." She wrote that it is "a flash of the hidden forces of nature" (*AR* 322). Sue Terry argues that Butts adapted "mana" from the classical scholar Jane Ellen Harrison, who described "mana" as a world of unseen power lying behind the visible universe" (205). Butts saw it as a subtle force or energy behind all things that occasionally became manifest, especially in certain special places. For Butts it is a "non-moral, beautiful, subtle energy in man and everything else" that may become evident in certain places. (*AR* 328). Eleusis, the site of the Eleusinian Mysteries in ancient Attica, was such a site. The mysteries were celebrated there for more than a thousand years (Bowen 34).[13] It was a "temenos" where one would be initiated into the mysteries. There is little to be found in written records about the ancient Greek mystery religions, but the thought is that initiates underwent a transformative experience that connected them in some way to another energy in nature. In such places, people might connect with the cosmic "outside the observation of their senses" (*AR* 349).

The character Dick Tressider searches London for "mana" in the story "Widdershins"[14] (1924). As a former soldier, Tressider "knew what war was" (*CS* 120). This story illustrates the "generational war-wound" that Sue Terry claims can be found in several of Butts's works (208). Due to his war experience, Tressider is now disillusioned about

13. Arthur Machen's first work was the poem *Eleusinia* (1881), which creatively depicted the ancient Greek mystery religion of Demeter and her daughter Kore through the experience of initiands in the Eleusinian mysteries.
14. "Widdershins" was first published in Ford Madox Ford's *Transatlantic Review* (March 1924) under the title "Deosil" (Foy, "'Brightness Falls'" 384). Desosil is a variant of deasil and deisal, which derives from the Gaelic *deiseil.* It means in the direction of the sun's apparent motion or movement in a clockwise direction.

everything. Butts may have been suggesting that disenchantment is like being shellshocked. As in "Brightness Falls," this story explores the differing responses to or attitudes of males and females toward that elusive sense of cosmic connectedness. The word "widdershins" originates from the Middle Low German and is defined as in a direction contrary to the apparent course of the sun (considered unlucky or associated with occult rites). Tressider is searching for meaning in London, but he did not understand that "what he wanted was magic" (*CS* 117), "what he needed was magic" (*CS* 118). He vaguely remembers that "moment of pure being" wherein he experienced "under the hills" on the Shap moors (*CS* 118). But that moment is gone. He is unable to have that moment of "peculiar quality" that would deliver him from the progress of mankind, that is, to experience enchantment (*CS* 118). He is an angry, damaged, egotistical man. He represents *la génération perdue* (the lost generation) wandering the "dreadful place" (*CE* 318) of the "war-shattered and disillusioned world" (*CE* 315). Everything that is said to propel progress, that is, industrialization and technology, does not overcome his "empty days" (*CS* 118).

Tressider wanders through Holborn (an area of central London) to become one with "cosmic consciousness" (*CS* 119), so he claims. But he seems unable to connect to people or nature, to forget the cosmos. In the British Museum he meets an old friend whom he regales with the cosmic significance of the artifacts. That friend, Brooks, thinks Tressider is madder than ever. This suggests that Tressider suffers from shellshock or PTSD. World War I and material progress have disenchanted his sense of the world.

He visits Daphne, a woman he once loved. She appears dressed in green, crystals, and silver as if a sorceress, someone who is attuned to nature. She is happy and amusing in contrast to his anger and resentment. He thinks she appears "like a tree in glory," but he wants to "hit her" (*CS* 124), expressing his rage at the world. She sets a "wreath of bright green leaves" on her head, "leaves of no earthly laurel"[15] (*CS* 124). She is nature and myth personified.

At the end of the story, Daphne leaves Tressider on the London street enmeshed in his egoism, wounds, and anger. Daphne seems attuned myth, nature, and magic. Here there is an extreme contrast between male and female, where the woman has a connection to the cosmos, while the man is vainly seeking a connection to something that will alleviate his sense of loss, suffering, and isolation. Tressider, wounded and longing, wants "[n]ature to knock the nonsense out of him and the memories" (*CS* 125). But as the wind roars past, he sees Daphne sail away into a world he longs for but cannot enter. Tressider represents those interned in the alienating, disillusioning, violent, and materialistic world. This is a strange story with an undercurrent of longing destroyed by war memory. It is a longing that is symbolized by Daphne disappearing through a tall golden arch, while Tressider stands forlorn on a London Street.

Butts's phenomenal places are akin to Charles Taylor's "interspaces," which are resonant spaces where human beings and the world intersect outside of the ontological and the psychological domains (52). It is another domain where humans and certain spaces interact in a fashion that can only be expressed through a work of art. He sees these as "'human related' realities" because they exist only where there are humans (55). This space is the creative, phenomenal space of arts that links humans to the underlying mystery and majesty of the universe (62).

Another supernatural story by Butts, "With and Without Buttons,"[16] suggests that the enchanted world is not always marvelous but also fraught with danger. It is a simple story on one level, but there is a fascinating repeated phrase that keeps sounding throughout, which keeps a focus on the sensory (auditory, tactile,

---

15. Here Butts alluded to the myth of Apollo hunting Daphne, who refused to accept his advances, and at the moment he touched her, she changed into a laurel tree.
16. This story was first published in Butts's collection *Last Stories* (1938), after her death.

and olfactory). One sister is the narrator of the story; the other sister is the ringleader of a plot to give their male neighbor, Trenchard, who irritated them with "his pseudo rationalization" (*CS* 332), "a nightmare" (*CS* 333). They live in adjoining cottages in a remote village in Kent. The plotting sister uses women's gloves as a stimulant to the haunting of their neighbor. Of the gloves, the sister says "[s]ome have all the buttons and some have one and some have none" (*CS* 335). The narrator sister listens to this chant, this "rune," so many times she cannot remember the count, and then she repeats "with and without," and she cannot remember how many times she had chanted it (*CS* 335). This rune, with its allusive and potent sounds, stir the story beyond its setting, beyond its ordinary occasion. As the story progresses, the two sisters appear to be taken over by some power arising from this recurring set of words.

These repetitions with variations throughout the story hint at the power and limitations of language to hide or reveal the nature of the world. Butts was interested in re-enchanting our sense of the world. This story suggests that experiencing that enchanted sense may be perilous, especially if it is a frivolous or malicious attempt to use unseen powers. This story may also reflect Butts's abandoned interest in occult practices because she found them worthless and used by some individuals to gain authority over people. Here she seems to be mocking the occult.

In the story, the "rune" may call up something that is hard to put back down or away, as the two young girls discover. Mellissa Edmundson suggests that this story emphasizes "gender anxiety and female power" (xix), which is absent in many of the strange tales written by men of the era. As with "Brightness Falls," two women seem arrayed against a male. But here the experience is not one of wonder but of danger. The story is filled with a sense of materiality (unwanted touching), the repetition of sounds, and the smell of things, especially the scent of those old gloves, which at the end are the dreadful smell of death to Trenchard.

The young girls form a coven of sorts with a plan for power over the male of the story, yet the most powerful thing in the story is what they cannot control. This is the power that takes control of the appearance of gloves, as they "feed themselves" across the cottages of the sisters and Trenchard (*CS* 338), spreading their feel and odor. They spread like an infection of slugs everywhere, carrying that odor of "[d]ead skin" (*CS* 341). At the end, the sisters consider they "came off lightly," but Trenchard seemed cursed by the experience because he "cannot think what he used to think, and he does not know what else there is that he might think" (*CS* 332). The experience has deformed his conceptual view of the world. Now he is lost between two worlds, the visible and the invisible.

In "Friendship Garland" (1925), Butts contrasts two views of the world, one of wonder, the other of the everyday. Cesca, the narrator, and her friend Zoe strive to stay in a state of natural wonder, mystery, and magic while warding off the chains of a society determined to conform them to its needs. This story reads like an allegory about the insidious effects of the disenchantment of the modern human experience.

The two women rebel against the "intelligences without imagination" whose prime "virtuosity" was "in the creation of pain" (*CS* 181). This story contrasts the material versus the magical, logic versus imagination, reason versus exhilaration, age versus youth, disenchantment versus enchantment, and the wasteland against nature's garden. The story exhibits many of Butts's unusual similes, for example: the staircase of a "house was like the easy stairs you fall down in dreams" (*CS* 182). Her style is elusive at times, as if she were trying to induce a feeling of disorientation akin to what the characters are experiencing in their mutable environs. Cesca's magical world is the world of nature and its mysteries in contrast to the world of The Craven, the embodiment of the disenchanted. In *Warning to Hikers,*[17] Butts cautioned about the loss of a sense of

17. Butts's pamphlet reads, in part, as a warning about the continuing destruction of nature and its ultimate impact on humans.

myth and the resulting ruination of nature underway by human beings because of that loss. In the story, she expresses this as where the quiet infects the woods and the faint "noise of harp runs down the trunks [of trees] into the earth. *And no birds sing*" [18] (*AR* 295).

The Craven is where there is "no nature" (*CS* 182). The atmosphere is like a "stale quiet whose murmur was like the tuning-up of birds that would never begin to sing" (*CS* 183). It is a temple of the modern dynamic "to be rich—to be *rangé* [19]—to be cute; to cut your friends—to suffer for nothing—to be a cad" (*CS* 186). Much of the action in the temple consists of bits of conversations among the characters that at times are confusing and disorienting, purposely perhaps, as it reflects the sensations of Cesca, who wanted to hide because part of her soul was being drained by modern society.

Cesca flees The Craven, as if leaving the disenchanted world to return to her enchanted home. In contrast to The Craven, Cesca's home appears an hallucination of wonders. It is a place where every room had its own tune; upstairs there was a mummy, seven glass balls for the seven planets hung in another room, and a cat that "threaded the rooms"; in one room lived "the most beautiful child in the world" (*CS* 187).

The story reads as if the character is on LSD. Cesca becomes one with the cosmos and experiences "the movement of the earth through space" (*CS* 187). The balcony becomes re-enchanted as the house transforms into a ship plunging through the seas. She has a mystical experience; it is a rebirth, because Cesca "looked like a child that has been dipped in dew" (*CS* 188), akin to Parmys and Cynthia in "Brightness Falls." She has made a cosmic connection or

---

18. This last phrase is from "La Belle Dame sans Merci" (1819) by John Keats. The phrase may also anticipate Rachel Carson's *Silent Spring* (1962), as noted by Foy in *Ritual, Myth, and Mysticism in the Work of Mary Butts* (93). David Matless disputes this notion, arguing that harp sounds helped to protect Vanna on a stone at the center of the ancient rings in *Ashe of Rings*.

19. French for: to be set, to be tidy, to conform.

experienced a moment of pure being that frees her from the wasteland of materialistic society. Butts contrasted a mechanical, regimented, merciless society against one of innocence and youth through a character receptive to enchantment and not consumed by material society. Nature was the gateway to enchantment for her, away from the cultural decay of "new barbarians" inured to the "vibrating roar" and "street shrieks" of industrial cities (*AR* 279). This tale is more of a paean to the glory of nature than a story.

Mary Butts also wrote a few supernatural stories that vary in theme from her enchantment ones. "After the Funeral" (1938) features a ghost who never appears except in the sorrow, thoughts, fears, and hopes of the characters. This ghost is haunted by the living. For the start of the story, Butts composed a scene of extreme grief and sadness at the loss of a friend. It started in an "ice-dark, star-pieced church" (*CS* 346), where mourners awaited the arrival of the coffin. Their grief was palpable, as a man sobbed and sobbed, another fell to his knees in his pew, and the narrator dreaded the arrival of "that, that, that which had been her" (*CS* 346). Sorrow itself came alive in the church as it "hid behind a pillar on which mildew had drawn green scrawls, lounged against it and watched us where we sat, slender and very tall, as the body we were waiting for," as if the dead Clair awaited her body along with the others lined up in their pews (*CS* 346). In one of the pews a painter friend sketched. It is a sketch of "Clair. Clair. Clair" (*CS* 348)[20] that will return later in the story, as if it is her.

Later, in the spring at a party, the narrator suddenly remembers her tall friend as someone who had been "like a tree moving in the wind" (*CS* 349) and a short poem forms in her head. The ghost appears in the effects it had on others. At another party, a male friend of Clair shows a sketch of her. He stares at the drawing until he seems to become "invisible" (*CS* 350), perhaps expressing his longing to see her or to join her. At yet another party, the narrator finds a friend in the garden with an April "moon pouring down into

20. Words are repeatedly stated three times in the story, akin to a lament.

it" (*CS* 351). He is staring at a drawing of Clair flooded by the light of that moon. He cries, "Clair, Clair Clair," as if saying it three times would be magic. She lives in the thoughts and memories of her friends, and that is enough for this ghost.

Another ghost story is titled "Look Homeward, Angel" (1938), after a phrase from John Milton's "Lycidas" (1638).[21] It is a sentimental ghost story laden with references to Milton's poem and to the perilous sea that takes everything at the end. The story abounds in foreshadowing, but the elegant phrasing conveys the story out of the realm of the commonplace. The sea seems sentient; it has blinded the night with its sea-fog crawling on the waters up through the moors above to the "dreadful hills with their standing stones" (*CS* 255). The house of Julian and Cynthia (character names used in other stories by Butts) is near Nanquidno in west Cornwall. It is an isolated area, where they watch giant liners go by "blazing at night as if they were on fire" (*CS* 226). The setting is near Pendeen lighthouse and the Longships Lighthouse (erected to warn ships away from the treacherous coastline) off Land's End. These sentinels speak to each other through a siren and gun that the sea has muffled into "voices from the other side of death" (*CS* 225). The couple await their friend Fergus, who is traveling on one of those giant ships, "passing [them] now, tonight" (*CS* 226). They are anxious for him to arrive because they both sense he has something special he wants to tell them. Cynthia thinks of the ultimate west where the sun sets into the "Baths of the Ocean" (227).[22] And Julian stands by the mist-clouded window speaking fragments from Milton's poem that the sea has whispered to him. It seems they are already mourning the death of their friend.

The story is short, as if it were a commentary on Milton's poem or

21. A eulogy for his friend Edward King, a fellow student at Cambridge who drowned in 1637.

22. Oceanus (Okeanos) is the son of Uranus and Gaia and is the guardian of the river that circled the earth. "Baths of Ocean" is from Samuel Butler's translations of the *Iliad* (18.489) and *Odyssey* (5.275–80).

an adulation of it. Perhaps Fergus stands for Milton's friend who drowned. But the story does evoke the power and terror of the "eternally angry seas" with their "death and resurrection" while the thunder roars and a "dreadful moan" replies as if a "vast cry of pain" (*CS* 227-228). Those seas allow Fergus to drag "his bones [. . .] out of the flood" and be "the first with his news" (*CS* 230) at that isolated cottage where the sea's icy dark water runs on the floor so "dark it might be blood" (CS 229). It is a story of someone lost and found at sea.

The idea of nature as sentient appears across Butts's work. "The Warning" (1938) expresses hers awareness that the wonder of nature is too often ignored in daily life. In this story, characters do not notice the natural marvels surrounding them because they become lost in petty squabbles about an invitation to tea getting mixed up. The house at the center of the story stands on a cliff where below the sea "sang, swore, snored, shouted, whispered, yelled" (*CS* 267). Onto a reef, the sea "leaped in seven waves whose hairs shook out the prisms of seven rainbows" (*CS* 267). A rising tide shapes itself into a bull that staggers across the shore to face "the raving of the green water beasts" (*CS* 268). There the shore shifts from "lion-bright sand to skin-pale sand," and at night the sea may "whisper its stupendous secret which is the meaning of everything," if only "people would listen" (*CS* 268). The surrounding landscape features a "stone hedge beside a planting of willows," a site of enchantment for Butts (*CS* 268). Yet the owners of the house (another Julian and a Marcia), near these marvels, focus on the delicate harmonizing of the coming and going of their many guests. No matter; their focus does go awry as two guests, Caroline and Violanne, collide as if caused by "star-dust from the tail of a very different comet"[23] (*CS* 271). With jubilant prose Butts minutely describes the natural world

23. This may be an early instance of C. J. Jung's concept of synchronicity, originally published in 1952. For Jung, in some cases of seemingly no causal connection, there is a connection beyond the realm of mere coincidence. For him the patterns in life are not mere chance events but express a deep coherence and meaning.

of moths, snails, hedgehogs, and toads three hundred feet below near the purring sea while the guests in the terrace room buzz in conversation and clink their glasses and do not notice the incense on the "night breeze off the sea" (*CS* 272). And they miss the mystery of the night around the house where moths, snails, hedgehogs, and toads roam. The perfume of these night callers on the night breeze off the sea passes unnoticed on that terrace. The characters ignore these stirrings in nature because they squabble over a minor indiscretion of a newly divorced mother of two young children. As Julian remarks in the story, "[s]ometimes things crash out of the invisible into the visible world, but people do not see" (*CS* 274).

In many of her works, Butts invoked ancient mysteries and places, a characteristic that Jascha Kessler calls "modern primitivism" (212). Ancient images noted in "The Warning" and other works are Neolithic monuments such as mounds, rings, barrows, or standing stones. In *Ashe of Rings,* an ancient British three-tiered earth-mound topped with stones becomes the center of a battle between its guardians and those set on its desecration. Three Mountains Press first published the novel in Paris in 1925, but parts of it were serialized in the *Little Review* in 1921. The novel presents a contest between the forces of enchantment and those of the disenchanted modern world. The Ashe family's ancestral manor is "a house crouched like a dragon on a saucer of jade" between the sea and that ancient sacred site of Rings (*AR* 5). Blondel says the novel aspires "to a condition of myth" (*AR* x). The Rings have an enduring history. In "Ghosties and Ghoulies," Butts wrote of a Neolithic earthwork in the south of England, which was a "temenos" (*AR* 349). And in the novel, the county history says that *"in the time of Arthur* [. . .] *Morgan le Fey* [. . .] *had dealings of an inconceivable nature"* at the Rings (*AR* 6). This ancient site is a long-standing revered place where the Ashes are the custodians.

Ashe of Rings is in three main parts. The first, set in 1892, starts with Anthony Ashe, the patriarch of the family, returning to the house after three years away, mourning the death of his son, Julian.

His aim is to sire an heir to continue the guardianship of the holy site. Anthony marries a local woman, Muriel Butler, but forces her to change her first name to Melitta.[24] She has a daughter, Vanna Elizabeth Ashe. Anthony and Melitta's marriage is not wholesome. Melitta is a representative of those arrayed against the mysteries of the mound and of nature, which seems to sense her hostility and is ready to combat her. While on a walk along a path, she "struggled with the sun. [. . .] The turf closed round empty shells. The path was sharp with flints, the heat like an army with banners" (*AR* 15). Melitta views the monument of earth and stone as merely that and fit to defile as she does by having sex on the rings with her lover, Morice Amburton, a local squire. She has a son, but it is not clear at first who is the father. Anthony dies soon after. Morice and Melitta wed, and Vanna is sent off to a boarding school and offered an allowance to discourage her from returning to the family house. At the conclusion of the first part, it seems that the dead Anthony Ashe departs in the form of a light that "rolled down the seven stairs [. . .] flew up to the ceiling, and broke into a storm of gold [. . .] quivered into a mist, and dissolved again into the unspeakable quiet" (*AR* 54).

The second part of the novel is set in London and features Vanna (also called Van) and a group of her young friends trying to establish a meaningful life. This section of the novel seems to be an analysis of the lost generation struggling to find meaning in a world shattered by war, the erosion of values, and economic upheaval. Vanna stays with the character Judy Marston, who plays a role in the final part of the novel. Judy becomes involved with Peter Amburton, the son of Morice Amburton and Vanna's mother, who plays a significant role in the final section of the novel.

In the third part of the novel, Vanna returns to the Rings, where the struggle over the ancient site occurs. Vanna shoulders the onus on the Ashe family to protect and guard that ancient set of rings,

---

24. Foy notes that "Melitta" is Greek and suggests "bees and the sweetness of honey [. . .] the implication is that Melitta is chosen because of her fertile childbearing abilities" (*Ritual* 38).

which is connected to ancient Eleusinian mysteries. She is attuned to the natural and marvelous and needs to stop her mother and her allies, who personify the evil of the disenchanted world. As if one of the Eumolpidae, Vanna returns to carry on their sacred duty. This is symbolized by a confrontation on the megalithic site at night, where the Rings' stones save Vanna. At the ancient monument, Peter Amburton attempts to rape Vanna. But the stones thwart her attacker. Amburton cries, "I won't touch that stone. It's alive" (*AR* 189). He flees. The site appears sentient and powerful. Early in the novel, Anthony Ashe warned that "once one starts disturbing old things, one raises something one did not know was there to be disturbed" (*AR* 18). Vanna's return may have activated the ancient power of this *temenos* site, as it reacquires its supernatural status.

In *Armed with Madness,* Butts revives another ancient myth as an elemental power within the British landscape riddled with "[r]ough barrow-haunted places" (*TN* 116). A discovered "odd cup of some greenish stone," a cup that may be the holy grail, is at the core of the novel (*TN* 22). Sue Terry documents Mary Butts's interest in and fascination with the grail legend and her reading of such books as A. E. Waite's *The Holy Grail* (1909)[25] and Jessie L. Weston's *From Ritual to Romance* (1920). Weston's study, which is somewhat discredited today, argued that the root of the grail legend could be traced back to "ancient ritual, having for its ultimate object initiation into the sources of Life, physical and spiritual" (191). Butts was also familiar with the work of Arthur Machen, who had a keen interest in the grail legend and wrote essays on the subject, including "The Secret of the Sangraal" (1907),[26] and embedded the notion of the

---

25. Butts reviewed Waite's book in the *Bookman* in 1933. The review is included in *Collected Essays* 162–63. In 1936, she reviewed *The Story of Parzival and the Graal* as related by Wolfram von Eschenbach, interpreted and discussed by Margaret Fitzgerald Richey (Oxford: Basil Blackwell, 1936) (*CE* 100–101).

26. This essay headlines a Tartarus Press collection of his essays, *The Secret of the Sangraal* (1994).

grail in the novella *The Great Return* (1915) and the novel *The Secret Glory* (1922). In "The Wonder from Wales" (1934), Machen wrote that the grail legend carried a "sense of enchantment," setting it "apart, and high above all other legends" (187–88). William A. Nitze argued the grail legend exhibited agrarian and mystic features. He compared the grail ceremony to the Eleusinian Mysteries, which fascinated Butts.[27] Nitze claimed that the quest for the grail was similar to an initiation in order to "ensure the life of the vegetation spirit always in danger of extinction and to admit the 'qualified' mortal into its mysteries" (394). Butts's search for enchantment was a lifelong quest, as if she believed that humanity had become sick on materialism and needed a new initiation into the mysteries of nature.

Armed with Madness starts in the environs of the house of Scylla[28] and Felix Taverner (sister and brother) "in which they could not afford to live" (*TN* 13). It is a country home on land between deep woods and the sea in the rural coastal village of Gault, Dorset. The other central characters in the novel include their friend Ross; Dudley Carston, an American visitor and war veteran; and Clarence Lake (a painter), who with Picus Tracy (a sculptor in clay) are two war veterans sharing a cottage but who have come to stay at the house. The reason is that their well became polluted. That well is where the mystery object is found. That "small jade cup" was "fished [. . .] out with a spear" (*TN* 22–23), hinting at the lance that appears in legend. Is it the holy grail? The novel again exhibits Butts's Modernist method of reinvigorating ancient myth and legend, in this

27. Weston argued that the association of the grail legend with the Eleusinian Mystery was a mistake because the Greek and Christian religious conceptions varied too widely from each other (133).
28. Scylla may be a reference to the Scylla of myth. In the novel, the character's actual name is Drusilla. Sue Terry suggests that the use of "Scylla" indicates her relationship with Hecate, who is thought of by some as the mother of Scylla (215). Hecate is considered the goddess of witchcraft and magic. Scylla was called a "witch" in the novel (*TN* 18). Robin Blaser explores the complexity of Butts's mythic references using "Scylla" in the novel (315).

case, the holy grail, to illustrate current social issues during her time.

The novel may suggest that the cup, as the grail, is a mode of enchanted healing in the midst of the 1920s post–World War I wasteland of the lost generation, who felt an emptiness and hopelessness in a world devastated by brutality and death and the rising of totalitarianism. Violence and death haunt the novel. The war veterans have all witnessed violence. After a meal, Ross tells a story about lambs "mewing in the dark" before the "shepherd exits with his hands covered with blood" (*TN* 33). During a trek through the woods, Picus discovers a "skeleton of a man" (*TN* 58). Death is brought onto center stage late in the novel when a shipwreck leaves twenty-three dead Danish sailors (*TN* 95).

Early in the novel, Scylla, who is "ash-fair tree-tall" and whom Carston thinks "the wood and the woman [Scylla] might be interchangeable" (*TN* 20), muses:

> everywhere there was a sense of broken continuity, a dis-ease. The end of an age [. . .]. Discovery of a new value, a different way of apprehending everything. She wished the earth would not suddenly look fragile [. . .]. There was something wrong with all of them, or with their world. A moment missed, a moment to come. Or not coming. Or either or both. Shove it off on the war; but that did not help. (*TN* 17–18)

In this interior monologue, Scylla (or Butts) expresses the anxiety and hopelessness about the future of the world, the lingering horror of the war, the feeling of something being amiss with or drained from life, and the wasteland that the human world has become. Robin Blaser calls this a "haunted passage" that sums up the "modern predicament" of loss (316). It was Butts's lament over the war and for the loss of a sense of a common connection of people with the earth, with the tradition of a mythic nature, and hope for a better future. In *Death of Felicity Taverner,* Butts extends this lament of the loss of a mythic view of life to increasing materialism and industrialization:

> The timeless active life of lover and sister and brother had been changed—for something which seemed to them to be like the cold arms and legs and abstractions of machinery [. . .]. For the realities that held them in activity and in vision, realities of the blood and the nerves and the senses and what is meant by the spirit, was to be substituted contact with the chill, the purpose, the strength of a machine, and of the impure values begotten by the machine upon raw human nature and re-begotten by them in turn. (*TN* 252)

This loss pervades *Armed with Madness.*

In the novel, the image of the grail suggests a possible return to a more mystical landscape. At first, the image of the grail seems to be lodged in that found object, but as the novel progresses it may be that the idea of the grail is as an ethereal presence found in enchanted landscapes, as Mark Valentine suggests in "Arthur Machen and the Mysteries of the Grail." Although the grail has a physical presence in a found object, it keeps shifting its form as if it is elusive and figurative and not substantial. That cup is treated with respect by some of the characters and mocked by others. It is viewed as an old English altar vessel, an ashtray, a spitting cup, or a poison cup out of the East. It is called a "shallow little green dish" (*TN* 23), a cup with "Keltic twiddles [. . .] round the rim" (*TN* 22), a "chalice" (*TN* 33), a " rajah's poison cup" (*TN* 81), a "mischief-making cup" (*TN* 118), and a "piece of worn jade" (*TN* 123). It may be all or none of these. The manifestations to different characters show who is and who is not receptive to its power and wonder. For some, the cup "might have been made out of star material" (*TN* 23–24) and may be the "cup of the Sanc-Grail" (*TN* 26). But not for others who "know what despair is" and are forever emotionally blighted (*TN* 35). The true nature of the cup, as a symbol of healing and regeneration, seems to withstand the negative views of some of the characters. But we never know whether the green cup is the Sanc-Grail, because that is not the point of the novel. These "grail knights" are all wounded (*TN* 125), not just the Fisher King in this "adventure of the cup" (*TN* 89).

In the novel, Scylla recognizes the lurking invisible power of the cup, but she is also confused by it. Scylla senses the cup's "mystery" as a sacred relic yet also knows it is cloaked in uncertainty (*TN* 81). She wonders if it is a covert transmitter of "mana." But she feels the emptiness of her disenchanted era. Scylla muses that "[i]f the materialists' universe is true . . . we are a set of blind factors in a machine. And no passion has any validity . . . They are just little tricks of the machine . . . If you stick to the facts as we have them, life is a horror and an insult" (*TN* 85). To Scylla, the presence of that cup seems to be made manifest, not as a physical presence, but as portal to "mana." However, the cup as an instantiation of enchantment is not understood by other characters. Most characters view it as meaningless, for example, Felix Taverner. Talking with Ross, he says, "You're looking for something. I'm not. And I hope when you get it, you'll like it. Looking for the Sanc-Grail. It's always the same story. The Golden Fleece or the philosopher's stone, or perpetual motion, or Atlantis or the lost tribes or God. All ways of walking into the same trap" (*TN* 121).

The final sections of the novel tell of the disintegration of the group that had congregated at Gault House. The grail quest becomes "complicated, violent, inconclusive" (*TN* 89). There are no longer chapters. The short sections follow each person on a different quest away from Gault House. This represents the fragmentation of the round table, which may be a microcosm of Butts's view of the state of the modern world.[29] In a section headed, "CLARENCE AND SCYLLA" (*TN* 126), Clarence, "dazed with violence and grief" and possessed by despair and loss, viciously attacks Scylla (*TN* 127). There is no miracle healing for the war-scarred in a land disenchanted.

The cup that could "transmit power from the past of myth to the present" is ignored and lost again, as it is eventually thrown back

29. Jennifer Kroll suggests that Butts may have been following Thomas Malory's *Le Morte d'Arthur* (1485), where the appearance of the grail disperses the Round Table.

into the well in the concluding sections of the novel (*TN* 27).[30] The story of the grail eventually becomes a "horror" (*TN* 116). At the novel's end, the knights return with no grail and no enlightenment. The violence and darkness of the world have broken their bond. There is no mythic wonder in the landscape. Max Weber thought that the modern disenchanted world was destiny and there was no return to enchantment. The "modern rational world was an 'iron cage'" (Angus 141). The ending note from *Armed with Madness* may be that the transformative energy of enchantment cannot be completely restored from the mythic past to the instrumentalist present. In her works, Mary Butts imaginatively portrayed a return of enchantment to modern times. But the "Sanc-Grail did not call on everyone," especially those who were trapped in the violent, disenchanted world (*TN* 27). *Armed for Madness* may express her sense of the cruel possibility of the continuation of the "bitter world" that characterizes modern technological societies of war, materialism, and division where enchantment is lost (*TN* 120). The wasteland persists.[31] The violence of Clarence, whose body was "branded with shrapnel and bullet and bayonet thrust," toward Scylla near the end of the novel suggests this may be so (*TN* 115).

Like other modernist artists, Butts's *Armed with Madness* and *Ashe of Rings* looks back to the past of myth to help express the human condition in the early twentieth century. It was an attempt to rebirth a mythic past in a desiccated present. *Ulysses* (1922), *The Waste Land* (1922), and *To the Lighthouse* (1927) are prime examples. Butts reanimated ancient legends and myths to reshape the representation of the current state of humans—a state that Schiller, Weber, and Taylor concluded was an increasing one of fragmentation, where people were cut off from nature, others, and themselves. Butts included ancient mythic elements in her works to

30. There are other tales about the provenance of this cup in the novel.
31. Butts ends her 1933 review of *A Modern Prelude* (1933) by Hugh I'Anson Fausset with a doubt whether "The Sanc Grail [...] will turn the Waste Land into a garden again? One is not quite sure" (*CE* 321).

illustrate her hope for a return to a wholeness within an enchanted nature. Her fiction is not nostalgic or sentimental about nature; rather, she expressed its power and terror, along with its beauty and wonder. Her fiction expresses her ongoing quest to reopen the doors of perception to enchantment. An element of strangeness, of something out of place, of something elusive haunts her work. Her fiction portrays how people's lives move into, through, and out of the mythical (or terrifying) world and how they are or are not affected by that experience. Butts seemed genuinely to have believed that there was another plane of existence beyond our normal perception.

Mary Butts shaped her life around an awareness of the myth and mystery beyond the materialism of the modern world. She wrote to surface the numinous from the confines of the ordinary world, that is, to overcome the boundaries of our ordinary language. She searched for ways to express that consciousness through her art. Her fiction and essays document that quest for an old mythic world of enchantment—a worldview that would reconnect people to the cosmic. There are two major aspects of her writings. One was her attempt to recapture the wonder of enchantment that she experienced in her home environs near the Badbury Mounds in Dorset and in the works of William Blake in her childhood home. The second was to recapture our symbiotic relationship with nature, which had been ruptured, or severed, by the focus on the exploitation of all aspects of nature for the insular use of human beings, which has been based on a view that we as a species are separate from the planet we inhabit, that we have no meaningful, no cosmic connection to nature. Her art worked to re-enchant the world for readers and release them from the cage of our ordinary language. That is why her style is challenging. As Wittgenstein wrote, the mystical is beyond our everyday language. Butts constructed unusual similes, used varying voices, altered the conventional flow of action, violated grammatical rules, resurrected ancient myths and places, and attempted to have nature speak in order to disrupt the standard reading experience of readers. She struggled to break our language-constructed view of the universe with the very language that bounded it. She hoped to reveal the wondrous in the universe.

That is what Charles Taylor tries to recover from the works of the Romantic poets. He searched through their works to identify how their poetry created an interspace where a cosmic connection broke through our language-ordered universe. This was the quest that Butts undertook in her tumultuous life and in her writing. At first she searched through drink, drugs, and occult practices, but she found these faulty and deceptive. What inspired her the most was her experience in the ancient mounds and stones and rural landscapes of Britain, where she was able to experience that phenomenal interspace. She found a connection and strived to convey it in her works. She wrote to express the synergetic connection between human beings, nature, and myth through an inadequate language. For her, nature was not to be conceived mechanistically. As Taylor argues the Romantic poets did, Butts rebelled "against a dead, mechanical view of Nature" (5). She saw nature as a living organism with human beings as an intrinsic element. But humans were increasingly alienated from nature, others, and themselves. She wanted her art, writing, to intensify our resonance with nature and, by doing so, to re-enchant our life and, as Taylor urges, to re-establish our "cosmic connectedness" (595). Mary Butts worked to awaken an "awareness and conviction and memory" of something more radiant in the world and found not just in nature but in a cityscape as well (*AR* 335). Her quest of the supernatural was a sacramental mission of a world becoming enchanted again.

Works Cited

Angus, Ian H. "Disenchantment and Modernity: The Mirror of Technique." *Human Studies* 6 (1983): 141–66.

Armstrong, Karen. *A Short History of Myth.* London: Cannongate, 2005.

Ashbery, John. "Preface." In *The Complete Stories of Mary Butts.* Kingston, NY: McPherson, 2014. 7–12.

Blackwood, Algernon. "Introduction to the 1938 Edition." In *Best Ghost Stories of Algernon Blackwood.* Ed. E. F. Bleiler. New York: Dover, 1973. xii–xviii.

Blake, William. *The Marriage of Heaven and Hell.* In *The Early Illuminated Books.* (William Blake's Illuminated Books, Volume 3.) Ed. Morris Eaves, Robert N. Essick, and Joseph Viscomi. London: Tate Gallery Publications for the William Blake Trust, 1998. 133–222.

Blaser, Robin. "*Imaginary Letters* by Mary Butts: Afterword." In *The Fire: Collected Essays of Robin Blaser.* Ed. Miriam Nichols. Berkeley: University of California Press, 2006. 164–78.

Blondel, Nathalie. "Preface." In *Ashe of Rings and Other Writings* by Mary Butts. Kingston, NY: McPherson, 1998. vii–xvii.

Bowen, Hugh. *Mystery Cults in the Ancient World.* London: Thames & Hudson, 2023.

Butts, Mary. *Ashe of Rings and Other Writings.* Kingston, NY: McPherson, 1998. [Abbreviated in the text as *AR*.]

———. *The Collected Essays of Mary Butts.* Ed. Joel Hawkes and Bruce R. McPherson. Kingston, NY: McPherson, 2021. [Abbreviated in text as *CE*.]

———. *The Complete Stories.* Ed. Bruce R. McPherson. Kingston, NY: McPherson, 2014. [Abbreviated in the text as *CS*.]

———. *The Taverner Novels.* Kingston, NY: McPherson, 2018. [Abbreviated in text as *TN*.]

Clukey, Amy. "Enchanting Modernism: Mary Butts, Decadence, and the Ethics of Occultism." *Modern Fiction Studies* 60 (2014): 78–107.

Dijksterhuis, E. J. *The Mechanization of the World Picture.* 1950. Tr. C. Dikshorn. London: Oxford University Press, 1961.

Edmundson, Melissa. "Introduction." In *Women's Weird: Strange Stories by Women, 1890–1940.* Ed. Melissa Edmundson. Bath, UK: Handheld Press, 2019. vii–xxiv.

Foy, Roslyn Reso. "'Brightness Falls': Magic in the Short Stories of Mary Butts." *Studies in Short Fiction* 36 (1999): 381–99.

———. *Ritual, Myth, and Mysticism in the Work of Mary Butts.* Fayetteville: University of Arkansas Press, 2000.

Greenstein, George. *Quantum Strangeness: Wrestling with Bell's Theorem and the Ultimate Nature of Reality.* Cambridge, MA: MIT Press, 2019.

Jung, C. S. *Synchronicity: An Acausal Connecting Principle.* Tr. R. F. C. Hull. Princeton, NJ: Princeton University Press: 1973.

Kessler, Jascha. "Mary Butts: Lost . . . and Found." *Kenyon Review* 17 (1995): 206–18.

Kroll, Jennifer. "Mary Butts's 'Unrest Cure' for the Waste Land." *Twentieth Century Literature* 45 (1999): 159–73.

Lees, James. "A New Introduction to Niels Bohr and Max Planck." In *Quantum Theory* by Niels Bohr and Max Plank. London: Flame Tree, 2023. 6–45.

Lyons, Sara. "The Disenchantment/Re-Enchantment of the World: Aesthetics, Secularization, and the Gods of Greece from Friedrich Schiller to Walter Pater." *Modern Language Review* 109 (2014): 873–95.

Machen, Arthur. *The Hill of Dreams.* In Machen's *Collected Fiction, Volume 2: 1896–1910.* Ed. S. T. Joshi. New York: Hippocampus Press, 2019. 9–156.

———. "Introduction." In Machen's *Notes and Queries.* London: Spurr & Swift, 1926. ix–xx.

———. "The Wonder from Wales." In Machen's *Hieroglyphics and Other Essays.* Ed. S. T. Joshi. New York: Hippocampus Press, 2022. 183–88.

Matless, David. "A Geography of Ghosts: The Spectral Landscapes of Mary Butts." *Cultural Geographies* 15 (2008): 335–57.

Nitze, William A. "The Fisher King in the Grail Romances." *Publications of the Modern Language Association* 24 (1909): 365–418.

Radford, Andrew. "Defending Nature's Holy Shrine: Mary Butts, Englishness, and the Persephone Myth." *Journal of Modern*

Literature 29 (2006): 126–49.

Rainey, Lawrence. "Good Things: Pederasty and Jazz and Opium and Research." *London Review of Books* 20 (16 July 1998): 14-17.

Schiller, Friedrich. *On the Aesthetic Education of Man.* 1791. Tr. Keith Tribe. London: Penguin Random House, 2016.

Swedberg, Richard, and Ola Agevall. *The Max Weber Dictionary: Key Words and Central Concepts.* Stanford, CA: Stanford Social Sciences, 2016.

Taylor, Charles. *Cosmic Connections: Poetry in the Age of Disenchantment.* Cambridge, MA: Harvard University Press, 2024.

Terry, Sue. "The Myth of Family: Friendship and Sexual Impropriety in the Feminist Occult Grail Narratives of Mary Butts's *Armed with Madness* (1928)." *English Studies* 105 (2023): 203–21.

Valentine, Mark. "Arthur Machen and The Mysteries of the Grail." *Wormwoodia* (6 February 2022). wormwoodiana.blogspot.com/2022/02/arthur-machen-and-mysteries-of-grail.html#:~:text=A%20keen%20insight%20that%20Machen,eg%20of%20healing%20or%20prophecy. Accessed on 20 November 2024.

———. "Inner Bohemia: The Mystical Fiction of Mary Butts." In Valentine's *Haunted by Books.* Leyburn, UK: Tartarus Press, 2015. 27–37.

Waugh, Evelyn. *The Diaries of Evelyn Waugh.* Ed. Michael Davie. London: Weidenfeld & Nicolson, 1976.

Weber, Max. *Charisma and Disenchantment: The Vocation Lectures.* Tr. Daimon Searls. Ed. Paul Reitter and Chad Wellmon. New York: New York Review Books, 2020.

Weston Jessie, L. *From Ritual to Romance.* 1920. Mineola, NY: Dover, 1997.

Wittgenstein, Ludwig. "A Lecture on Ethics." 1965. In *Philosophical Occasions 1912–1951.* Ed. James Klagge and Alfred Nordmann. Cambridge: Hackett, 1993. 37–44.

———. *Tractatus Logic-Philosophicus.* 1921. Tr. D. F. Pears and B. F. McGuinness. London: Routledge & Kegan Paul, 1974.

Death Would Steal My Voice

Darrell Schweitzer

Death would steal my voice,
but still I'm shouting
that Death is a fraud,
that there's no grim but alluring specter,
no beautiful angel with dark wings,
no velvety voice whispering of mysteries,
none of that, not even a kiss
when the last act of love may be changing a diaper.
I call out my challenge:
Show yourself, spirit!
Show your pale face and shrouded cloak!
Speak mysteries!
But there is only silence, nothing romantic
about it, no breath on my glasses
when I place them under her nose,
just a mouth stuck open because
rigor mortis has set in.
Then, after a while, an empty room.

Danse Macabre

Lee Weinstein

The landscape was devoid of life. There were only a few nondescript wooden structures, half buried, like the crumbling remains of a ghost town; and here and there the twisted, gnarly silhouettes of long-dead trees interspersed with a few slab-like rocks, worn and eroded. Aside from these bastions not yet succumbed to time and decay, there was nothing. Only endless stretches of moldering soil, dank and lifeless as a forgotten cellar, basking in eternal dusk.

I gazed about my surroundings, trying to ignore the oppressiveness of the air. It was heavy with moisture and laden with foul odors. The closest wooden structures appeared to be large boxes or crates of some sort, protruding above the damp earth, except for one particularly large one that was apparently the remains of a shanty.

I became aware of a faint rhythmical creaking, as of wooden frameworks in the wind. There was no wind. The gray air hung like a heavy foggy curtain.

The creaking grew steadily in volume, and one by one the lids of the crates rose, the rusty nails pulled from the rotted wood.

One by one the inhabitants of the crates stood, pushing the lids aside. They were skeleton figures, garbed in rotting flesh that dripped from them like melting wax, exposing the bone and sinew.

I stared transfixed, fascinated, as I became aware of a slow, macabre chant that had been wafting through my head from nowhere.

They were all swaying in silent motion to the chant. As I watched the grinning fleshless faces I realized that they were its source.

Their movements, which at first seemed almost graceful, now had become rigid and jerky as they moved about in a grim mockery of dance.

As the chanting became more intense, there suddenly arose a shrill new voice, picking up the persistent melody, carrying it to frantic heights, and letting it fall through the depths of my numbed senses. Its source was what appeared to be a dried corpse of a woman, old, shriveled, and putrid with corruption.

The apparition jerked its way toward me, singing its hypnotic song. It collapsed at my feet, and its open mouth clamped onto my leg like a vice.

I awoke with a start. It had been a dream. Had it been a dream? The persistent melody was still with me. I threw aside the bedcovers and parted the curtains. The day was overcast; the dark edges of the clouds were tinged with gold. I realized that my leg was still throbbing. The skin was broken where I had imagined I'd been bitten. A closer examination revealed the blackish edges of the wound. They appeared necrotic. A shudder ran through me.

I dressed hurriedly. I had to make it to a doctor before the poison spread. There was no point calling for an appointment; I was racing against a seed of death that was even now germinating in my flesh and sending out its rootlets.

The corridor of the apartment building was dim and dusty. I descended the well-worn wooden steps and emerged into daylight. The sun was still feebly attempting to show itself; the street itself was nearly deserted. An odd thing, I thought, for it was already fairly late in the morning; I had slept quite late.

There was no pain in my leg now; instead, a throbbing numbness that I could feel diffusing through my tissues. I decided to go down Arnold Street for a block, and out diagonally through Lincoln Park.

The shops along Arnold Street were all open, but there were few people inside. A woman with a little girl was standing by the counter in the bakery; next door in the laundromat an old woman hunched on one of the seats looked up as I went by. A faint thrill of repulsion passed through me, for the huddled figure reminded me momentarily of the nightmare.

I became aware as I hurried on that I was limping. My leg had lost most of its feeling. A few curious onlookers watched from half-shuttered windows as I set out across the cobblestoned street, a relic of the city's older days.

A thin mist had begun to descend, and I could see that the grass at the park's edge was already beginning to acquire a dewy dampness. For some reason I thought of snake venom, exuded slowly in crystal droplets, beautiful and deadly.

The stillness of the park was disquieting. Not the twitter of a bird nor the chirp of an insect penetrated the silent gloom of the place. A few acorns scattered about the roots of the trees made conspicuous the absence of their furry predators. The numbness had spread through my hips by now and showed no indication of stopping or slowing its inexorable spread.

The mist had been gradually thickening, and the park had become quite foggy. There was a dank and somewhat fetid smell in the air, as though there were a dead animal nearby. Perhaps a squirrel had been killed by some of the urchins who often frequent the park, and left to rot.

Ahead of me, about a hundred yards down the path, I thought I saw someone sitting on a bench. As I approached, the apparition seemed to become the corpse-lady of my nightmare, but resolved itself into a rock formation on closer inspection. The swirling fog was beginning to play tricks on my eyes. From what I could see of my surroundings now, things were beginning to look somewhat unfamiliar. I passed a fountain that I did not remember, and the path itself had taken on a marble-like sheen, probably from the dampness.

The numbness had spread up through my abdomen and entered my chest, lying upon it like a lead weight. My limp had disappeared, although both legs were now without feeling. I suddenly realized that I was no longer breathing. I could no longer feel my heartbeat. The absurdity and impossibility of the situation was almost funny, yet I did not laugh. Nor did I cry; all feeling had been drained from me. Realization of my plight had finally taken hold; I had known from the beginning, but only now was belief manifest in reality. My body was dead.

Only my flesh, for I was still able to think. The corruption of death was upon me, dissolving the flesh from the bones. My movements became rigid and jerky as the vise of rigor mortis set in, staying my progress. The fog was lifting now, and I saw about me the marble slabs of multitudinous graves.

I raised with an effort my decomposing hands to a black sky as I sank into a thick foul mush. Before me was a headstone bearing my name; seated upon it was the grim mockery of humanity that had sent me to this fate. I knew her now; I had never really doubted it. Was she not an avatar of the primal Great Goddess, progenitor of the malignant? Was she not Yva, come to Earth again, even as she had before the days of men? Darkness flowed over me like black slime as her mad laughter resounded in the eternal night. And I knew I could never die.

Frank Belknap Long, Jr.: Fantasist of Multiple Dimensions

Perry M. Grayson

During the formative years of twentieth-century fantastic literature there was one author whose diverse talent and style allowed him to help mold the genres of weird fiction, fantasy, and science fiction (SF) and push their boundaries. Frank Belknap Long, born in New York on 27 April 1901, began his writing career in amateur journalism as a poet and teller of strange tales similar in vein to Poe, which sparked his professional publication in the world's first exclusively macabre/fantasy magazine, *Weird Tales*.

With sales to *Weird Tales,* Long's opportunities in the ever-expanding American fiction magazine scene began to increase. Pseudo-scientific stories in *Weird Tales* were followed by acceptances in the science fiction pulp magazines in the 1930s, first with publisher/editor Hugo Gernsback's *Science Wonder Stories Quarterly.* Long transitioned from the supernatural weird tale to the science fiction story, and his style changed with the availability of potential markets. As the SF magazines gradually began to dominate the newsstands, stories of this nature began to take over the bulk of Long's literary work.

What Gernsback dubbed "scientifiction" became what the public today knows as science fiction. Long continued to write for the SF magazines throughout the 1930s. In an autobiographical column in the Summer 1945 issue of *Startling Stories,* Long told of lending his hand to writing for the comic books, along with other writers such as Edmond Hamilton and Henry Kuttner ("Meet the Author: Frank Belknap Long" 96); the comics included *Superman, Green Lantern,* and *Captain Marvel.* The most groundbreaking of Long's comic book scripts were to be found in the world's very first horror comic anthology, *Adventures into the Unknown* (published by ACG in Fall 1948). Long enthused about this volume in his letters to friend and Arkham House publisher August Derleth. He told of penning every story in the inaugural issue, which preceded the popular EC horror comics (starting with *Tales from the Crypt*) by two years.

Long's adaptability allowed him to stay on as a grizzled veteran in the literary arena when the so-called Golden Age of SF began in 1939, with the publication of *Astounding Science Fiction,* edited by John W. Campbell, Jr.

In a career that spanned seven decades, Long's dream-quest brought him through the revolution of modern fantasy and horror in *Weird Tales* and later *Unknown/Unknown Worlds* (the fantasy companion of *Astounding Science Fiction*). Long was instrumental in blazing a path from the seedling Gernsback SF pulps to SF's Golden Age (under the reins of exacting editor John W. Campbell), through the decline of the pulp magazines in the mid-1950s.

Long also wrote more than thirty books under his byline. He also made more than 100 anthology appearances in both hardcover and paperback. It was during the upsurge in paperback publishing from 1949 onward that saw the advent of many sociological developments, discoveries, and technological advances prophesied in the stories of Long and his peers in the 1920s and 1930s.

The legacy of Frank Long lives on in his works, which are still being reprinted well into the twenty-first century. The floodgates reopened in the months following his death on 2 January 1994. For example, his tale "Second Night Out" (first published under the title "The Black, Dead Thing" in *Weird Tales,* October 1933), was selected for inclusion in the 1994 anthology *Sea-Cursed,* and is a favorite among anthologists and scholars of weird fiction. What Long attested to was that the aforementioned technological advances had little to do with the stories themselves, and he maintained a sense of both cosmicism and romanticism in regard to plight of the human being in the universe throughout his entire body of work. The depth and scope of the concepts woven into Long's tales illustrate how weird fiction (fantasy included) and SF travel far beyond the stock gadgetry and giant insects that many critics have grown accustomed to associating with the realms of the fantastic. Though the remittance for his tremendous service in producing thought-provoking stories was only a small monetary one, Long is regarded highly by fans of weird and science fiction. For eighty years people thrilled to the parallel fantastic worlds of Frank Belknap Long—from the weird and earthbound terrors to the wonders and revelations that lie in the cosmic scales where earth is but a dust-mote.

At the age of seventeen, Frank Long entered and won an essay writing contest in a magazine called the *Boy's World*. This brought Long an invitation to join the United Amateur Press Association (UAPA), where Long's first two weird stories, "Dr. Whitlock's Price" (March 1920) and "The Eye Above the Mantel" (March 1921), would strike the interest of H. P. Lovecraft from the pages of the official organ, the *United Amateur*. These events were, without a doubt, the single most relevant development that led to Long's decision to become an author; before that, he had dreamed of becoming a naturalist (*The Early Long* 15), and it was only with the aid and support of Lovecraft that he chose to follow his literary pursuits.

The two literary men had much in common where favorite authors were concerned, and Long would introduce Arthur Machen to Lovecraft, while the two discussed major works of the late nineteenth and early twentieth centuries by such authors as M. P. Shiel, William Hope Hodgson, Ambrose Bierce, Robert W. Chambers, and Leonard Cline (author of *The Dark Chamber*).

The correspondence between the young Long and Lovecraft was the impetus for Long's first professional story sales, but this was only made possible through Lovecraft's regard for "The Eye Above the Mantel" and a third amateur story, "In the Tomb of Semenses" (*United Amateur*, November 1921), which Lovecraft called "an Egyptian phantasy filled with musical and rhythmical phrases, and opiate visions of 'multi-coloured lights and the clanging to of brazen portcullises', which proclaimed the genuine poet beneath a dress of prose" (*Collected Essays* 2.80). Lovecraft saw in Long the influence of Poe, not only in his prose but in his verse. With three stories in the amateur journals and numerous poems in verse and prose, such as "Felis" (an ode to Long's cat of that name in the *Conservative,* July 1923) and "The Migration of Birds" (*United Amateur,* March 1922), Long garnered Lovecraft's laudatory critical essay, "The Work of Frank Belknap Long, Jr." (*United Amateur,* March 1924).

"The Eye Above the Mantel" struck a chord with L because it spoke of ancient horrors and forbidden knowledge of this Earth and dimensions lurking outside. Stylistically "The Eye Above the Mantel" is somewhat different from other early Long stories in that its narrative is a passionate and swiftly moving force, overpowering the atmosphere entirely. It is an indication of Long's preoccupation with foreign cultures and their histories, especially Egypt, Greece, and Rome. "The Eye Above the Mantel" showed qualities and ideas Lovecraft had used and would go on to use himself, chronicling the death of a race of people and the superior species that would replace humanity. Gazing from the mantel, the protagonist seems to enter into a hallucinogenic voyage through eons and multiple levels of dimension, watching the earth become a wasteland. The tale bears the same feverish dimensional horror as one of Long's most memorable stories, "The Hounds of Tindalos." The tone is slanted more toward terror than the scientific, but the concept of evolution still remains, aside from an air of witchery and sorcery.

Soon after, with the creation of *Weird Tales* in 1923, Lovecraft would recommend Long to the publisher, J. C. Henneberger, editor Edwin Baird, and his successor, Farnsworth Wright. With the help of Lovecraft and his friends James F. Morton, a museum curator, and W. Paul Cook, a small press publisher, Long would see his rise to professional publication in 1924, at the age of twenty-three.

From 1924 to 1937, Frank Belknap Long found *Weird Tales* to be the most congenial market for his manuscripts. His first story in *Weird Tales* (November 1924) was "The Desert Lich," a straightforward Middle Eastern horror story that exhibited his love for strange facets of the lands of the ancient world. The same would prove true for African tales ("The Red Fetish" and "The Devil-God"), Egyptian horrors ("The Dog-Eared God" and "A Visitor from Egypt"), and Haiti ("You Can't Kill a Ghost"). Discarding some of his zest for these foreign cultures, Long began to take more of a scientific slant, recognizing the popularity of the new science fiction magazine *Amazing Stories,* founded in 1926. Leading up to Long's immersion in the scientific were the stories "The Space-Eaters" (*Weird Tales,* July 1928) and "The Hounds of Tindalos" (*Weird Tales,* March 1929). These two gave bare hints at what was to come in 1930, with Long's sale of "The Thought Materializer" to Gernsback's *Science Wonder Stories Quarterly,* followed by several sales to editor F. Orlin Tremaine for the popular Street & Smith magazine *Astounding Stories.*

"The Space-Eaters" deals with an alien invasion of creatures who attach themselves to the human skull and bore into the brain. Long perpetrated an in-joke by using the names Frank and Howard for the two central characters; one was the author, while the other was a caricature of Howard Phillips Lovecraft, the author's best friend. Though many stories of its type have been written and adapted for film and television, Long's story is among the first of this type of alien intruder narrative, where a parasitic organism attaches itself to a human body to control it. "The Space-Eaters" was lauded heavily by readers in the *Weird Tales* letter department ("The Eyrie"), and a peer of Long and Lovecraft, Clark Ashton Smith, wrote a story, "The Vaults of Yoh-Vombis," with a similar concept. Robert A. Heinlein's *The Puppet Masters* and the film *Alien* also drew influence from Long's story, as well as Smith's.

Thirty-five years before the drug-experimentation waves of the 1960s, Frank Long wrote "The Hounds of Tindalos," in which a researcher takes consciousness-expanding drugs and inadvertently unleashes rabid creatures, the Hounds of Tindalos, from the fourth dimension. Though owing something to Lovecraft's "From Beyond," "The Hounds of Tindalos" touches areas of cosmic terror that were previously unexplored. Throughout the tale, Long maintains the same straight and strict scientific manner that allowed Lovecraft to make successes out of stories such as *At the Mountains of Madness* and "The Whisperer in Darkness."

With brief forays back to the horrors of the ancient world, Long's pseudo-scientific side returned to the pages of *Weird Tales* in the February 1935 issue, with "The Body-Masters," which Long himself acknowledged as one of his best stories. This story hints at what was to come in the so-called New Wave of science fiction of the 1960s. One of the earliest risqué science fiction tales, "The Body-Masters" told of android lovers used to occupy bored husbands—*and* wives. Maintaining a serious tone throughout, it displays a controversial theme of artificial intelligence and human love, refraining from indulgences into the sort of heavy breathing one would expect from a "true confession" story of the same period. It predated Ray Bradbury's similar robotic tale "Marionettes Inc." (*Startling Stories,* March 1949) by nearly fifteen years, and Philip K. Dick's dystopian 1968 novel *Do Androids Dream of Electric Sheep?* (filmed as *Blade Runner*) by more than thirty years.

Lovecraft's influence on Long rarely strayed from support and aid, and at this point, 1935, Long had already carved out his own style. Whether dealing with the horrors of a world long forgotten, a land on the far side of the map, or a future Earth or the void of space, Long's romanticism and regard for the human condition were readily apparent. By 1939, in the story "Escape from Tomorrow," he exhibited men and women assailing the barriers of governmental restriction, wrestling with the vagaries of their own relationships, and trying to recognize their place in the universe. This tale marked a hiatus from *Weird Tales* for Long, who had begun selling stories to the bulk of newly emerged science fiction pulp magazines.

It took a span of four years for Long to sell a second scientific tale to a strictly science fiction magazine after "The Thought Materializer" debuted in *Science Wonder Quarterly*. By 1934, he had blasted through the screens that held him back from publication in the expanding SF markets. "The Last Men" appeared in the August

1934 issue of *Astounding Stories,* and it began a cycle of three tales Long wrote around the future of an Earth in which human beings were reduced in size and stature and enslaved by gargantuan emissaries of the animal kingdom, including insects. A stereotype surrounding science fiction since the earliest days, emphasized by its firmest detractors, was that the stories all centered on giant cockroaches, ants, grasshoppers, etc. This generalization did not prove true, not even in Long's three stories of the tiny humans against evolution, "The Last Men," "Green Glory," and "The Great Cold"—all of which appeared in *Astounding Stories.* Much more than just "that Buck Rogers stuff," as many put it when Long was a budding science fiction writer, these stories commented on the environment and humanity's treatment of the planet. Long's own opinion was that "At least a dozen establishment critics of major stature—as such criteria go—have ceased to draw any distinction between the best of science fiction in a literary sense and novels in other categories" (*Autobiographical Memoir* 16).

Frank Long was only a boy when he read one of the earliest stories of evolution gone awry (especially involving insects), H. G. Wells's *The Food of the Gods,* but it influenced him into his third decade (*Early Long* 14). Long's naturalistic whims shone through in nearly everything he wrote, and they took him from the triad of tiny men yarns to a series of stories on John Carstairs, a botanical space detective in *Startling Stories* and its companion *Thrilling Wonder Stories.* Long continued to write for *Astounding Stories* into 1936, and soon began selling stories to the new Standard Magazines pulps *Startling Stories* and *Thrilling Wonder Stories,* while still placing a few with *Weird Tales.* With Lovecraft's death and that of editor Farnsworth Wright, however, *Weird Tales* began to flounder, and Long committed himself almost entirely to science fiction, while selling detective and 'weird menace' stories on the side. Before Asimov, Heinlein, and Sturgeon ever entered the field, Long and his peers had helped point science fiction in a new direction.

With the onset of 1938, a revolution in science fiction publishing struck the scene: *Astounding Stories* changed editorial hands from F. Orlin Tremaine to John W. Campbell, Jr. and became *Astounding Science Fiction*. In the interim of this shift, Long steadily sold material to the two Standard Magazines SF pulps, Tremaine's new magazine *Comet Stories, Science Fiction Stories,* and *Astonishing Stories,* as well as Standard's weird menace magazine *Thrilling Mystery*. It took a total of almost two and a half years until Long broke through Campbell's rigorous editorial policies.

In 1938, the Golden Age of science fiction began with Campbell at the reins of its flagship, *Astounding Science Fiction*. In 1939, he read a novel manuscript by Eric Frank Russell called *Sinister Barrier* and, based upon its merit, decided to create a new fantasy magazine. *Unknown* was published by Street & Smith as a companion to *Astounding* and featured many of its popular authors, including titans such as Theodore Sturgeon, Robert A. Heinlein, A. E. van Vogt, Fritz Leiber, and future *Galaxy* editor Horace L. Gold. In 1939, Long sent a story for consideration to *Astounding*, "Dark Vision." He was surprised only days later when Campbell responded by saying that it wouldn't be right for the science fiction magazine, but it would work well alongside Russell's novel in Vol. 1, No. 1 of *Unknown* in March 1939 (*Early Long* 155–56). This put Long's foot in the door and paved the way for his first story acceptance in *Astounding Science Fiction,* "Brown," in July 1941.

Though *Startling Stories* and *Thrilling Wonder Stories* would prove to be as congenial a marketplace for Long as *Weird Tales* once was, Long sold twelve stories to Campbell for *Astounding* and made ten appearances in *Unknown*/*Unknown Worlds*. These twenty-two total sales to Campbell were all stories of high caliber. Long's fantasies in *Unknown*/*Unknown Worlds* were filled with wild events and abstract imagery. "Dark Vision" is a story of a reporter who falls into an active line at a power plant and ends up gaining a power of insight into the thoughts and emotions of other people. It is the sort of tale that does not decline with age. Along similar lines, George

Clayton Johnson and Rod Serling co-wrote a teleplay for the *Twilight Zone* episode "A Penny for Your Thoughts," first televised in October 1959. It was a topic that Frank Long dwelled on in "Flame of Life" (*Science Fiction Stories,* October 1939), but the realization of the inner and brutal thoughts of human beings was more apparent in "Dark Vision," in which the protagonist was able to see through the façade to what others truly felt. Though a fantasy, "Dark Vision" used a scientific explanation, and it proved that some science fiction is merely a fantasy of another world, while some earthbound weird stories are science fictional in their methods.

In the region of Golden Age science fiction, one of Frank Long's finest contributions to *Astounding Science Fiction* was "To Follow Knowledge" (December 1942), an attempt to illustrate how the events in the life of the universe, the planet, and the human being live in frames of time that coexist side-by-side. "To Follow Knowledge" maintained the same abstract mood of Long's previous *Unknown* stories and tugged at the emotions of the reader. The ceaseless loop of events in the lives of the characters brings "To Follow Knowledge" to a warming in the layers of time at a river, where the protagonist watches a friend who was once his peer cast away as an old man.

Throughout the years 1939 to 1950, Frank Long contributed to the same magazines that the acknowledged masters of science fiction did, and he shared the same pages as Isaac Asimov, Robert A. Heinlein, Theodore Sturgeon, A. E. van Vogt, L. Ron Hubbard, and Henry Kuttner. In reality, Frank Belknap Long was the elder science fictioneer to all the aforementioned authors.

Professional book publication began for Frank Long in 1946 with the Arkham House volume *The Hounds of Tindalos,* a story collection featuring twenty-one of Long's triumphs from *Weird Tales, Astounding Science Fiction, Unknown, Marvel Tales, Startling Stories,* and *Thrilling Wonder Stories.* Although it was issued partially as a favor to Long by friend, fellow author, and Lovecraft correspondent August Derleth, *The Hounds of Tindalos* fared well for the first specialty publisher of weird fiction. Though the collection did not garner much in royalties, it did serve to bring Long a critical response from the literary arena. Renowned author Eudora Welty even commented that the volume displayed "unusual excellence." Reviews showed up in the *New York Times,* and despite low payment, Long's name was thrust further into the eyes of publishers and readers alike. Today, the Arkham House hardcover of *The Hounds of Tindalos* commands a value of over $500. Enthusiasts of fantasy and science fiction treasure the book, and at least fifteen of its stories have been widely anthologized by editors all over the globe. *The Hounds of Tindalos* packed nearly all Long's finest stories from *Unknown* together between one cover. Long himself felt that, to a great extent, none of these have been overtaken by the effects of time (*Early Long* 23).

In the aftermath of *The Hounds of Tindalos,* Frank Long watched the gradual demise of magazine science fiction. The field narrowed from dozens of periodicals to approximately one dozen, and time professed that Long would have to move onwards with the change.

In 1949, Frederick Fell published Frank Long's first hardcover science fiction "novel," *John Carstairs, Space Detective.* Truly, this volume was a fix-up novel consisting of six of the eight stories in the magazine cycle of separate tales involving John Carstairs, the manager of a botanical garden who uses alien plants as a means of foiling mysteries. Considering the humorous tone, the blend of the hard-boiled detective yarn and science fiction, *John Carstairs, Space Detective* represents one of the first successful hybrids. He explored areas beyond Edmond Hamilton's space-mystery "The Space-Rocket Murders" (*Amazing Stories,* October 1932). Not only were the scattered John Carstairs stories of the early to mid-1940s well liked by readers of *Startling Stories* and *Thrilling Wonder Stories;* the book proved enthralling enough to be picked up for a British edition, as was *The Hounds of Tindalos.*

As the magazine market began to shrink, science fiction books began to crop up in their place—and though few volumes had been published years earlier, the blooming era of the paperback book brought forth the birth of the paperback science fiction anthology. The first of its kind, *The Girl with the Hungry Eyes and Other Stories* (1949), an original SF anthology in paperback, was edited by writer/editor/publisher Donald A. Wollheim for Avon Books. Among the authors included were the *Weird Tales* and *Unknown* veterans Fritz Leiber, Manly Wade Wellman, William Tenn, and Frank Belknap Long, whose "Maturity Night" was printed therein for the first and only time anywhere. To say that "Maturity Night" resembles Long's work for *Unknown* is an understatement, and leads one to wonder if the tale hadn't been written several years earlier, before *Unknown* ceased publication.

The continuing growth of paperback science fiction and fantasy brought forth still more anthology appearances for Frank Long. And it was not long after that his first real science fiction novel was purchased by the largest publisher of American SF in the pocketbook format, Ace Books (Donald A. Wollheim, senior editor). In a letter to August Derleth dated 19 October 1958, Long notes: "My Ace paperback *Space Station No. 1* has been doing very well—close to 100,000 copies in the first six months." Though no in-depth studies have been made of sales on Long's books, *Space Station No. 1* may well be the book with highest exposure to the public. The novel itself was a gripping story of stellar intrigue, revolving around the first orbital station and the spread of human colonization to Mars. Long deftly wove *Space Station No. 1* with a concern for elements of mystery, science fiction, and the gripping psychological tension of horror. The mysterious use of form-fitting masks in the novel serves to bring about anxiety in the reader, and the interplanetary conspiracy is unearthed by the combined strength of a young space officer and his fiancée. From his stories of the mid-1930s to his novels and final short stories, women have always played a large role in Frank Long's work. He showed their inner strength and the workings of their relationships with men in *Space Station No. 1,* and also wistfully in *John Carstairs, Space Detective*—not to mention earlier stories such as "Flame of Life."

While *Space Station No. 1* was being printed a second time by Ace, Frank Long sold a suspense novel, *The Horror Expert,* to Belmont Books. While the noirish *The Horror Expert* established a market for further Long books, he also sold two risqué SF novels to the softcore men's entertainment publisher Chariot Books. *Woman from Another Planet* (1960) and *The Mating Center* (1961) were disregarded because of their lurid cover art and the reputation of the publisher, but both maintain a serious manner toward sex similar to that of Philip Jose Farmer's *The Lovers* (Ballantine Books, 1961).

Another paperback SF novel appeared in 1962, *Mars Is My Destination* (published by Pyramid). It followed a similar formula to *Space Station No. 1,* but also had its own qualities. In *Mars Is My Destination* Frank Long again combined mystery and science fiction for tension and powerful storytelling that appeals to more than one type of reader. Then, in 1963, Arkham House solidified a deal to have Belmont reprint *The Hounds of Tindalos* in paperback in two volumes. This happened at the same time August Derleth published Long's 1931 *Weird Tales* short novel *The Horror from the Hills* under the Arkham House imprint.

A flurry of book publishing greeted Long between 1963 and 1964. Before Belmont issued a paperback reprint of *The Horror from the Hills* as part of a collection called *Odd Science Fiction* (1964), Long's novel from *Future* magazine, "Made to Order," was revised and lengthened for publication by Belmont, retitled as *It Was the Day of the Robot* (1963). This is a story of governmental control of people by computers in the far future; it bore effective traits that likened it to *1984.* Also revealed in *It Was the Day of the Robot* was Long's early preoccupation with the android or robot with a human-like brain, which was used in the *Weird Tales* stories "The Body-Masters" and "He Came at Dusk."

Throughout the 1960s, Belmont issued more of Long's science fiction and horror, twice in anthologies. Of all his novels of this period, *Journey into Darkness* (1967) presents the most experimental and harrowing vision. Here the invasion of an outside alien agency is discovered to be perpetrated by the individual human beings themselves, buried in their subconscious, which was given power to emerge from the psychiatric patients' minds through similar drug-induced consciousness-expanding experimentation that Long used in "The Hounds of Tindalos." Closing out this period, Long wrote . . . *And Others Shall Be Born* (Belmont, 1968), which combined a sense of horror from within the common and prosaic area of the Midwest U.S. and the cosmic implications of humanity's place in a universe large enough to contain races more advanced than they are. The final line of . . . *And Others Shall Be Born* invokes the rationalist/materialist and agnostic/atheistic philosophies held by both Long and his mentor Lovecraft: "How much did anything that took place on earth really matter, when weighed in cosmic scales that spanned the universe or stars?" (172).

By 1970, Frank Long had written three modern gothic novels, two of which were written under the pseudonym Lyda Belknap Long (his wife's name was Lyda Arco Long), due to the publisher's insistence that all good gothics were written by women. In addition to continuing his career in weird fiction and SF, Long wrote a total of nine gothics, eight as by Lyda Belknap Long. These gothics used facets of weird fiction and mystery throughout, and they are equally as compelling and important in the study of Frank Long's work as are his fantastic stories. Frank Long's aforementioned work in the weird menace pulp magazines, such as *Thrilling Mystery*, *Mystery Novels,* and *Short Stories,* is extremely relevant to his modern gothic paperback work; the formula for both markets involved plotting a story so that what seemed to be a supernatural phenomenon is explained away as a natural occurrence at the conclusion. For example, *So Dark a Heritage* (Lancer, 1966) detailed voodoo, held a dark and brooding atmosphere in the deep South, and involved a mystery of drug smugglers—which effectively blotted out the implications of supernatural voodoo. Omnipresent in the gothics were Frank Long's portrayals of strong-willed female characters.

Science fiction under Long's byline continued rise into the decade of the 1970s. The third short story collection by Long, *The Rim of the Unknown* (Arkham House, 1972), presented fine stories that had been bypassed in *The Hounds of Tindalos,* as did *Night Fear* (Zebra, 1979); they drew from sources of quality, mainly *Weird Tales, Astounding Science Fiction,* and *Fantastic Universe* (one of the many magazines Long had a hand in as an associate editor). *The Three Faces of Time* (Tower, 1969), *Monster from out of Time* (Popular Library, 1971), and *Survival World* (Lancer, 1971) were all novels involving the evolution of humanity and involved displacement of people in both space and time. The savagery in depicting dawn men in *Monster from out of Time* and *Survival World* is similar to that in "Willie" (*Astounding Science Fiction,* October 1943), and the predicament of men and women caught between time and dimensions compliments "To Follow Knowledge" (*Astounding Science Fiction,* December 1942).

Though Long saw a slightly abridged reprint of *The Hounds of Tindalos* published under the title *The Early Long* (Doubleday, 1975) and *Night Fear,* he ceased active production of SF and weird novels after writing *The Night of the Wolf* (1972). His final novel was a gothic, *The Lemoyne Heritage* (Zebra, 1977). From 1972 until his death in 1994, Long's output consisted of his memories of his friend, *Howard Phillips Lovecraft: Dreamer on the Nightside* (Arkham House, 1975), the last of the gothic paperbacks, his *Autobiographical Memoir* (Necronomicon Press, 1985), and a handful of stories in magazines.

Throughout the 1970s and early 1980s, a growing sense of nostalgia for Lovecraft and his compatriot Long surfaced in such periodicals as *Twilight Zone, Nyctalops, Crypt of Cthulhu,* and *Whispers.* Long's final ten stories appeared as follows: "Cottage Tenant" in *Fantastic* (April 1975); "Autumn Visitors" in *Twilight Zone* (January 1982); "Problem Child" in *Fantasy Macabre* 4 (1983); "Woodland Burial" in the Doubleday anthology *Whispers III* (1983); "Diploma Time" in the Doubleday anthology *Whispers IV* (1983); "Homecoming" in the paperback incarnation of the magazine *Weird Tales* No. 4 (Summer 1983); "Gateway to Forever" in *Crypt of Cthulhu* No. 25

(1984); "Discovery Time" in *Crypt of Cthulhu* No. 31 (1985); "Lover in the Wildwood" in the Doubleday anthology *Halloween Horrors* (1986); "The Soaring" and "Sauce for the Gander" in a companion to *Crypt of Cthulhu, Astro-Adventures* Nos. 1 and 3 respectively (January 1987 and January 1988).

With the help of anthology editors such as Stefan Dziemianowicz, Robert Weinberg, and S. T. Joshi, a continuous stream of Long stories were reprinted in themed hardcover and paperback volumes. In his eighth decade, despite frequent illnesses, Long did more than sit back and watch editors select his stories for publication in their anthologies.

"Cottage Tenant" was the longest of Long's later works. Editor Roy Torgeson gave first mention of a final novel by Long in 1979: "Presently he is working on a new novel and a number of short stories which are scheduled to appear in the newly revived paperback magazine *Weird Tales*" (*Night Fear* 9). Though the newly reincarnated *Weird Tales* died a quick death, Long continued to submit work to other markets. Out of all his last stories, including the science fictional "Discovery Time" and "Sauce for the Gander," Long felt "Cottage Tenant" to be his finest work in years. It is no surprise that evidence has been unearthed substantiating that Long was working on a new novel at the time of his death, a revised and lengthened version of "Cottage Tenant," which had appeared in two anthologies. Long made a comment about how much he enjoyed the story in his afterword in *Masters of Darkness II:* "'Cottage Tenant' was the first of this new, quite recent twelvesome, and it is the one I most fear to dwell on in the chill hours just preceding dawn" (94). Whether or not "Cottage Tenant" can be salvaged as a short novel, it is certain that Long lived a capacious existence and thrilled readers with more than thirty books and nearly three hundred stories.

Frank Belknap Long was unjustly given low payment for his work, spurned by the masses who saw him as a hack pulp writer, and remembered not for his own literary triumphs, but for his association with H. P. Lovecraft. With these jaded public opinions, the World

Fantasy Lifetime Achievement Awards holder's work languished out of print for nearly two decades. Willing readers can now discover more than 100 magazine stories by Long that have not previously appeared in book form. With this in mind, the next major event for Frank Long came in the years following his death on 2 January 1994. Though an indigent Long was initially buried in potter's field, Necronomicon Press publisher Marc A. Michaud spearheaded an auction to raise funds for a reburial. By early 1995 he was interred in the Long family plot at Woodlawn Cemetery in New York with the aid of loyal friends and readers. The Lifetime Achievement Bram Stoker Award–winning author now rests in peace.

Justice has been served, and Frank Belknap Long's work has again seen the brilliant light of publication. A memorial story collection chapbook, *Escape from Tomorrow,* featuring three tales neglected since their first appearance in *Weird Tales,* was published by Necronomicon Press in 1995. In 2022, Centipede Press issued a massive 800+-page compendium in its Library of Weird Fiction, edited and introduced by noted Lovecraftian scholar S. T. Joshi. *When Chaugnar Wakes,* Long's collected poems combined with other important short works, was published by Tsathoggua Press in 2024. These efforts and others like it have ensured a place for Frank Long among the twentieth century's masters of fantastic literature under the eternal veil of stars.

Works Cited

Etchison, Dennis, ed. *Masters of Darkness II.* New York: Tor, 1988

Long, Frank Belknap. *Autobiographical Memoir.* West Warwick, RI: Necronomicon Press, 1985.

———. *The Early Long.* New York: Doubleday, 1975.

———. "Meet the Author: Frank Belknap Long." *Startling Stories* 12, No. 2 (Summer 1945): 95–96.

———. *Night Fear.* New York: Zebra, 1979.

Lovecraft, H. P. *Collected Essays.* Ed. S. T. Joshi. New York: Hippocampus Press, 2004–06. 5 vols.

To Ishtar

Dmitri Akers

O Queen of every dreamer's inner world,
Whose Beauty gleams as bright as any moon,
Thy luscious locks may flow—as vines unfurl'd—,
As planets change their course to magick's boon;
Thy hair is flowing past thine ebon horns
And droops along thy marble skin and flesh
Of purest hue. Thy horns are wild, a fawn's!
Thy lips may pry to kiss, to suck, to thresh
The minds of dreamers! Ishtar, break the sleep
Of every god and every dreamer's sire;
The skies and stars begin to break with flames
To sounds of screaming stars and horrid lyre,
As beasts of dread begin to lope and creep
Across the mantled Earth with swords and shields,
To conquer lands of kings, and all their claims—
With cries to stir the gods of death and plight.
Within the Heav'ns that burn with azure light,
I see this horrid sight that never yields:
The shade of bifurcated horns so black
That pierces moons with whate'er light may lack!

Birthday Party

Harley Carnell

By the time three o'clock came, I was almost in tears.

"It's the summer holidays, everyone's probably away," my mother tried to console me. "School starts in a week, they're busy getting ready for it, buying all their clothes and stationery."

While I didn't have the word for it then, or fully understand the concept, this was the first time I was ever conscious of being humoured; or, to put it more bluntly, bullshitted. I knew that my mother was lying, and lying to protect my feelings. I was also introduced to another concept, that of being the sort of person pathetic enough to require such protection.

I still hadn't cried, but what finally set me off was a chance look over at the table. At the sight of the mounds of uneaten food and undrunk drink, the stack of unworn party hats and unpopped party poppers, the tears came. Through my stained eyes I could see my mother's concern. She was mired in indecision, not knowing what to do. This utter helplessness was another new concept to me. It dismantled my conception of adult perfection, maternal omniscience. Then the doorbell rang. My mother froze; my tears were derailed. We both looked at each other, and then my mother laughed.

"See," she said, "what did I tell you!" She grinned and headed out to answer the door. When she did so, I waited eagerly, wondering what classmate's voice I would hear. Or classmate*s*'. Perhaps they had all travelled together and were all late.

"Hello, thanks so much for coming!" my mother said cheerfully. Then there was a pause: "Oh, where are your mum and dad, sweetheart?"

"Dunno, came on my own, innit." I knew immediately I did not know this voice. It was gruff and harsh, the sort of voice you'd get after shouting for a prolonged period or when severely dehydrated. Did one of the kids have a cold? Had the six weeks of summer been long enough for their voice to alter into unfamiliarity?

"Oh, right," my mother said. "Well, I guess you better come in then! Paul's right through here."

All my questions were dispelled immediately on seeing the boy, whom I definitely did not know. My mother had sent out invitations to everyone in my class, as well as the other class in my year. I supposed it was not impossible one could have slipped into the hands of a kid from another class or year, but I had never seen this boy around the school or playground either.

"Look, Paul," my mother said, "I told you people were coming."

"I don't know him," I said immediately.

"Paul!" my mother said, gasping almost comically, "that's very rude. You can't expect to make friends if you're rude to people, can you? Please forgive Paul, sweetheart, he forgets his manners sometimes. Oh, and I didn't catch your name, darling."

"Alan," the boy said.

"Alan, it's very nice to meet you, and Paul's happy to see you too even if he's too impolite to show it. Now, did you want something to eat, Alan? We've got loads of food here."

Alan nodded hungrily and scuttled over to the table. He began piling a plate up with food until it resembled a Scooby Doo sandwich. He then grabbed an entire bottle of limeade and sat down at the table.

"Oh, Alan, sweetheart, that drink is for everyone, and maybe—"

But Alan had already opened the bottle and was downing it. He took a long drink, inexplicably draining half the bottle without a breath, and then let out a loud burp. In another circumstance this would have had me breathless with laughter, but not today. I did not know Alan, but knew I did not like him. There was something odd about him; something *off* about him. As he ate, he breathed through his nose loud enough for me to hear at the other end of the room. And, I realised, he did not so much eat as slam the food into his mouth. He didn't even look as if he swallowed, yet must have done in order to accommodate the next onslaught of food.

When I turned to my mother, I could see that she shared a little of this disgust. I was hoping that she would back me up and ask Alan to leave, but instead she raised her eyebrows and tilted her head, indicating I should speak to him. When I didn't, she turned to Alan and smiled.

"So, Alan, where do your parents live? Are they from around here?"

At this point Alan's mouth was bulging with food. Speaking through it—another thing that would have been hysterical under other circumstances—he said, "Peacevale."

For the first time, my mother's facial expression matched my own. She frowned, although I didn't know why. I had never heard of the place.

"Peacevale?" my mother said cautiously. "The only Peacevale around here is—"

"That's right, they're dead."

"Oh," said my mother. "Oh, darling, I'm so sorry."

Alan shrugged, grabbing a slice of congealed pepperoni pizza.

"Don't be," he said. "People die. We all do. *He'll* die." He pointed at me without looking in my direction.

He scraped off the pizza's toppings with the top of his surprisingly sharp teeth, and then used his tongue to scoop them into his mouth. This didn't make me quite as sick as the tongue itself, which looked dry and almost grey, although that might have been the lighting in the room. He chucked the shorn bread onto the table and began dismantling another slice. I could see that my mother wanted to admonish him for this, but she didn't, probably feeling sorry for him after what he'd just revealed.

"So do you live with relatives then?"

Alan shrugged again. "Don't live with no one, innit."

My mother was a teacher, and under normal circumstances she would have been sent into paroxysms by the double-negative, let alone the “innit.” Now she seemed more concerned with the import of what he’d said.

“Well, you must live with someone, sweetheart,” she said.

“Don’t live nowhere.” Alan shrugged and drank some more limeade, wiping his mouth with his arm. There were a few seconds of awkward silence, and then my mother put her hand on my shoulder.

“Paul, why don’t you go and eat with Alan?”

I was about to refuse—I wanted to be nowhere near this boy—but then he looked at me. I thought of the bullies at my school. Right now I longed for them and knew they would never scare me again. I almost shuddered at the look Alan gave me. While my initial instinct was to be as far away from him as possible, I also didn’t want to anger him by refusing. Reluctantly, I went and sat next to him.

Aside from a small breakfast, I had not eaten all day as I fruitlessly waited for kids to arrive and the party to start. Despite this, I had no appetite as I sat next to Alan. I looked over at the bowl of cheese and onion crisps—the one thing he had left untouched—and grabbed a few for appearances’ sake.

“So, Alan,” my mother said, smiling, “how do you two know each other?”

I was about to interrupt and reiterate to my mother that we didn’t know each other, when Alan said, “Seen ’im.”

“Is that right?” she said, smiling. “So you know each other from school? Or the neighbourhood.”

“Seen ’im,” Alan repeated, shrugging.

“Oh, right,” she said, striving to keep her smile. “Well, um, well that’s nice, then.”

There was silence after this, punctuated by Alan’s disgusting eating. He ate intensely, as if he was one of the competitive eaters whose YouTube videos I lapped up. But even they displayed more decorum than he did.

I reached up for another crisp, when Alan’s hand shot forward and grabbed for the bowl. He scratched me in the process, with what I saw were long and filthy nails. I cried out and said, “What did you do that for?"

"Now, Paul," my mother said, "let's not overreact. I'm sure it was just an accident, wasn't it Alan?"

"Yup," Alan said, burping again and expelling a tang of limey cheddar from his mouth.

I knew that it was not an accident, although even if it was he still should have said sorry. At first I thought my mother's leniency with him was because he was the guest. Then I realised it was something else. Alan was the only one who had come to my party. If she told him off and he got upset, he might go, leaving me alone. And, perversely, her thinking was obviously that it was better to have him here, horrible as he was, than to have no one. It was a disheartening thought, but then I wondered if I should have been thinking it too. Was she right? Was it in fact better in life to have someone, even if it was a bad person, than to have no one?

"Right, well, I think that we should do presents now," my mother said.

The thought of presents swept away all my worries. My mother tended to wrap the moment she bought something, and for the past few weeks I had spent many agonised hours trying to work out what the various gifts in the hallway closet were. Although I knew a pair of Airpods or a new phone could come in small boxes, my kid-logic dictated that the large box contained the best and most expensive present.

I reached for it, thanking my mother, when I felt a hand on top of mine. Alan had reached for the present at the same time, his fingers sweating grease onto me and the wrapping paper. As scared as I was of him, this was my present, and I spoke up.

"Mum!" I said.

"Oh," my mum said awkwardly. "Um, Alan, sweetheart, this is Paul's present. I do have some little things I bought for guests, so I can give you them in a minute, but how about for now we let Paul open, okay?"

But it was evidently not okay. Alan did not move, except to

entwine his fingers further into mine. I looked at my mother, but she wasn't sure what to do. Not wanting his disgusting hands touching me anymore, I removed mine, leaving his hands on the present.

"Um, all right then, how about you help Paul open it, okay?" my mother said.

Alan ripped off the ribbon and then began clawing at the paper, his fingers moving with the alacrity of a spider's legs. He grunted as he did so, breathing heavily through his nose as he'd done while he ate. I was simultaneously upset, disgusted, and scared, until the final shred of paper was shorn and I knew what the present was.

"A water gun!" I cried out.

My mother grinned. I had been begging for one all summer, after seeing some of the kids in my neighbourhood playing with them.

But this was not just *a* water gun. I had been not so subtly hinting about wanting one for the past few months, but had specifically avoided mentioning this one whenever we passed the toy shop. I was not too young to know that it was prohibitively expensive, with all sorts of unique features such as an ability to rapid-fire water balloons, and an intricate system that allowed it to store two pints of water while remaining compact and manoeuvrable. I felt sorry for the kids who had decided not to come today, who had not got a chance to use it.

I ran to my mother and hugged her. She laughed and held me tightly in her arms. There was no Alan; there was no no-shows; there was only the water gun, and—

I felt myself being snatched away. Before I knew what had happened, Alan had wrenched me out of my mother's arms and was now hugging her. For a second my mother hesitated. It was clear she didn't want Alan hugging her. But then, whether through pity, or maybe fear, she embraced him back. She let him go quickly and then picked the water gun up from the table.

"I'm just going to fill this up for you two," she said, before walking off.

I did not want to be alone with Alan, but she was gone before I could say anything.

"This food is shit," Alan said.

Although it was by no means the first time I had heard another kid swear, this was the first time I had ever heard a swear word said with such venom. For the first time I knew why they were called "curse" words. Despite being scared of him, I responded:

"Hey, my mother made that!"

"No, she didn't. She bought it from some store. Banged it in the oven."

I couldn't argue with that.

"My mother was a much better cook. But she's dead now."

I suddenly felt sorry for him. My mother had always told me that if you got some tearaway kid at school, you had to think about their home situation. Maybe Alan was as horrible as he was because he'd had a horrible life. Maybe I should try to give him a bit of a chance.

"I'm sorry," I said.

"My dad as well, they're both dead."

"I'm sorry," I repeated, not knowing what else to say.

"I'm dead too."

I was about to ask what he was talking about, when my mother came in with the now-filled water gun. Alan stepped in front of me and took it from her. All my sympathy for his situation was washed away immediately.

"That's mine!" I shouted.

"Paul!" my mother said, shocked. "That's not how I brought you up, is it?" she added, in that way she had of getting me to participate in my own telling-off.

"No," I said. "But it's my b—"

"Alan is a guest here, and we always share with guests. You'll have plenty of time to play with the gun."

"But I don't *want* him to have the gun. I don't *want* him here."

My mother first widened, and then narrowed, her eyes, in a gesture that was the facial equivalent of "shut up, now." When I did, she spoke through gritted teeth:

"Now I'm going to finish the washing up, and when I come back I expect to see you two sharing properly, okay?" She then relaxed her expression and put her hand on Alan's shoulder. "I'm sorry about Paul," she said.

Alan nodded solemnly.

"Don't care," he said. "Used to people treating me like dirt."

Although I didn't know Alan, I knew what he was doing here. Kids, even those my age, could outsmart adults easily, playing them like puppets. I knew Alan wasn't as upset as he made out. I imagined he didn't care at all. But the way my mother was looking at him now, he may as well have been Anne Frank. My mother gave me a final scowl as she left the room. Any semblance that I might have misjudged Alan disappeared when he turned to face me with a wide grin. Then he sprayed me with the water gun, directly in the face.

"Hey!" I said, choking a little as the water had gone straight up my nose. "Hey, don't do that!"

"You're the boss," he said, shrugging, and then began walking over to the other side of the room. I wasn't sure what he was doing at first, but then realised that he was heading to my cat, Mr. Barlow. Mr. Barlow had been sleeping in his little corner, obscured by the table, and I had no idea how Alan even knew he was there. Before I could stop him, Alan had sprayed Mr. Barlow a few times with the water, causing him to jump up and hiss. Alan knelt down and, incredibly, hissed back at him. Mr. Barlow, a formidable Maine Coon who had the power to scare even my mother sometimes, shrank back and whimpered. Alan then growled at Mr. Barlow, causing him to run off rapidly in defiance of his massive size and ancient age.

I was about to call out for my mother, but Alan rushed over to me.

"Don't say nothing," he hissed, his face right up against mine. I nodded frantically, and he took a step back.

"I'm dead," he mumbled.

Although I was scared of him, I couldn't help blurting out, "You're not!"

"Oh, yeah? Watch this."

He lifted my water gun up high, and then threw it so hard on the floor it shattered against his feet. He was splashed with shards of plastic and water, so soaked you'd think he'd just emerged from a bath. I screamed and began crying, as my mother came rushing in the room.

"Mum, look what—"

"Paul!" she screamed. "What did you do?"

I was about to respond when I looked over at Alan and saw that he was bone-dry. I, on the other hand, was soaked head to toe, the remains of the water gun pooling around my feet.

"Do you have any idea how expensive that was?" my mother said. She was not angry, I noticed, but exasperated, distraught. I thought of all the hours she'd worked and money she'd saved to buy the gun.

"But Mum, it wasn't me, I—"

"Enough," she said. "I really don't know what's gotten into you, but please don't add lying on top of it. You know, sometimes it feels like you're not my child."

My mother had never hit me, but I would have welcomed a slap across the face compared to this. Not only the words, but the injustice of them, and the impossibility of her ever believing me. My mother began picking up the remnants of the water gun.

"You should go and get changed," she said to me coldly.

Not daring to argue, I nodded and went to my bedroom.

After getting out of my wet clothes, I dried off and put on new ones. I would have gone straight back out, but wanted to give my mother a little bit of time to calm down. I was also scared to go back out there.

I had no idea what had happened. Had I just thought Alan had thrown the gun at himself, when he'd actually thrown it at me? Had I just imagined it? Whatever had happened, the thought of being out there with him, even with my mother to protect me, was enough to keep me in my room.

I was thinking this when the door opened.

"Mum, I'm really—"

But I could tell from the size of the shadow in the door that it was not my mother. When I'd entered my bedroom, it was just about light enough to get changed without the light. Yet by now it had darkened further, and I was far back into the room. Still, I knew it was Alan. If nothing else, I would have known simply by hearing him, as he was breathing heavily through the back of his throat.

"It's not fair I died," Alan not so much said as growled.

"You're not dead," I said. "You're scaring me."

"And it's not fair that you're alive. That's not how things should work. No one likes you. No one wants you."

"That's not true. My mum wants me, she loves me."

"She hates you, just like everyone else. Do you know what you've done to her life? When I was alive, everyone loved me. Do you think I was like this when I was alive? No, I was nice. Everyone wanted me to be alive, and then I wasn't. It's not fair. When I died, it killed my mum and dad. It's the universe that decides these things, but the universe don't know nothing. If it did, it'd know it should be you out there with all the shadows and not me. No one came to your party but me, and I don't even exist."

His voice was laced with fury. He was breathing so hard that it sounded like he was choking.

"It's not true! It's not true!" I repeated, without being sure what part of what he said I was referring to.

Then Alan stepped out of the dark. There was something about the last dredges of light through the window that gave his skin a dull, grey quality. His eyes flamed with livid hate. I felt as if I could have seen them through the dark. When he walked towards me, I backed away until I hit the wall.

"Please," I said.

Alan took my hand in his. Then, using his fingernails, he began scraping against my palm. I was about to scream out when he placed his other hand over my mouth. It smelled disgusting, and I wanted to throw up, but was distracted by the pain as he continued to claw at my hand. I then felt the unmistakable squelch of drawn blood. He clasped my hand in his and squeezed it.

"You keep your mouth shut," he said. "It's not fair what happened. I shouldn't have died. The universe got it wrong, so it's only fair I make it right."

And with that, he let me go.

"Let's get back out," he said, shoving me forward towards the door.

I had to squint when we left my room, having been in the dark for so long. When we both entered the living room, my mother had picked up the last of the water gun and dropped it into the bin.

She looked over at me and Alan and said, "I think you should probably get going now, Alan. I really don't know what got into Paul today, but I want to thank you again for coming."

Alan then ran over to my mother, and wrapped his arms around her legs.

"I'm sorry about the water gun, Mum," he said. "I shouldn't have broken it."

I was expecting her to recoil, or to be frozen in confusion or shock, but instead she hugged Alan back and kissed him on the top of his head. Incredibly enough, she then laughed.

"Thank you for being honest, Paul," she said. "That's what hurts the most, the lying."

Alan stepped back from her, wiping a tear from his eye, and then my mother turned to me.

"Is there somewhere I can drop you, Alan?"

"But Mum," I said, "it's me, Paul."

My mother offered a strained smile.

"As I said, sweetheart, thank you again for coming, but it's late now. I work in a supermarket and have to get up really early tomorrow."

"But, Mu——"

"No, Mum," Alan said to her. "Alan said he'd make his own way home. I'll show him where to go." Then, before I could do anything, he was pushing me out of the door. He put his arm around my shoulder and surreptitiously squeezed it so hard that I could not speak.

"Bye, Alan! Hope you have a safe journey," my mother called out.

Once in the hall, Alan released me and pushed me towards the door.

"Now you'll know what it's like to be dead," he said. "See if you like it."

I didn't know what to do—whether to cry out or to fight. I went for the latter, leaping forward, but Alan was too quick and strong. He blocked my punch, and then twisted my arm around by my fist. A few inches more, and I suspected he would have ripped my shoulder out of its socket. He squeezed my shoulder again, leaving me breathless once more. Then, before I even knew what was happening, he had opened the door and shoved me outside. He slammed it behind me.

I was about to knock on the door, call through the letter box, when something caught my eye. Or, more accurately, nothing caught my eye. I turned around, and instead of my street, the main road in the distance, the neighbours to the side and across the road, I was standing in darkness. Complete, unrelenting darkness. I scoured my arms with my hands, feeling my flesh prickle against the cold of a late winter day. Everywhere I looked, and everywhere I tried to look, there was nothing but darkness.

I called out. At first I thought nothing came from my mouth. Then I realised I did make a sound, but the space around me was so expansive that the noise registered no more than a torch in a black hole.

Nor was there any other noise. I was in complete blackness; utter silence. That is, until I saw something out of the corner of my eye. I then heard something swishing past my ear, like a whisper travelling at a train's speed. Each time I turned to face the noise or sight, it would rush away, only at the corner of my perception or hearing.

And as these imperceptible, noiseless things swirled deafeningly around me, I remembered what Alan had said:

"It should be you out there with all the shadows."

Ramsey's Rant: Musical Musings II

Ramsey Campbell

Last time I rambled through my history of musical appreciation and threatened to continue. Having heard no protests, I muse anew.

Two BBC radio programmes invite a guest each week to choose their favourite music: *Desert Island Discs* on Radio 4 and *Private Passions* on Radio 3. The latter channel used to run a second similar show, on which I shared my preferences decades ago. Alas, I no longer recall those or even the name of the series, but it may be nesting in an archive of the BBC. Years later the talented Angela Heslop, producer and creator of Radio Merseyside's much-missed cultural survey *Artwaves,* hosted a Liverpool equivalent. Is that archived too? I recall including Mahler, but that's all that comes to mind, which means I can mull my selections afresh.

In idle moments I've indulged in imagining which eight discs I'd take to the desert island. For the purpose of selection I assume the isolation would be literal, in which case I (timid fellow that I am, in some ways at any rate) wouldn't choose any music that might unnerve me too much, however favourite. The power of some works to disturb me has diminished with familiarity; for instance, the opening section of Berio's *Visage* (a work I continue to appreciate, but not with dread), and (although not entirely) Ravel's *La Valse,* where my initial encounter with von Karajan's account took me wholly and unsettlingly off guard. Some Janáček has lost none of its power. The first time I heard his *Sinfonietta* I found the final movement terrifying beyond words. Perhaps that shrieking piccolo derives from Beethoven's storm scene or Berlioz's witchy revels, but they alarm me more than either. At least, they do in the first recording I heard, by the Bavarian Radio Symphony Orchestra under Kubelik. At times the performance seems to teeter on an edge, though not in the way the Lindsay Quartet often does for me; I admit to finding their Beethoven recordings too frequently strained, conveying effort that borders on painful. Mackerras's account of the Janáček celebrates beauty of sound but restrains the terror; Serebrier's offers orchestral detail I have never heard elsewhere and discovers terror in the central movement. Still, I return most often to the Kubelik, and also to his recording of the Glagolitic Mass with the Bavarian forces. Is the orchestral response to the pleas of the Agnus Dei the voice of some implacable presence or just the icy reply of the void? In either case I find it too disquieting to invite to the island.

So how to select the eight pieces of music to keep me company? One tempting notion suggests taking eight different performances of a favourite substantial work—the *Mass in B Minor,* say, or one of Bach's Passions (stopping short of the Mendelssohn *St. Matthew* and the Schumann *St. John,* though both are worth a listen) or the *Missa Solemnis.* Another would involve restricting myself to a specific set of works, although would the Beethoven symphonies or Mahler's involve much restriction? The problem would rather be that there are nine of each. I could reluctantly drop Beethoven's first, charming and typically inventive though it is, and the choral is the Mahler symphony I find least approachable, although that could be a reason to spend more time with it and get to know it better. However, neither series quite competes with the Beethoven quartets, but selecting just half of those—that's a choice beyond my making. Four works each by the two greats, Bach and Beethoven? That's a decidedly alluring notion, but I'll be rigorous. Let's see how I fare with representing composers by one work each.

Bach, then. If we say just that name we may expect people to know who we mean. Might this assume too much? After all, it was quite a musical clan. For that matter, Mendelssohn might refer to Fanny, Schumann to Clara now that both highly talented sisters have emerged from the fraternal shadows. But yes, I have Johann Sebastian in mind, where there's barely room for his vast achievement. What to take? Perhaps one of the Passions, and just now I especially appreciate John Butt's way with the Dunedin Consort, reducing the forces for extra clarity but by no means reducing their expressive power. To me some of Bach seems to presage how eternity might feel, in the best sense: some of the Goldberg episodes, sections of the *Musical Offering.* Above all the *Art of Fugue* conveys this, and so that's my choice. What a task (however pleasant) it will be to select a single version! Hewitt? Rachel Podger and the Brecon Baroque? Suzuki? I've hardly begun.

Some of our readers may feel I've been unfair to Mozart by failing to admit him to the peak. Perhaps I have, and he's entirely welcome on the island. For longer than embarrassment permits me to admit, I used to mistake movements of the Jupiter for Beethoven if I heard them on the radio. (While driving I like to listen to Radio 3—the BBC's classical music station, no longer what it was, but better than none—and guess which composer I've switched on.) This mistake makes me think I've underrated him, and further exploration confirms his importance. While no quartets in my experience equal Beethoven's, several of Mozart's significantly advance the form (and now, having been reminded of their roots in Haydn, I realise he too shouldn't be left off the island). That said, the operas represent some of Mozart's most substantial work, and my island doesn't ban videos, in which case I have a range of possibilities: Losey's opulent *Don Giovanni,* Hanake's disturbingly bleak *Cosí Fan Tutte,* Bergman's magical *Magic Flute?* If the opera itself takes precedence, I think *Giovanni* just pips to competition.

I'm fond of many a Haydn symphony, especially the cycle conducted by Giovanni Antonini, and I think the operas are unjustly neglected—Dorati recorded them all early this century. However, Beethoven admired *The Creation* (though he also claimed to have learned nothing from the older composer, a contention we may dispute), and who am I to argue? I'll take McCreesh's exhilarating version with the Gabrieli Consort and regret leaving Harnoncourt's German-language performance behind.

And so to Beethoven. I especially value performances that convey the shock the premieres must have brought to their audience. A BBC film starring Ian Hart as the composer confronts us with the *Eroica* in a ferocious account conducted by John Eliot Gardiner, and if that's more thoroughly rehearsed than the first performance would have been, surely the point it makes is more important. No work by Beethoven can be said to sum him up, but the sixth symphony goes some way towards it: the prodigious inventiveness, the lyricism, the humour, the drama, the aspiration to the numinous are all there. I'm drawn to the quartets but find it impossible to choose just one. For many years I couldn't grasp *Fidelio,* until it occurred to me that it begins as Mozart and ends as Beethoven, but I'll take another piece I always feel I haven't wholly comprehended, the *Missa Solemnis.* That's one of the works of which I could easily take eight different versions, and I hope I may be forgiven for not specifying one now.

For pure pleasure I often turn to Italian opera. I don't mean braving Monteverdi, though I do find *Orfeo* variously appealing; to my ear *L'Incoronazione de Poppea* is almost as unrewarding as *The Rake's Progress* (whereas I relish much of Stravinsky, if mostly his music up to the neoclassical). Instead, what of Rossini? His irrepressibility—which he can't entirely suppress even in the *Stabat Mater*—would be a welcome companion. The *Petite Messe Solonelle* (which my spellcheck suggests is called the *Petite Messe Salmonella*) sounds startlingly modern to my ear, but I've promised myself an opera. *Guillaume Tell* comes to mind, not least for its extraordinary overture that's so much more than the section everybody knows. Still, I think the barber has it, given how hirsute I'm liable to grow in isolation.

Lord, that's already more than half of the permitted number. I can't do without Mahler, not least for how his musical language straddles the centuries. The second symphony uplifts us towards awe, while *Das Lied von der Erde* gives us a poignant glimpse of eternity (for me nowhere more so than in the recording with the splendid Alice Coote). The sixth symphony can and arguably should be devastating; certainly Tennstedt's version is. If I plump for the third it's only partly because it was the first work by Mahler I heard. The opening pages sound like the breaths of some vast entity or something even more substantial roused by the opening fanfare, and surely announce a new direction in music. None of his symphonies contains a greater range, and I doubt I would ever tire of it.

In the interest of potential comprehension I'm tempted to take Schoenberg, specifically his first quartet. Since the score confounded Mahler, I don't think I need to be ashamed of my bemusement. I originally encountered the work on Deutsche Grammophon vinyl, and was so bewildered by the first two movements that I didn't even turn the disc over. Oddly or otherwise, I find the later quartets more approachable, partly because of a sense (however illusory) that their composer remains drawn towards tonality, even if he never quite reverts. By contrast, to me the first quartet feels as though he's struggling to escape the tonal in every direction but has yet to break free, instead constructing a hugely elaborate prison in which I'm fumbling to find my way. Perhaps direction may dawn.

But could I honestly forego Tchaikovsky? I can't be so ruthless with myself. My indulgence, by no means a guilty one, shall be the complete *Nutcracker,* that bountiful fount of melody and brilliant orchestration. And Schoenberg must yield to Britten as my final choice. The song cycles are unfailingly eloquent, while the *War Requiem* stands high among English choral works, but I'll content myself with my favourite Britten opera, *A Midsummer Night's Dream,* which encompasses magic and the mysteries of sleep and, when it turns comic, remains one of the few operas that are genuinely funny, not least in the music.

Quick, strand me before I change my mind! Other composers are clamouring for inclusion: Telemann for prodigious inventiveness; Biber for the awesomely massive *Missa Salisburgensis* and the intimate fertility of the violin sonatas, not least the astonishing Rosary cycle; Handel for melodic and structural fecundity applied to many different forms; Schubert for *Winterreise* and the equally devastating Unfinished, not to mention his String Quintet; Berlioz, competing with that Biber mass but appealing operatically to me even more (*Les Troyens* is an epic favourite); Verdi, dislodged only and barely by Rossini; Bruckner and his monumental numinous symphonies; Richard Strauss, for me the greatest late Romantic composer (the *Alpine Symphony,* the *Four Last Songs* but by no means only those); Shostakovich's often harrowingly personal saga of living under and either side of Stalinism . . . I see I could have assembled an alternative list, but they'll do for the next island.

Montgomery-Amis operas.

Take Cage if he keeps quiet.

Dazzle Comes for Death

Scott Bradfield

Eventually, the concept of death arrived in Dazzle's life like an unwelcome houseguest. It unpacked its bags, spilled messy toiletries and dripping ointments all over the bathroom, and, despite every promise it made to the contrary, exhibited no intention of leaving. Ever.

"Like I just sat up in my cave last night," Dazzle told his father, "and was suddenly struck with this terrible sense of permeability. It never hit me that hard before—but the fact of the matter is I'm gonna *die*. Me, Dazzle, this extraordinarily powerful and immutable force. (In my private universe, anyway.) And when I'm gone, I'll fade away into the pointless eternity of every dog who ever lived. Even my scent will be erased from the rocks and trees I love, and nobody will care how valiantly I fought to achieve a few good brief things in this world, such as our self-sustaining community of scruffy dogs out here in the woods, or the time I bit that glamping Pharma exec on the ass in front of his stupid wife and kids. Even the trees and clouds and sky won't last forever. We're all going away, and there's nothing any of us can do about it."

Dazzle had hardly touched his salad of night-blooming mushrooms, new potatoes, and heirloom carrots—which he had desultorily plucked that morning from the communal garden. But Dazzle's dad preferred store-bought (or "store-stolen," more accurately) cinnamon and raisin flapjacks, which he chewed daintily with his loose, cavity-strewn molars.

"Life's a bitch and then you die," Dazzle's dad said. "I wish I could provide more comfort than that, son, but it's the only story Mother Nature ever wrote. Best advice I can give is to stop thinking about it. Take longer naps. Count the stars or clouds in the sky.

And try some of this fine fermented grape juice I've been brewing in that black trash bag in the woods. It's pretty diverting."

Around the encampment, dogs were awakening in their own sweet time, snacking on carrots from the vegetable bin, or dried dog food from the food buckets that were posted around the campfire like crude, dwarf-sized totems. But others loped off freely into the woods to scout for rats, mice, and squirrels. For years Dazzle had tried to promote an all-veggie diet among his overextended family, as well as a higher sense of moral purpose. But 'moral purpose' was a tricky concept for dogs, who seemed to figure that eating whatever allowed itself to be eaten was 'moral purpose' enough.

"I've done the fermented grape juice thing, Dad. I've even tried Jack Daniel's, Peppermint Schnapps, TM, and some stress-reduction exercises I read about in an old *Vogue* somebody dumped on the freeway. But no matter how hard I try, I can't get over this increasingly inescapable feeling that I don't have any choice in the matter. Pretty soon—and probably much sooner than I dare speculate—that hoary old Grandmaster Death is coming for me. And there's not enough fermented grape juice in all of Big Sur to help me forget it."

For years Dazzle had enjoyed a near-anonymous existence in small towns along PCH. But ever since the Lifetime biopic based on Dazzle's two-sentence "treatment"—not to mention three decreasingly competent sequels—he had learned to live with a sort of (if you'll pardon the expression) dog-eared celebrity.

"How's it hangin', doggy-dude? Wanna whiff of this righteous weed we got?"

Or: "Hey, mutt! Why not spend some of your movie-money on postcards here at the Big Sur Whale Shack? Or what about this mighty fine plastic pair of binoculars for only ten-ninety-nine?"

"Mr. Dazzle! Can I have your autograph? It's not for me—it's for my pet Weimaraner, Bruce!"

"Go back to the woods from whence you came, Dirtbag! Some

of us are sick of hearing you complain about human beings—you gotta lotta nerve!"

Dazzle had never sought this level of renown, but over the years, as if it were a recurring rash, he had learned to abide it. When it came to human beings, a little went a long way; but when he needed things only human beings could provide—such as a soothing voice filled with beatific platitudes, or long sharp nails for scratching behind each of his ears—he headed straight for Suzy Sandwich's Mental Well-Being Emporium on Main Street.

"Wow, if it isn't my hairy little angel-magnet, Dazzle the dog! I dreamed about you last night. We were bathing in this splendiferous cosmic heart-storm that manifested itself down by the beach. I never felt closer to another spiritual entity in my life—at least not since my hamster Petey died. You want some green tea, Dazz? Or how about some righteous Lotus Zinger I just got in from Tibet, along with a whole-bran carrot muffin I baked myself? The lotus root cleans out your chakra, and from what I can tell, honey, your chakra can use all the cleansing it can get."

Suzy was the sort of girl who appreciated the animal simplicity of a creature like Dazzle. Which meant he could say whatever was on his mind, whether it was in conventional human-sounding language or not.

"Woof," he said simply, nosing aimlessly at a revolving wire-rack display of cut-crystal mood-necklaces. "Woof woof."

"They're energy-formulator crystal-necklaces, hon. You wear 'em round your neck and they protect you from disharmony."

It all seemed so futile, Dazzle thought. There was just too much disharmony in the universe to be warded off by a five-dollar trinket.

"Woof," Dazzle said.

"Of course we all go eventually, hon. It's part of the Process."

"Woof."

"No, I don't believe it'll hurt. We just gotta recalibrate our pain-comprehension mechanisms. And keep a handful of depolarizing blue earth-stones close to us at all times."

"Woof woof."

"Ginseng *can* help. So long as it's hand-picked."

"Woof?"

"I like this music, too. It sounds like Enya, only goes on a lot longer. It makes me feel spiritually balanced, like the company of peace-loving animals such as yourself. 'Cause if there's one thing I know about you, Dazz, it's that you're peace-loving. Which, unfortunately, isn't the same thing as being at peace. But then, everybody knows that, right?"

The worst part of these slow declining days in the winter of life was how much they made Dazzle feel unlike himself. His carefree life didn't feel so carefree anymore. It felt more like grieving for a serenity he could never get back.

"Most of all," Dazzle confessed to his dad one morning, "I'm just ashamed of myself and all I ever believed in. After all, what did any of my much-vaunted ambitions ever amount to? A planet burning down around me. A bunch of pups all grown up and gone to live in the woods where they howl with wolves. Even those stupid Lifetime movies I was credited for testify to nothing more than an ability to sell out cheap. Regret much? Boy, do I. Sometimes, late at night, I even think about the Davenports, this perfectly well-intentioned family who raised me through the first years of my life. What did I ever do for them? And when they least expected it, I just went pissing off down the road and never wrote or called to let them know I was okay. I keep thinking of little Jennifer, this sweet but sort of moronic blonde kid who was always squeezing the breath out of me, or dressing me up for these afternoon 'teas' we'd have with her friends. When I was young, I thought the sun shone out of little Jennifer's ass. She was my dream of a good life fulfilled, and I can't help wondering, you know, what if she needed me sometimes, or called out my name in the dark when I wasn't there? What sort of dog does that to a little girl who loves it? I don't. . . . I don't think I can bear to live with myself anymore, and when I think about it I just start crying, you know, and *splurf,* oh no, it's starting again, it's, it's—"

At which point Dazzle lay down in the dirt and sobbed like a lost puppy in the woods who had been betrayed by everyone he had ever loved.

The tide of grief lifted him up and brought him down again, sunlight waned and moonlight returned, and soon the warm morning sun was rousing him from a soft dream of infinite graveyards filled with mournful daisies weeping into tiny silk handkerchiefs. And then he felt a feeling he couldn't recall feeling before. It carried with it a sense of bristly warmth, and a distant odor of sour breath and stale shrimp that reminded Dazzle of a garbage bin outside a seafood restaurant he used to frequent. What can smell that bad and taste that good? he asked himself.

And of course it could only be one thing.

"Give yourself a break, son," Dazzle's dad said. "And once you've caught your breath, get your act together, buckle up, and march yourself into those Gnarly Woods and give that Grandmaster Death a little of the old what-for. The way Death operates, see, is that He spends existence hunting down everybody one at a time and never expects one of us to go looking for Him. And one more thing. When you tell that noseless bastard what you think of him, make sure he knows it goes for me double."

In all his aimless wanderings, Dazzle had never explored this part of Big Sur. The trees rose up in every direction, brooding and nebulous like shadows of their former selves. The brittle leaves at his feet grew increasingly fractured until they formed a gritty orange sand that whispered against his paws like tiny souls frightened of being born.

The silence was so deep it resounded. There were no birds, no clouds, and in a funny way that Dazzle couldn't understand, no sky. And yet everything was illuminated by a weird interior glow. Go figure, Dazzle thought. It's not like the end of anything out here. It's more like the beginning of everything else.

"Dazzle the dog! Well, I never!" Death stood alone in a wide clearing, entangled by leafy spiderwebs that joined him in a colloquy of dead trees. In a funny way, he looked like a form of darkness that had emerged from itself. "You're early. What brings you to these parts? I thought you were an antisocial character who disliked company. Which, come to think of it, means you've come to the right place. You might even say I'm *dying* to be alone. Get it? Dying? To be alone? Anyway, enough chitchat. What were we talking about? Who are you again? Oh, I know! You're Dazzle the dog! You'll have to come back later! I don't have time for you right now."

Death, as anybody might expect, was wearing a calfskin knee-length overcoat and black rubber galoshes. Dazzle figured the overcoat was a means of delineating the undefined force of his nature; and the galoshes stabilized him amid the shifting currents of dead leaves. He held a tattered yellow loose-leaf legal notebook in one hand, a black felt tip pen in another, and in what appeared to be several additional digits, some tattered, loosely flapping road maps, the sort Dazzle had picked up at random gas stations in the years before SatNav and, after unfolding, had never been able to refold properly again.

"The trick is to follow the creases," Death said, flapping what looked like an Asian mountain range in Dazzle's direction. "But enough about me. What can I do you for, Dazz? I'm almost flattered you came visiting before I went looking for you. Who does that? And so far as roadmaps, follow the creases. But enough about me. There must be other places we both need to be."

Dazzle had never sought confrontation with anything or anybody, but confrontation always seemed to find him. And now that he stood facing the one adversary that could never be beaten, what could he do? Say something pithy? Curse Death to His face?

What could you say to Him that hadn't been said before? Nothing seemed appropriate—either to say or to not say.

Dazzle's silence lifted up out of his misty breath and settled down flatly in the orange leaves. It wasn't an utterance. It was more like an emanation.

Dazzle and Death looked at it. Then they looked at each other.

With one long bony appendage that resembled a finger, Death reached up and ruminatively scratched what resembled a forehead.

"Dazzle . . . the dog . . . I know you . . . Maybe you could come back later? I'm sure we both have places we need to be . . ."

Dazzle couldn't help recalling Emily Dickinson's poem about how, when she hadn't stopped for Death, Death had kindly stopped for her. The main thing wasn't who did the stopping; the main thing was that whoever stopped for whom, don't get Death started talking. Once that happened, it was impossible to shut Him up.

"The most annoying thing about sentient creatures is how special they all think they are," Death said, flipping gently through the pages of his yellow loose-leaf notebook as if trying to locate his own name in a crowded ledger. "It's the same story with every living creature I meet. 'Sorry, I can't go right this minute! I'm very busy!' As if I've got all eternity to wait for them to achieve their pointless plans. They act as if they're the only creatures on earth who deserve a special dispensation. 'I was nice to my mother in the hospital!' Or: 'I was the world's best dad!' Or maybe they gave something to charity, or were working to end world hunger, they all think they're better than me when, as you know, I'm actually a lot better than everybody else. I never meant to be the Bringer of Destruction and the Obliterator of All Earthly Joys. I just sort of fell into it. In fact, what I wanted was to become a poet, but my parents refused to send me to a liberal arts college, which meant the end of *those* dreams. In fact, now I remember what it was I wanted to talk to you about. I've been working on a screenplay, and it's a lot better than the screenplay everybody always *tells* you they're working on. It's about this guy, see, who grows up wanting to be a poet, and then decides to be the Bringer of Unhappiness and Destroyer of All Earthly Joys. It's a coming-of-age story with a strong romantic element, though I haven't worked out the romantic part yet. Think of the finished movie sort of like, oh, like *Avatar* meets *Titanic*. Or *Spider Man: Always Coming Home* meets *Spider Man: Homecoming*. So do you want to hear my pitch? It's far from perfect, but I could use the advice of an experienced pro like yourself, especially when it comes to punctuation. Maybe you could help with that colon and semicolon stuff and who knows, I might win the Academy Award."

By this point, Dazzle sat down in the gritty orange dust and began to lick himself in places he always thought dogs shouldn't lick. (It made them look so much like dogs!) But here at the end of time, or the beginning of despair, or the midway point between one state of existence and none at all, Dazzle couldn't for the life of him think of a better thing worth doing. It certainly wasn't worse than the normal organic rudeness of everyday animal life.

"The main character is this really smart, attractive young man or woman who lives in a city that's economical for filming, like maybe they offer tax breaks or stuff like that. He or she wants to be a doctor or lawyer or veterinarian, but then they fall in love with this rich boy or girl from the other side of the tracks. He has some funny sidekick sort of friends who make lots of jokes at his expense (we need to hire somebody to write the jokes), and some dramatic issues with his or her family (do you know any good dramatists?), and then a plot arises that will need to be hashed out with a good plot man. The main part of the story is that the young man or woman has these dreams of achieving great success as a poet or screenwriter or any sort of profession that doesn't require them to slaughter living creatures by the zillions and so, when they go home at night, they don't feel as if everybody hates them. Which is one of the things people don't think about when you're Death. Like you just want to go home at night and not feel like some mass murdering s.o.b., which is how everybody else thinks about you."

Now Dazzle was not a forward-thinking dog—which was probably why he had come journeying to Death's door without any idea how to proceed once he got here. Dimly he had imagined himself telling Death off or, borrowing a page from his long-deceased mate, Edwina, taking a big bite out of his ass. He had imagined reciting a list of grievances and even negotiating some sort of agreement. ("Okay, so I get that you have to take everybody's life—but can't we do it without the pain and suffering? And what about childhood cancer, or cluster bombs near schools and hospitals? Can't we at least eliminate *them?* I'll swap you, say, prematurely excruciating demises to all our corporate lawyers, junk bond dealers, and munitions manufacturers. You can do whatever you want to *those* pricks. In exchange, you leave the kids and pups alone.")

But now that Dazzle found himself face-to-not-face with the most formidable entity in existence, all these vague, half-formulated plans vanished with the odorless breeze. What possible revenge could any simple creature raise against an entity like . . . *Him?*

Unless, of course, you were talking about giving somebody what they wished for. And them giving you some of what you wished for right back.

Six weeks later, while Dazzle was trying to teach some of the grandpups how to swim at a nearby creek, he heard the steady *thrum, thrum* of a cell phone he had almost forgotten he still owned. And by the time he found it buried under some old soup bones near the campfire, its scratchy, diamond-scarred screen was flashing a sequence of "Missed Calls."

"Dazz, baby!" Bunny Fairchild's voice rattled through the fractured speaker like a mouse racing around the inside of a metal castanet. "Long time no *capisce!* This not-so-young prospect you sent me is tearing up the lunch circuit, and my phone's ringing off the hook. Sure, his work stinks, but so far we've greenlighted his live-action remake of *Bambi,* a live-action remake of *The Nightmare Before Christmas,* and animated musical family versions of both *Seven* and

The Hills Have Eyes. (Personally, I plan to be buying a lot of popcorn for those two.) Anyway, I know you're too good for the real world, so I'll let you get back to whatever it is you call "business" these days, which is probably licking your . . . Oops, snide remark. What I mean to say is stay safe, Dazz, and if we can find a couple of easy projects to bump up your Guild pension, will do. Turns out it's "cool" to hire non-bipedal gender benders these days, and you're all we got."

It was as close to a perfect winter as winter usually got. For this brief time, everybody seemed surprisingly healthy and happy; Dazzle's dad didn't lose his temper with the pups as much as usual; and even Dazzle didn't obsess about the things he normally obsessed about, such as the pointlessness of living and the imminence of his own demise. Instead, he enjoyed the winter sun lying flat across the encampment like a resident force, and the unusually animated splash of fish in the nearby creeks and ponds.

Until, of course, that brief respite ended—along with Death's screenwriting career.

Sometime after the New Year, when the apostrophes of dead birds could again be found punctuating the forest's vast rippled pages of snow, Dazzle received a letter from his former mistress, Jennifer, which arrived care of General Delivery at the Big Sur Post Office, where Dazzle stopped every month to pick up his pension check. The letter went as follows:

> Dear Dazzle,
>
> Don't ask how I got your address, it's just one of those funny things.
>
> Getting used to the funny way things happen has been a big part of growing up since you went away when I was three years old. Often I blamed myself for being a bad mistress, but other times I blamed you for being a bad dog. And if you think about it, what does it matter? We live our lives the best we can and then we die.
>
> So now for the newsy part of my letter which goes like this:
>
> I was a mother and now I'm a grandma and I was married and then I was divorced and then I married again. Whenever they

showed one of those movies about your adventures on Lifetime I would get together with the other moms in my neighborhood and we would watch with about two Margaritas apiece, and while the movies weren't particularly good it was nice knowing you got paid for them.

And now for the more serious part of my letter, being that I had cancer and beat it, but then last week it turns out I have cancer again. So go figure.

Guilt is one of those things that gets heavier as we get older and I figure it must be the same for dogs, so don't feel bad that you never visited or wrote and you can go on feeling not guilty about writing me or visiting me now. I won't mind.

Love from the little girl who loved you when you were a puppy.

Jennifer

P.S. I can probably live with everything about getting old accept the learning to accept death part. How about you?

It was the sort of question that left Dazzle lying disconsolately bedside the campfire for almost an hour until he realized there was only one answer left to give.

And so the next morning he packed his gray knapsack, recharged an old SatNav he kept for emergencies, and set off to visit his oldest friend in the San Fernando Valley, where Dazzle's life once began and might well begin again someday—at least so long as that noseless bastard Death wasn't watching too closely.

The Transient's Dream

Verde Valley, Arizona, April 30, 19—

Manuel Arenas

The transient trudged aimlessly down the dirt road, kicking up a cloud of dust with each step. He had failed to find any gainful employment in Sedona and had wandered afield looking for somewhere safe to pass the night till he could move on to Flagstaff. Coming across a sleepy little settlement on the outskirts, he spent his last dime on a cup of joe at the local greasy spoon, though what he really could use now was a stiff drink. The waitress at the diner was a sloe-eyed dollface with pouty lips and sleek hair that fell on her narrow shoulders like a pall of black satin. He spotted her nametag, which read *Bella,* and tried to chat her up, but she wouldn't give him anything beyond a cold shoulder and a hot cup of bitter bistre brew.

While nursing his ego and his coffee, he overheard some locals talking about a nearby abandoned mission at the edge of town that was rumored to be haunted by a group of miscreant monks who were burned at the stake in 1820 for their myriad blasphemies. To Brenton, who didn't believe in such hokum, this meant that no one would probably care if he spent the night there, providing he could find a way in. It would be a welcome change from sleeping under cover of the moon in the inhospitable desert, as he had been doing for the last few days.

The path leading up to the mission was long and winding, but he hotfooted up the trail and eventually reached the portal. He was a bit spooked by the ornamentation surrounding the doorway, which gave the impression of a massive mouth. Steeling himself, he tried the door, surprised to find it unlocked. The interior was dark, but by the waning light outside he could see a candelabrum sitting on an ornate table in the vestibule. Entering, he set his bindle stick on the tabletop and drew out a tinderbox to retrieve a lucifer to light the candles.

Candelabrum in hand, he entered the church and was surprised to see that, save for a thin layer of dust and the odd cobweb, the interior was relatively intact. The walls were whitewashed; but, upon closer inspection, ghostly outlines hinted at something grotesque just beneath the surface. The longer he looked at it, the clearer their lineaments became. He felt a pull toward the mural but snapped out of it when he heard the clack of his bindle stick resounding as it slipped from his slackened grip and fell to the ground. Shaking his head clear, he picked up his pack and worked his way toward the altar, where he abruptly halted when the feeble candlelight revealed a reredos of diabolic ornamentation, the centerpiece being an inverted crucifix surrounded by winged devils and myriad sacrilegious scenes. Brenton wasn't an overtly religious man, but he did consider himself a Christian, and this appalling display made him uneasy.

A faint creak resounding from somewhere behind him sent a ripple of goose flesh up his lanky torso. Out of the corner of his eye he noticed a door that stood ajar to his left. Wanting to put some distance between himself and the impious altar, he resolved to see where it led. Stepping through, he found a stairwell that descended into a dark passage. Candelabrum stretched out at arm's length before him, he plunged into the tenebrous depths. Upon reaching the bottom, he tried the first heavy door to his left, hoping to find some accommodation. What he found instead appeared to be a wine cellar, stocked with several butts of Spanish Oloroso. With a little exertion he opened the tap and, after a quick test with the tin cup from his pack to see if it was palatable, availed himself of several cupfuls of the dark sherry.

Sated and slightly sotted, he nodded off, allowing the candelabrum to gutter. He dreamt he was a mendicant, seeking sanctuary at the mission. They spoke to him in an archaic form of Spanish, which he somehow understood, welcomed him, and led him to a dining hall with a hearth where a young indigenous woman in a blanket dress, who looked remarkably like the waitress from the diner, gave him a glass of reddish sweet juice and a bowl of porridge with what appeared to be some kind of docandoberry.

Hesitant at first, he soon cleaned the bowl. Hunger temporarily stayed, he paused to observe his surroundings. The walls, which had been whitewashed on his initial entry to the mission, were free of their censoring blot and revealed more unhallowed imagery, which reinforced his prior sense of unease. The woman, returning, cleared away the table as a bearded monk clad in a black robe entered the room and chided her for giving him such a paltry meal. "Come now, Nizhóní, bring our guest a slice of *bistec!*" He introduced himself as Dimas and offered Brenton a chalice filled with dark sherry. He gulped it down greedily, had barely set down the goblet before he was offered another. Soon the monk joined him in his swilling while the woman, coyly smiling as her counterpart at the eatery would not, kept the cups coming. Nizhóní set a plate with a thick slice of perfectly cooked beef before him, and the monk nudged his elbow as he ogled the young woman and winked his eye. This caused the tipsy Brenton to utter a weak and self-conscious laugh before he dug hungrily into the meat. Soon the surprisingly dissipated monk began exchanging ribald tales of libidinous exploits with Brenton, which further loosened him up. Before long they were singing bawdy songs in between lewd observances about the young woman.

Eventually, Dimas threw his arm around Brenton, calling him *hermano* (brother), and told him he wished to share a secret. As often happens in dreams, there was a shift in scenery then, and Brenton abruptly found himself descending the same stairwell he'd taken when awake. The monk led the way, candelabrum in hand, past the familiar wine cellar, showing him into an oddly cold and darkened room. The monk closed the door after him and used the candelabrum to light two large candles on an altar. Once his eyes adjusted to their lambency, he noticed they bore cabalistic insignia of some kind. Between them was a dais with a large wooden chest. The monk uttered an invocation and ceremoniously unfastened the lid. Lifting it, he backed away and genuflected before the gruesome relic enclosed therein.

Resting on a cushion of red velvet lay a mummified head, its sallow, desiccated skin stretching tightly over the contours of the skull like butcher paper. Its livid lips curled away from bared teeth, and its dead, opaque eyes regarded him surreptitiously from half-closed lids. Entranced, Brenton couldn't look away. Then, to his horror, it spoke. Furthering his astonishment, it addressed him, not in the classical Spanish of the monk, but in honest-to-goodness American English!

"Did you like the sherry? And the squaw: powerful purdy, huh? Yeah, she's a dish. You know, you can have her, and the steaks, and all the hooch you care to drink, if you join the brotherhood. All you have to do is sign your name in this book . . ."

At this point the genuflecting monk held out a black book to the transient. Behind him approached the young woman, clad in a loose-fitting black robe like the monk, but which clung to her lissome figure enticingly. She proffered him a poniard. Brenton stared at the offerings, then back at the head, then at Nizhóní, whose inky gaze drew him in like a lure.

"All you have to do is prick your finger with the end of the dagger and sign the book," the head uttered in a voice that sounded too clear to have come from the wizened skull in the box. "Then you can have all you desire, and more . . . much more."

He looked again at the book, then the poniard, then at Nizhóní, who smirked knowingly as his gaze lingered. Just as his hands reached for the dagger, the enchantment was broken by a pounding on the mission door, followed by a tumult without the walls. Men could be heard shouting as the portal was breached and a skirmish ensued. Glass was broken and shots were fired, Spanish troops stormed the mission. The girl, grabbing the poniard to strike at a soldier as he rushed into the room, was bayonetted and pushed aside to bleed out on the floor. Meanwhile the monk was grabbed and detained by soldiers.

A priest entered the hall, making the sign of the cross and rattling off a sacramental oath in Latin. He then ordered the box to be closed and confiscated. Behind him stood a wide-eyed Mexican boy with shiny black hair and dusky cast, dressed in a cassock and holding aloft a golden crucifix. He gaped, aghast, at the young woman expiring on the floor, and a rill of tears streamed quietly down his face.

The transient was accosted by a soldier and held at gunpoint while the priest asked him what his business was with these malefactors. Dimas looked him in the eyes but said nothing. Brenton, flustered, broke his gaze. He looked down at his feet, then at the young woman expelling her lifeblood with hitched gasps. Raising his eyes meekly to regard the priest, he claimed he was just a beggar looking for shelter for the night and had no idea he was calling on a house of sinners.

Would the priest buy it? Brenton pleaded for the mercy of the church and to be forgiven and spared for his ignorance. Warily, the priest looked him in the eyes for a moment, then made a sign of the cross and perfunctorily uttered *"Ego te absolvo,"* and told the soldiers to take him outside, but to keep him apart from the denizens of the mission.

Again the scene shifted. Now he was in a crowd looking at a hastily constructed stage where the monks, thirteen in all, were being tried and sentenced in an *auto-da-fé*. They were clad in *sanbenitos* and tied to stakes. The attendants of the mission, a divers mixture of indigenous peoples and odd locals ostensibly cleared of charges of devilry, were made to carry firewood from the mission storage along with dried desert flora to place at the foot of the accumulating pyre. From behind the crowd Brenton scanned the stage for his host. He needn't have bothered, for when he finally spied Dimas amongst his compeers, the monk was already staring at him fixedly. When Brenton locked in on his fiery gaze the devil worshipper mouthed something, but Brenton could not make it out, the soldiers blocking his view as they ignited the kindling.

All thirteen monks simultaneously commenced to chant darkly as the flames took hold. Concurrently, Dimas held Brenton's gaze as the flames traveled up his ceremonial raiment, singeing his whiskers and searing his flesh. The transient, horrified, turned to flee back into the mission.

The darksome chant of the maleficent monks still ringing in his ears, the transient groggily opened his eyes onto the chill black room. Sensing a presence, he made to rise when cold hands seized him by the shoulders and embraced him, a familiar voice whispering *hermano* into his ear as he burst into flames. The still desert night was unruffled by the ensuing muted screams.

Requiem: 2085 A.D.

Carl E. Reed

The wind whistles darkly—
        hallowed, hollowed: heads of foe
pike-mounted 'gainst the sky,
        winter-washed in moonlit glow.

Shriek of flutes, rhythmic drumbeats
        Hyah! Hyah!—round the fire;
drug-fueled chants, feverish cries
        circle woodsmoke, climbing higher.

Behind the dancing warriors
        a grim horizon: crumpled mounds
of steel & concrete, stone & brick
        town turned burial ground.

Blistered glass, blackened masonry
        patrolling wolves, corpses strewn—
Man returned to savage beast
        howling in his ruin.

Dead Reckonings

RAMSEY CAMPBELL. *An Echo of Children.* London & New York: Flame Tree Press, 2025. 245 pp. $26.95 (US), £20.00 (UK) hc. Reviewed by S. T. Joshi.

For decades Ramsey Campbell has been concerned with the fate of children who are victims—or, more rarely, perpetrators—of terror, supernatural or otherwise. One of his earliest tales, "The Interloper," is a harrowing account of schoolboys plagued by a teacher who may not be fully human. Other powerful tales—"The Chimney," "The Man in the Underpass," "Mackintosh Willy"—gain much of their poignancy because children are the targets of incomprehensible horror. *The House on Nazareth Hill* (1996), one of the greatest haunted house novels ever written, focuses on the fraught relationship between a single father and his wayward teenage daughter. In a non-supernatural vein, *The Last Voice They Hear* (1998) and *Silent Children* (1999) derive much of their power from their focus on the plight of children.

And so we come to *An Echo of Children.* Here we are confronted with intergenerational conflict, as the parents of Allan and Coral Clarendon (Thom and Jude Clarendon and Kendrick and Leigh Benton, respectively) are at loggerheads over each other and, especially, over their offspring as the young couple move to a fictitious town in northern England, Barnwall, along with their six-year-old son, Dean. Dean's treatment at the hands of both his parents and his grandparents is etched in an agonising fashion in a novel that, even if sparing in its depiction of explicit horror, will engender an enormous impact even in those of us who are childless.

At the outset, Thom and Jude learn that Dean has an apparently imaginary playmate, which his parents believe is named Eddie but is in fact named Heady. What could this possibly mean? Jude, staying at the Barnwall house (of relatively new construction), thinks she hears children in or near her room at night. She is worried that Dean's parents have become uncharacteristically overprotective—and she thinks the parents are themselves worried about what Dean might say or do out of their presence. Coral's parents gently scoff at Jude's worries, causing Jude to feel isolated and paranoid, as she senses that her own husband is insufficiently supportive of her.

But Thom has a change of heart when, one night, he detects a presence in their bedroom—a presence that possibly took hold of his hand. Jude, purchasing a new computer, quickly discovers that the name Barnwall is derived from Old Norse roots meaning "child" and "field." More disturbingly, she learns that the name comes "from all the children who were slaughtered here." The Vikings had executed people, including children, by decapitating them. Could Dean's ominously named playmate be the ghost of one of these children? Jude asks a local priest why some ghosts seem to linger in the places where they once lived. He responds, "Perhaps the way they left this world was so traumatic it traps them where it took place." Leigh suggests an exorcism, but the priest is hesitant about involving the church; he instead recommends a local owner of a shop called Crystal Distillations, who performs some sort of ritual that seems to alleviate the difficulty.

Jude, however, is puzzled over one critical point: if hundreds of children had been killed centuries ago on the spot where Allan and Coral's house now stands, why is only one ghost plaguing Dean? But she then learns of a case of much greater recency that may have relevance to the whole situation. A couple named Day had subjected their adopted son (who, like Dean, was six years old) to increasingly harsh "discipline" that amounted to torture, finally killing him in the belief that he was possessed by some demonic entity. The house in which the Days lived was on the very spot occupied by Allan and Coral's house. There had even been difficulties when the Days' house had been torn down and pulverised. People had attempted to snatch portions of the bricks to keep as macabre curios, and the dust generated by the demolition process may have caused sickness—and worse.

To Jude's increasing horror, Allan and Coral are now punishing their son for real or imagined peccadillos (recalling the comment that a subsequent owner of the Days' house had made to Jude—that living in the house was "making us intolerant of every little thing they [their children] got wrong and even some they didn't") and are also actively trying to exclude Thom and Jude from contact with themselves and especially with Dean. They take him out of school, determined to educate him themselves. They suddenly become religious, instilling a particularly rigid and dogmatic form of fundamentalist Christianity into Dean—and others—at every opportunity. Jude feels she has no option but to take drastic measures. "We have to get them away from that house," she declares—and strives to do just that.

An Echo of Children is one of Ramsey Campbell's most intense novels, precisely because it is one of his most intimate. It is as far as can be from the awe-inspiring cosmicism of the Daoloth Trilogy, and its unrelenting focus on the hapless little boy who is victimised by his own parents creates a sense of wrenching torment that requires no dollops of sensationalised grue for its grim effectiveness. There is no doubt that Campbell has set up the supernatural premise—the lingering effects of child abuse, perhaps stretching back to the Druids and continuing on through the Vikings and the Puritans, but most keenly evident in the wretched death of the Days' child—as a symbol for the mistreatment of children, with a secondary condemnation of the religious fanaticism that has become so prevalent in some corners of Anglo-American society. And if the conclusion of the novel lacks the blood-and-thunder denouement that some readers might wish, the supernatural substratum of the novel is always present and is repeatedly invoked as the ultimate source of the novel's terrors, lifting it far beyond a mere portrayal of domestic conflict.

It cannot be stated too often that the power of Campbell's work extends far beyond his ingenious and innovative scenarios. He has evolved a prose style that, in its suppleness, subtlety, and emotive power places him close to the ranks of those great novelists—from Vladimir Nabokov to Graham Greene—whose work he absorbed after writing his Lovecraftian pastiches in the early 1960s. What he learned from these prose masters has stuck with him for all the subsequent decades of his career, lifting his work so far beyond mere "horror fiction" as to be a contribution to literature as a whole. A single sentence describing a carousel in an amusement park—"a horse bared its glossy painted teeth while it elevated Dean and bore him away at a paralysed canter"—is so well crafted that one can only stop and admire it. Every word, every sentence in this novel contributes to its overall impact, and every one of its characters—including Dean himself, desperately seeking his parents' approval by mouthing the excessively polite phrases (such as "Please and thank you!") they have inculcated in him, but also sensing that his parents are insidiously becoming something other than what they were or should be ("They aren't my mummy and daddy")—is vividly and poignantly depicted. Thom Clarendon, struggling with the physical and mental ailments common to advancing age, is also a crisply realised figure; and it is his actions, while overcoming the difficulties that afflict so many of his generation, that form the capstone of this book.

Ramsey Campbell recently celebrated his eightieth birthday, but he shows no signs of letting up on his incredible production of fiction, short and long. *An Echo of Children* can take its place among those of his works that create an ever-increasing sense of unease that may ultimately be far more potent than overt displays of bloodshed or flamboyant supernaturalism. All devotees of weird fiction must hope that the literary creativity that flowered in Campbell more than six decades ago continues to flourish for years to come.

JOHN LANGAN. *Lost in the Dark and Other Excursions.* Petaluma, CA: Word Horde, 2025. 292 pp. $21.99 tpb. Reviewed by Darrell Schweitzer.

There's no doubt about it: John Langan is a powerful writer, one I find rapidly rising in my list of favorites. No one who has read it can possibly forget the relentless title story in his first collection, *Mr.*

Gaunt and Other Uneasy Encounters (2008). I need to find time to read more of his work. I am sure it will all be a treat, as is this latest, his sixth collection.

We see that Langan is a tricky writer. He can make effective stories out of what would be, in the hands of most, mere apparatus and stunts. He starts off with "Madame Painte: For Sale," which is—I kid you not—about a killer garden gnome. He also likes to play with form, telling stories shaped like something else. "Errata" seems to be a letter to a publisher about typos in a book, but it manages to deliver an M. R. Jamesian fright in just a few pages. "My Father, Dr. Frankenstein" tells a science fiction story (Cold War, altering humans to survive nuclear war, nanotechnology) as a series of notes to a review of an imaginary book.

Much more complicated is the title story, one of two novellas in this collection. "Lost in the Dark" starts with Langan, as journalist, interviewing a movie director who has made a film about a sinister legend, something on the order of *The Blair Witch Project,* at which point it is clear that if Langan had been in charge of *The Blair Witch Project* it would have been a much better film. We get a summary of the film allegedly taken from the Internet Movie Database, analysis, an account of what happened during the shooting and afterwards, which all builds up an increasingly creepy vision of one Bad Agatha, who may be the ghost of a possessed woman imprisoned in a mine by the Catholic Church, and who may have gotten out of control and killed her captors. "Fiction" and "truth" are inextricably woven together. The legend is firmly left in the reader's mind, even if we are not totally sure which if any of the narrators are reliable.

A little less ambiguous but no less mysterious is "Natalya, Queen of the Hungry Dogs" (the other very long story), in which a man visits a dying friend, they get drunk together, the guy seems to have already died before anybody knows it, they are haunted by a long-dead sister, and there is a passage into more than one afterworld including the sister's private universe. It is very convoluted and ghostly, but told in the third person, and presumably Langan himself is a reliable narrator, even if some of his characters are not.

Another spectacular stunt is "Haak," which could have been just an in-joke, written to cheer a colleague who was suffering ill-health, but also manages to involve the god Pan, diminished and mad in modern times, a lost ship from the Spanish Armada, sirens, and an absolutely deadpan account (told by a college professor, which Langan is in real life) about a bizarre incident in the life of Joseph Conrad.

Beyond this we are treated to nautical horrors, another sinister siren, and the story of a professor and a lamia, told as an analysis of an imaginary novel. Plenty of riches here. Not all gimmicks and apparatus. Langan is the real deal.

CHUCK McKENZIE. *The Dark Man, By Referral and Less Pleasant Tales.* Melbourne: Daft Notions, 2024. 180 pp. tpb. $25.00 tpb; Kindle ebook $4.99. Reviewed by Leigh Blackmore.

Chuck McKenzie, a well-known Australian speculative fictioneer, has previously published the science fiction novel *Worlds Apart* (1999) and the speculative collection *Confessions of a Pod Person* (2005), which includes his riff on H. P. Lovecraft, "The Shadow over Bexley." He has also coedited the Ditmar-nominated anthology *AustrAlien Absurdities* (2002; with Tansy Rayner Roberts). As a blogger in the realm of horror fiction (especially zombies), essayist, playwright, podcaster, club dj, former bookstore owner, and well-known local ring-in for the first Master from Dr. Who, McKenzie always brings a vivid imagination and frequently a darkly comic sense of humor to his fiction. Simultaneous with the release of the volume under review, McKenzie has released another collection (focusing on his often highly amusing SF short stories and novellas), *Daily Grind and Other Astounding Stories of Mundane Matters* (Daft Notions, 2024). His other recent releases include several other books of oddball SF and detective noir, some featuring cats (talking and otherwise).

The Dark Man, By Referral (McKenzie's first horror collection, with evocative cover art by the accomplished Greg Chapman) gathers his darker work, with tales of zombies, kaiju, alien invaders, visits to hell, Lovecraftian entities, and spectral terrors. Most have previously appeared in Antipodean venues, though one tale, "The Gift," is original to this collection. The flash fiction piece "Howler" previously appeared in *Confessions of a Pod Person,* as did the tale that gave that first collection its title. There are several other flash fictions here, which (like the one-idea "Schrödinger's Catastrophe"), while inconsequential, are of commendable brevity, nicely conceived and executed.

In these macabre tales McKenzie, one of the most purely entertaining writers around, evidences his strong command of his genre craft. (If you want a sampler first, the title story of this collection is also available as a standalone chapbook.) The collection's lead story has overtones of Bradbury, Stephen King, and "Slenderman," with its mysterious supernatural figure who presents children in the town of Stanhope with special "toys" (nature not specified here) to help transform their suffering lives. Parental domestic violence toward children is a strong theme, and McKenzie handles it powerfully, drawing convincing adult and youthful characters through crisp realistic dialogue. In the author's afternotes, "Where Do Horrors Come From?" McKenzie admits that one of his deepest personal triggers is Bad Things Happening to Kids. "The Dark Man, By Referral" thematically reflects on that issue, but within the narrative it is only the Dark Man who is able to offer Stanhope's abused children some hoped resilience, and, yes, comeuppance.

A majority of the tales were sparked by various forms of personal trauma (psychological, personal, medical)—trauma that McKenzie documents in his story notes with an openness approaching Ramsey Campbell's famous autobiographical foreword and afterword to the restored text (1983) of the novel *The Face That Must Die.* Personal domestic violence forms the substratum of the effective zombie tale "Bad Meat." "Tagged" delves into voodoo and railway graffiti, a combination I find irresistible. The taut "Scotoma Fatalis" embodies

McKenzie's apt use of inspiration from the everyday, in this case eye surgery. "The Gift" is a thoroughly convincing short ghost story arising from notions of elderly parents fading from their earlier lives. "Eight-Beat Bar" is a short and nasty tale drawing on the author's DJing experience, "Daddy's Always Right" a brief apocalyptic shocker. "Chrysalis," though thematically conventional, packs a horrific punch. "A Bug Underfoot," a giant monster tale, shows off McKenzie's enviable knack for black comedy. It is in the longer tales, where the author has a chance to stretch out, that his horror fiction is at his most chillingly affecting, as in the title story and in "The Mark of His Hands," which investigates horror in the context of the Crucifixion.

Lovecraft fans are not ignored. "The Second-Hand Bookshop of Alhazred" is brief but funny—the first Mythos tale I've read where such forbidden tomes as *The Ponape Scriptures* exist in Reader's Digest editions. "The Shadow over Bexley" is a full-on Cthulhu Mythos tale, told with a lighthearted touch worthy of a Darrell Schweitzer, as a member of the Marsh family sways the members of the (Christian) Lodge of the Mottled Gecko toward human sacrifice and Dagon-worship.

The Dark Man, By Referral and Less Pleasant Tales is both a classic instance of the author's dark muse assisting him through his own troubled personal times, and a thoroughly entertaining volume of wicked horror fiction. If his tongue is never far out of his cheek, McKenzie proves both that horror and humor can work well together in skilled hands, and that some stories are simply too close to the bone to be told with anything other than brutal frankness.

SONIA H. DAVIS. *Two Hearts That Beat as One: An Autobiography.* Edited by Monica Wasserman. N.p.: Helios House Press, 2024. 252 pp. $62.50 hc. Reviewed by Peter Cannon.

In this welcome compilation of her autobiographical writings, Sonia H. Davis, the erstwhile Mrs. H. P. Lovecraft, tells her life story, starting with her childhood in Ukraine, then part of the Russian empire. Her maternal grandfather, Moisieh Haft, was an Orthodox Jew who disapproved of his daughter Racille's marriage to Simyon Shafirkin, who apparently observed only the Jewish faith's major holidays. The young couple soon parted after Sonia's birth on 16 March 1883, because her father, who was about to turn twenty-one, had to start his mandatory three years' service in the tsar's army.

That Sonia was too young or otherwise not a firsthand observer of family interactions doesn't stop her from describing not only what people said but how they felt, as this exchange from Chapter One between her father and grandfather illustrates:

> With tears in his eyes and a quavering voice [Simyon] added, "Three years! Three long years of hell!"
>
> Moisieh was ruminating in his mind on how to console him, although he knew there were no words that could be effective. Then, again after a short silence, the older man made an attempt to speak. Slowly he said, "Yes, my son, I know."

After Simyon's departure, baby Sonia and her mother moved into her grandparents' house, where she was their "favorite."

When Simyon finally returned home, he ceased to attend synagogue and "once more gravitated to the sort of companions who were more literary and artistic rather than those of a religious bent," according to a stray autobiographical piece quoted in editor Wasserman's introduction that's not in the main narrative. Following Simyon's decision to seek work outside Ukraine, Moisieh made Simyon and Racille divorce for what he considered practical reasons. Simyon hoped that one day he and Racille would remarry, but they lost touch and never reunited. Harm from antisemitic neighbors was a constant threat. Further imagined dialogue enlivens Sonia's accounts of the troubles leading up to the move with her mother to England and later to America, where they adopted Haft as their last name.

For the reader's convenience, a timeline, "The Life & Legacy of Sonia H. Davis," charts the main events and people in her personal history. More than four hundred footnotes provide context and additional information. In a note on editing the text, Wasserman explains that she has honored Sonia's request, originally made to a niece, then a potential editor for her autobiography, to convert all first-person references to herself to third person for publication.

A "Key to Sources in the Manuscript" identifies extracts from such items as Sonia's memoir *The Private Life of H. P. Lovecraft,* her travelogue *European Glimpses,* and letters in the collection of Brown University's John Hay Library. These color-coded extracts are inserted into the main text where chronologically appropriate, depicted as separate sheets affixed with pieces of tape, for a pleasing scrapbook effect.

This volume is indeed a visual delight, with decorative color fonts and pictures of Sonia and her family and friends, mostly from her later years. A ladies' hat such as Sonia might have designed graces the front cover. Most striking are three views of Sonia from her youth. One is a "composite photo sketch," another a formal head-and-shoulders shot. Both are full page and date to 1906. The book's frontispiece, an undated color drawing, could have been based on the other two. As many of those who knew her have attested, if not Lovecraft, she was a beauty.

In a paragraph from Chapter Nine, Sonia displays no false modesty in assessing her own appearance:

> As Sonia entered the ballroom on the arm of an admirer with whom she had spent the earlier part of the evening, one was almost spellbound by her youthful and innocent beauty. Hers was a face such as Da Vinci would have loved to have painted. Brilliant lights reflected from eyes that looked like large brown velvet pools overshadowed by long, dark lashes, set in a delicate face of milk and roses. Her mouth was rather large, with full red lips that gave the appearance of bright, ripe cherries. Though tall, her figure was slight, with the promise of delightful young womanhood in the offing. Chestnut hair slightly covered her ears and wound into a coil on her neck. Upon first meeting her, the first thing that dazzled the beholder most was her luminous eyes.

Her admirer was Samuel Greene, "a salesman in one of the largest wholesale woolen houses," whom she met "at a dance and benefit banquet in Passaic, New Jersey," on Christmas Eve 1898. At the time Sonia was fifteen.

In a particularly harrowing incident from Chapter Ten, she recounts how Samuel, who was ten years her senior, came close to raping her in a New York hotel room one night. Uncertain whether she loved Samuel, Sonia nonetheless married him in December 1899. They had two children, a son who died in infancy and a daughter, Florence, from whom Sonia would become estranged. About 1908, Sonia divorced the jealous and controlling Samuel, though she credits him with introducing her "to the best English writers." In particular, "She loved Lord Byron's poetry, William Shakespeare, Alfred Tennyson, Robert Browning, especially Elizabeth Barrett (Mrs. Browning)." She also read the French and Russian classics.

Sonia's self-education equipped her well for her later involvement in amateur journalism, to which she was introduced by Lovecraft's friend James F. Morton, whom she met in 1917. In early 1921, by then a buyer for the millinery firm of Ferle Heller, she consulted a vocational advisor at Columbia University "about a course of studies that might procure her a professional degree." She was advised to keep her job and take a cultural course, which would include such subjects as "Early colonial and American history" and "Latin and Greek literature in translation."

It is no surprise that she and Lovecraft hit it off intellectually when they met at a National Amateur Press Association convention in Boston in July 1921. The material in the chapters about Lovecraft "doesn't really shed much new light" on their marriage, as Sean Branney and Andrew Leman of the H. P. Lovecraft Historical Society note in the book's foreword, but it is refreshing to see Sonia take center stage, an attractive, self-assured businesswoman, with Lovecraft in a supporting role, as yet another unsuitable man.

Sonia finally found a compatible mate in Dr. Nathaniel Abraham Davis, a sixty-eight-year-old widower, whom she met at a board of education lecture in Los Angeles in 1936. It was a case of love at first sight for Nathaniel. A Sephardic Jew born in Brazil with a Ph.D. in philosophy from Yale, he soon won over an initially skeptical Sonia. Her account of their courtship is enhanced by convincing dialogue, as shown in this excerpt from Chapter Twenty-Five:

> After exchanging a few banalities, he said, "I can't stay very long but I'd like to ask you a few questions."
>
> Sonia thought, *well! he surely has cheek!*
>
> "If they are very personal . . ." she said, and then smiled ever so slightly. "I may not wish to answer them."
>
> "Well, that's up to you. They *are* personal."
>
> She kept smiling and said, "Shoot."
>
> [He asks about her name and surname.]
>
> "One more, and I won't ask you any more to-day," Dr. Davis said. "Are you Gentile or Jew?"
>
> Sonia was flabbergasted!
>
> "What difference does it make?" she hesitated.
>
> "*Are* you?" he asked.
>
> While smiling enigmatically, she countered, "What are you?"
>
> "I am a Jew."
>
> "So am I."
>
> He rose from his chair, folded his hands in prayer, and raised them aloft as he looked toward the ceiling and said, "Thank God!"

The two married within a month. Nathaniel died nine years later, "the only man who truly ever loved her." The book's epigraph, taken from a nineteenth-century play called *The Son of the Wilderness,* sums up their union: "Two souls with but a single thought, two hearts that beat as one."

At the close of her acknowledgments, Wasserman refers to Sonia H. Davis as "this phenomenal woman." Readers of this labor of love are sure to agree with her judgment.

Notes on Contributors

Dmitri Akers is a writer of the weird and photography student, living on Kaurna country (Adelaide, Australia). An avid reader of H. P. Lovecraft since high school, Dmitri finds solace in cosmic dread and the Decadents. His poesy and prose haunt *Penumbra, Spectral Realms, The Deadlands, Spawn II,* and *Skull & Laurel.* Dmitri's first series, FORLORN—photographs reflecting on the paradoxes of life and death—is exhibiting at Gallery 42 in December 2026.

Manuel Arenas is a writer of verse and prose in the Gothic Horror tradition. His work has appeared in various anthologies and journals including *Spectral Realms* and *Penumbra,* as well as *Weird Fiction Quarterly.* He has two collections of prose and poetry, available from Jackanapes Press: *Book of Shadows* (2021) and *The Burning Ember Mission of Helldorado* (2024). He is seasonal poem "Greetings from Krampus" is available as an illustrated chapbook from Fluke Publishing.

Leigh Blackmore is author of two weird verse collections: *Spores from Sharnoth and Other Madnesses* (P'rea Press, 3rd ed. 2013) and *Azathoth and Other Horrors* (IFWG, 2023), plus the weird fiction collection *Nightmare Logic* (IFWG, 2024). He currently reviews for *SF Commentary* and *Penumbra.* A long-term devotee of Sherlockiana and of Derleth's Solar Pons, Leigh is assistant editor of the thrice-annual *Passengers' Log* (Sydney Sherlock Holmes Society) and has received investiture into the PSI (Praed Street Irregulars; Pons organization). His current projects involve research on authors including Blackwood, Bloch, W. H. Hodgson, Machen, Joseph Payne Brennan and Lovecraft.

Scott Bradfield is a novelist, short story writer, and critic, and former Professor of American Literature and Creative Writing at the University of Connecticut. Works include *The History of Luminous Motion, Dazzle Resplendent: Adventures of a Misanthropic Dog, The Millennial's Guide to Death: Stories,* and *The People Who Watched Her Pass By*. Stories and reviews have appeared in *Triquarterly*, the *Magazine of Fantasy & Science Fiction,* the *New York Times Book Review,* the *New Republic,* the *Baffler,* and numerous "best of" anthologies. His new novel, *The Season of My Forgiveness,* will appear in April from Phantasmagoria Press.

The *Oxford Companion to English Literature* calls **Ramsey Campbell** "Britain's most respected living horror writer," and the *Washington Post* sums up his work as "one of the monumental accomplishments of modern popular fiction." His latest novels are *Fellstones, The Lonely Lands, The Incubations, An Echo of Children,* and *Ancestral.* His Brichester Mythos trilogy consists of *The Searching Dead, Born to the Dark,* and *The Way of the Worm.* His most recent collections are *Fearful Implications,* a two-volume retrospective roundup (*Phantasmagorical Stories*), and *The Village Killings and Other Novellas.* His nonfiction is collected as *Ramsey Campbell, Probably* and *Ramsey Campbell, Certainly.*

Harley Carnell lives and writes in London. His fiction, which has been nominated for the Pushcart Prize, appears in *Blue Earth Review, Confrontation, Riptide Journal,* and *Shooter Literary,* among others. His nonfiction appears in the *Lovecraft Annual, Gamut, L'Espirit Literary,* and *Aurealis.*

Scott J. Couturier is a Rhysling Award–nominated poet and prose writer of the weird, liminal, and darkly fantastic. His work has appeared in numerous venues, including *The Audient Void, Spectral Realms, Space and Time, Cosmic Horror Monthly, Weirdbook,* and *Eternal Haunted Summer.* His most recent publication is a collection of weird horror verse, *Nightmuse: Poems of Speculative Darkness,* released by Jackanapes Press in 2025. Couturier lives an obscure reverie in the wilds of northern Michigan with his partner/live-in editor and two cats.

Wade German's most recent full-length poetry collection is *Psalms and Sorceries* (Hippocampus Press, 2022). His first collection, *Dreams from a Black Nebula,* is also available from Hippocampus Press. Other titles include several slim volumes of his selected poems with Portuguese translation, most recently the chapbook *Noctivagations* (Raphus Press, 2024). His work has appeared widely in speculative magazines, journals, and anthologies, and has received many nominations for poetry awards.

James Goho is a researcher and writer with many publications on dark fiction. In 2014, Rowman & Littlefield published his *Journeys into Darkness: Critical Essays on Gothic Horror*. McFarland published his *Caitlín R. Kiernan: A Critical Study of Her Dark Fiction* in 2020. His higher education research is found in academic journals, and his infrequent short stories appear in literary magazines. He lives in Winnipeg, Canada.

Perry M. Grayson's writing career began in 1994 for SilentRadio. Perry was copywriter and production coordinator for Sampson Advertising for a decade. He founded Tsathoggua Press in 1994 and has edited several volumes by Frank Belknap Long. He was a staff writer for *Metal Maniacs* from 1999 to 2009. As a pro guitarist, bassist, and vocalist, he has played in Destiny's End, Artisan, Falcon, Isen Torr and Pale Divine. He lives in Sydney, Australia, with his wife and two cats.

Ellen J. Greenham is an interdisciplinary humanities lecturer at Murdoch University in Perth, Australia, working at the intersection of science fiction, futures thinking, and data ethics. She is the author of *After Engulfment: Cosmicism and Neocosmicism in H. P Lovecraft, Philip K. Dick, Robert A. Heinlein, and Frank Herbert,* published by

Hippocampus Press in 2022, and several papers on Jim Morrison, neocosmic apocalypse, and American and Russian science fiction.

Edward Guimont is Chair of the History and Cultural Studies Department of Bristol Community College in Fall River, Massachusetts. He is also head of the academic speaker track at NecronomiCon Providence; coauthor of *When the Stars Are Right: H. P. Lovecraft and Astronomy* (Hippocampus Press, 2023); and co-editor-in-chief of the history and philosophy of science journal *Endeavour.*

Mark Howard Jones lives and writes in Cardiff, the capital city of Wales. He is editor of the *Cthulhu Cymraeg: Lovecraftian Tales from Wales* anthology series, including the latest volume *Cthulhu Cymraeg: The Night Country* (Macabre Ink). His latest collections of weird fiction are *Star-Spawned: Lovecraftian Horrors* and *Strange Stories and Tales from The Rain: Early Weird Fiction* (both Macabre Ink).

Ben Keene is a British literary critic and writer who has won the Leicester Literary and Philosophical Society Award. He is the founder of Loughborough Creative Writing Society and holds a bachelor's degree in English from Loughborough University; his research interests include weird fiction, affect theory, animal studies, and political economy in literature.

Ngo Binh Anh Khoa is a teacher of English in Ho Chi Minh City, Vietnam. In his free time he enjoys daydreaming, reading, and occasionally writing poetry for personal entertainment. His speculative poems have appeared in NewMyths.com, *Heroic Fantasy Quarterly, The Audient Void,* and other venues.

Manuel Pérez-Campos writes poetry mostly in the tradition of the weird. Some of the venues in which his works have appeared are *Spectral Realms, Weird Fiction Review, Penumbra,* and even *Lovecraft*

Annual No. 15 for a sonnet cycle in which scholarly insight is on display. He lives in Bayamón, Puerto Rico.

Carl E. Reed has worked as a U.S.M.C. photographer, long-haul trucker, stage actor, cab driver, construction worker, and door-to-door encyclopedia salesman. His poetry has been published in the *Iconoclast, Spectral Realms, Black Petals,* and *Deathlehem: Holiday Horrors;* short stories in *Black Gate, newWitch, Sci-Fi Lampoon, Penumbra, Eldritch Tales,* and elsewhere. He is a member of Frank Coffman's Weird Poets Society. *Dark Matter: Weird Stories and Poetry* was published by Hippocampus Press in 2024.

Darrell Schweitzer has been publishing weird or fantastic poetry for decades. His two previous collections of (mostly weird) verse are *Groping toward the Light* (2000) and *Ghosts of Past and Future* (2008). Hippocampus Press issued a new volume of previously uncollected and selected poems, *Dancing Before Azathoth,* in 2025. His most recent story collection is *The Children of Chorazin* (Hippocampus Press, 2023) and his most recent anthology is *Weird Tales: The Best of the 1920s* (Centipede Press, 2025).

James Ulmer's collection of stories, *The Highway that Leads Beyond the World,* is forthcoming from Bridge House Publications. His previous collection, *The Fire Doll,* was awarded the George Garrett Fiction Prize from Texas Review Press. Recent stories have appeared in the *South Carolina Review*, the *Saturday Evening Post, Arkansas Review, Descant,* and elsewhere. Ulmer is Professor of English at Southern Arkansas University.

www.ingramcontent.com/pod-product-compliance
Lightning Source LLC
LaVergne TN
LVHW050629100826
845148LV00011B/1793

* 9 7 8 1 6 1 4 9 8 4 9 4 8 *